# Only You

Michaela Jean Taylor

**ONLY YOU**

Editor: Britt Tayler

Cover Designer: Catharine Pace

*For those who grow up without much love,*
*but who sure still know how to give it.*

# Chapter One

I slammed the hatch of my trunk down, praying to anyone listening that the stupid thing closed. I knew I'd overdone it with packing, but I wanted to get all of my things into my car so that I didn't have to come back here.

"Amelia, please! Just hold on a sec," Noah pleaded, reaching out to grab my hand. I yanked it away from his reach and marched back up the walkway and through his front door. I had one last bag of clothes and a box of books to get, and I hoped like hell they'd fit in the car.

I made it back into the main bedroom—the room Noah and I had shared for the last eight months—and decided to check the spacious walk-in closet one last time. Anything left behind I knew I would never get back. Not that Noah would refuse to; I just never planned on talking to him again after today.

After taking one last look through all the clothes, I was satisfied that I hadn't missed anything of mine. I went back to the large black duffle bag that was overflowing on the floor by the bed and worked to zip it closed before swinging it over my shoulder. With the weight against my back, I realized it was going to be difficult to pick up the heavy box of books in the living room. *I've got this. Almost there.*

Taking a deep breath, I walked down the hallway toward the living room, eyeing the brown cardboard box in the middle of the floor. I'd hastily thrown all my books from Noah's bookshelf into an old box I'd found in the garage. It definitely wasn't my finest packing—the books were overflowing from the top of the box in total disarray—but I'd been in a rush. I just needed to get everything to my brother's, and then I could exhale.

The straps from the heavy duffle bag on my back were digging painfully into my shoulder. I quickly readjusted it, and then did my best to squat down with a straight back so that I could pick up the box without straining a muscle. I tucked my fingers under the sides and almost dropped everything halfway up, but managed to get into a standing position, albeit a precarious one.

Pleased with myself, I blew a piece of loose hair out of my face and began taking steps back toward the front door and out to my car. I could see Noah standing out in the front yard with his hands on his head, waiting for me. I swiftly averted my eyes and, as confidently as possible, walked right past him to my car.

"Amelia. Stop. Just listen to me, *please.*" His voice cracked on that last word. Pathetic.

I tuned him out as I used my body to wedge the box between myself and my car, freeing my hand to open the back passenger side door and moving to set it down on the backseat.

I contemplated buckling it into the seat belt to keep paperbacks from flying around as I drove, but then realized that Noah would see. He'd always hated my book collection—"stupid romance novels" he'd called them—and I didn't want to give him the gratification of seeing me baby them.

Actually. Fuck that.

I pulled the strap down so that the lap belt sat across the box and clicked the buckle into place. *There.* Satisfaction swelled inside of me.

Now I just needed to figure out where to fit this duffle bag. My car was already packed full of my belongings. Everything I owned in the world.

I'd moved into Noah's house eight months ago after dating him for two years, and had just *finally* started feeling like I was settling in. His charming three-bedroom bungalow in the suburbs had felt so grown-up, so mature, and I'd been excited to take this next step in our lives together.

That was, until I walked in on him and some platinum-blonde girl last night when I came home early from work. They'd been on the couch watching a movie together, with his pants pulled down around his thighs and her mouth on his cheating dick.

Swinging the duffle bag down off of my shoulder, I moved to the passenger side of the car hoping I could get the monstrosity to fit in the front. A tub of all my toiletries already sat in the front seat, but I figured that I could Tetris it on top of the tub and it would hopefully balance and stay put.

It did not, in fact, stay put. Instead, over it went to the other side, toppling into the driver's seat.

*Well, I guess I'll just have to try to sit under it.*

Shutting the car door and walking back around to the driver's side, Noah launched himself in front of me. I avoided looking into his eyes, setting my sight on a neighbor's rose bush in the distance instead as I expelled a quick breath of air in annoyance.

"Amelia. You're acting so immature right now." His tone was condescending, as if I were a child throwing a tantrum in the middle of a crowded grocery store. "Just talk to me. I know we can work through this."

I told myself over and over last night that any confrontation wasn't going to be worth it. He'd already ruined our relationship beyond repair, and at this point there was nothing else to say or do except leave. But calling *me* immature?

I flicked my eyes to his face and looked at him with as much intensity as I could muster. It was the first time I let myself actually look at him since I'd walked in on him last night. I didn't recognize him anymore. In ten short hours, the man that I'd been in love with was gone, replaced with a swollen-faced loser with bags under his eyes.

His hair stuck up at odd angles and his shirt was crumpled. I guess that couch probably wasn't the most comfortable for him to sleep on all night, but he'd had no choice after I locked him out of the bedroom. "Excuse me? *I'm* immature?! Coming from the guy who couldn't keep his dick in his pants, acting like a horny sixteen-year-old!" I scoffed. "Get out of my way, Noah. I'm done with you."

He narrowed his eyes at me. "Fine. You know what? Have it your way. You want to leave all of this behind"—he motioned his arm toward his house—"go ahead."

Arrogant bastard.

"Great, thanks," I said, shaking my head and pushing past him to get into my car.

Noah abruptly ran in front of the car then and threw his

hands down on the hood, as if to stop the car from moving. "Amelia," he yelled, "wait! Give me another chance!" I rolled my eyes before shifting the car in reverse and stomping on the gas. Noah must have been leaning most of his weight on the car, because as it moved backward he lost his footing and fell into the street. His face immediately turned red and his eyes bulged. He never did well with his embarrassment. Seeing him like this filled me with so much pleasure, I almost smiled.

Before he had a chance to get back up on his feet, I shifted the car into drive, maneuvered around him, and got the hell out of there.

Twenty-five minutes later, I pulled my car into Adam's lot. The apartment building that he lived in was in a ritzier part of town, and the building amenities included an underground parking garage for residents and a friendly doorman named Charlie. It was *nice*, as my mother would say. Perks of being a surgeon.

In May, my brother completed his general surgery residency in Tucson and had moved back to Denver for a job at Saint Joseph Hospital. All of his hard work—and thirteen *years* of school—had definitely paid off for him. He was living out his dream of following in our father's footsteps, and my parents were beyond proud of him and his solid work ethic.

Not that I didn't have a good one myself, but I would never in a million years have committed to that much school or student loan debt. I knew my father helped Adam with his tuition, but my brother had been responsible for most of it on his own.

I'd chosen a more creative route for my own career and

graduated CU Denver with a degree in marketing and graphic design. I worked for a marketing agency downtown for two years after college before deciding to work as a freelancer for small businesses earlier in the year.

I was making decent money on my own, but it was the flexible schedule that I absolutely loved. At the agency, I'd hated sitting in an office all day. I wanted to work from coffee shops, libraries, or even from a restaurant patio when the weather was nice. I wanted to plan days off for long hikes in the mountains. I wanted to have extended vacation time during the holidays to be with my family. Agency life wasn't really conducive to those desires, so I worked my ass off to build my own brand and after landing a few steady clients, I quit the agency.

Even though I certainly felt confident in my own successes, I knew Adam would have never chosen a path like mine. He was a straight shooter with a twenty-five-year plan. He worked hard, always pushing the bar higher and higher for himself. It was admirable, really, but I still wouldn't trade lives with him.

I parked my car in an open spot close to the front doors and turned off the ignition. Glancing at the time on my phone, I saw that it was just after eight in the morning. I didn't even know if Adam would be home, but he worked nights so chances were that if he wasn't home now, he would be soon.

I decided to leave most of my stuff in the car and only grabbed my black leather tote bag. Aside from using it as a purse, it also held my laptop and charger, which pretty much went everywhere with me.

Locking the car, I walked through the parking lot toward the front door of the building. Charlie saw me approaching through the glass doors and gave me a bright smile as he opened one for me. "Good morning, Miss Campbell." His blue eyes twinkled in the morning sun, and he smelled like aftershave.

"Good morning, Charlie. How are you?"

"Very good, dear. How about yourself?"

"You know, Charlie, I've been better." I sighed.

His face turned to concern. "Is everything alright?"

"It will be. I caught my boyfriend—*ex-boyfriend* I should say, cheating on me last night." I hadn't told anyone about Noah yet, and it felt so weird to say the words out loud. Ex-boyfriend. I'd been cheated on. I was . . . *single.*

Charlie gasped as he shook his head. "Who on Earth would have the nerve to act so foolishly, especially with a girl like you?"

I shrugged and gave him a weak smile. "Yeah, he's an asshole. I'll be okay, though. Do you know if my brother's home?"

"I haven't seen Mr. Campbell leave today," he said as his eyes flitted up toward the ceiling, as if he could see all the way up to the sixth floor.

"Thanks," I said as I moved past him into the lobby. "I'll head up."

"I hope you have a better day, dear!" Charlie called after me.

"It can only go up from here," I called back, my smile strengthening.

I turned toward the elevators at the far end of the lobby and pressed the button.

As I waited for the car, I took a quick peek at my work email on my cell phone. A couple new messages were listed at the top of my inbox from a new client that I'd signed earlier this week, but the elevator chimed before I could read them.

When the doors opened, I stepped in and hit the button for the sixth floor on the selection panel.

Even the inside of the elevator was fancy. A small flatscreen TV was built into the metal wall, providing building residents with ample entertainment during their twenty second elevator ride.

When the doors opened again on Adam's floor, I tore my eyes away from the news story that was splayed on the TV screen and came face-to-face with a beautiful woman who was waiting in the hall. She was dressed in gorgeous, pleated business slacks and a silk white shirt underneath a dark blazer. She eyed me up and down before her lips flattened into a thin line of disdain as we made eye contact.

"Good morning," I said, smiling pleasantly.

She dipped her head in a curt acknowledgment, treating me to no further response, as if we were in high school and I was just some random nerd trying to make conversation with the most popular girl. *Rude bitch*, I thought to myself.

Dropping my smile, I moved out of the elevator and into the hall past her. As I walked toward my brother's apartment, I could hear her heels echo on the floor as she stepped inside of the elevator, but I waited until I heard the doors close before I allowed myself to look down at my own outfit.

I was wearing an oversized white T-shirt that I'd gotten as a souvenir in Cabo during my college graduation trip, faded pink sweatpants and my faithful Birkenstocks. Okay, so maybe I didn't exactly look like I belonged in this building.

Continuing my trek down the hall, I reached Adam's door and gave it a quick knock. He wasn't expecting me since I'd decided to just wait to tell him about Noah once I got here. I knew if I'd called him while I was still at the house, Adam would have raced over there to kick Noah's ass. He'd always been a protective older brother and I had full expectations that he was going to be furious when he found out about everything that had gone down.

Hopefully he didn't mind me staying here for a little while. At least until I could figure out what I was going to do next.

I heard shuffling on the other side of the door before it opened. Adam peeked his head out and saw me before opening the door wider, a worried expression lacing the lines on his face. "Amelia? Is everything okay?"

"Dude, you answer your door in your boxers?" I asked, zeroing in on his lower half and throwing him a look of exaggerated repulsion.

He looked down at the blue plaid cotton shorts he was wearing before looking back up at me. "*Dude.* It's still early. And I wasn't expecting company. What are you doing here?"

I sighed, finally feeling the weight of all my emotions starting to crack the firm foundation of resilience I'd been sporting since last night. I had been holding out on falling apart until I made it to Adam's, and now that I was here with him, I could feel the tears building in my eyes. "Can I stay with you for a while? I broke up with Noah."

His eyes softened. Opening the door wider, he beckoned me inside with a nod of his head. "What happened?"

I blew out the breath that I'd been holding in as I tried to fight my tears away. There was no use though. One by one, like a synchronized cascade, I felt them spill over onto my cheeks. "I had a work dinner last night with a client, and when I got home I caught Noah with another woman."

Adam's eyes flared with rage. "That *fucking asshole.* Are you okay?"

"Yeah, I locked him out of the bedroom all night so I could pack all of my things, and this morning I loaded everything into my car. I'm hoping I can crash with you until I figure out what to do next."

"Of course," he replied, reaching out to pull me into a hug. I wrapped my arms around him and let myself fall apart a little more. "Let me get dressed and I'll help you bring your stuff up. You can take the guest bedroom for as long as you need."

"Thank you. I really appreciate it."

"Adam?"

I froze at the unfamiliar woman's voice. Pulling back from our embrace, I looked up questioningly at my brother before turning in the direction the voice had come from. There was a woman standing at the entrance of the hallway, wearing nothing but her underwear and one of my brother's University of Arizona shirts.

Adam quickly let go of me and ran his hand through his short, dark hair. "Uh, Rachel . . . this is my sister, Amelia. Amelia, this is Rachel."

Rachel's confused face relaxed a bit at the word "sister." Despite the tears I still had in my eyes, I threw a smile on my face and walked over to her, putting a hand out. "I'm so sorry, I guess I caught my brother at a bad time. Are you his . . . date?" I'd known Adam to pick up a girl or two at bars during his undergrad years, but since he went off to med school I'd assumed his partying days would've died down. Apparently not.

A flash of animosity crossed her face as she took my hand in hers. "I'm his girlfriend," she said, clearly taking offense.

*Oh.* "I'm so sorry, I had no idea," I replied, throwing a look of daggers over my shoulder to Adam. I watched his cheek twitch—a nervous tick he'd had since we were kids.

We all stood there in silence looking at each other. Guilt crept into my mind—I definitely should have called first, should have given him a heads up. Why didn't he tell me he had a girlfriend? And how long had they been together?

After what felt like several minutes, Adam clapped his hands together as if to break apart our awkward huddle. "Alright. I'm going to go get dressed, and then we can go get your stuff and get you settled in."

"Right," I said. "I'll meet you down at the car."

## Chapter Two

It took us a total of five trips to bring all of my stuff up to Adam's apartment. Rachel took the opportunity to give us some "family time," saying she needed to run errands anyway.

"Does she live here?" I asked Adam as we carried the last load of bags through his front door.

"No, of course not."

"Does she know that?" I pondered out loud as I looked around his apartment. I hadn't been to Adam's place in nearly a month, but there were obvious signs of a woman's touch I could now see. The guest bathroom boasted a lush new towel set, a vase full of fresh peonies adorned the small dining room table in the kitchen, and a soft, yellow throw blanket had been expertly draped over the couch.

"She, uh . . . stays here sometimes."

"You don't say."

Adam cut me a narrowed glance as we brought my things

into the guest bedroom. "Go ahead. Spit out whatever's on your mind."

"I can't believe I didn't know you had a girlfriend!" I set down the heavy duffle bag on the foot of the guest bed. "Since when do you keep things like that from me?"

Adam rolled his eyes. "I was planning on telling everyone when I brought her to Breckenridge for Thanksgiving."

I'd completely forgotten that Thanksgiving was two days away. Adam and I would be making the trip out to Breckenridge like we'd done the last few years, ever since my parents had purchased a beautiful home there. I needed to call my mother soon and tell her that Noah would no longer be coming on that trip. Or any trip. Ever again.

"Do you need help unpacking any of this?" Adam asked, bringing me back to the present.

I looked around at all of the *stuff* on the floor of the room. Yikes. "No thanks, I can handle it." I sighed, suddenly feeling exhausted. "I'm actually pretty tired. I didn't sleep at all last night, so I might take a nap before I try to tackle anything else."

"Yeah, of course. Take all the time you need. Just let me know if I can help you with anything," Adam said, nudging me on the shoulder. "And hey, I'm glad you came here. Noah doesn't deserve you. I never liked that guy, anyway."

My heart swelled with love for my big brother. He was four years older than me and had always been there for me when shit hit the fan in my life. "Thanks. And *I* promise not to wear out my welcome. I'll find a place as soon as I can," I assured him.

"Don't worry about it, take your time. You can stay here as long as you need."

I threw my arms around him and squeezed. "I love you."

"Love you, too." He squeezed me back before stepping toward the bedroom door. "By the way, would you find any comfort or satisfaction in me going over to beat Noah's face to a pulp? Because honestly, just say the word," he growled.

A light laugh escaped from my mouth. "As much as I'd love to give you that opportunity, it's not worth it, Adam. You're a surgeon now. You're supposed to help people, not hurt them."

"Hm," was all he replied with before shutting the door behind him.

Closing my eyes, I took a deep breath of air into my lungs and let it sit in my expanded chest for a ten-second count before releasing it. The past twelve hours of my life had taken a serious left turn, and although I'd kept myself composed for the most part, I knew that my heart and mind were eventually going to catch up to the reality of the situation.

I'd been with Noah for almost three years, since meeting him at the agency that I worked at after college. When I first met him, he'd been a part of the business development team, focused on networking and bringing in more clients.

At the time, I was a part of the firm's account services team that handled the majority of the work for the clients once they were signed. Because we handled different phases of each client's journey, we rarely worked directly together. That didn't stop him from finding excuses to meet with me, though.

Eventually, he'd started asking me out. It took a few tries before I finally relented, but after a couple of great dates, things really started to heat up. It wasn't long before I was staying at his place more than my own.

After two good years, it had seemed like a no-brainer to move in together. Our lives were moving in the right direction —he'd been promoted to manage the development team at the agency, and my own company had started to take off. Our careers were in a good place, so we'd been thinking about logical next steps for ourselves and making plans for the future. Things like living together, marriage and maybe even a family.

Unfortunately for Noah, it would now seem, those plans did *not* include infidelity.

The eight months I'd spent living with him had been solid, all things considered. But as I closed the shutters in Adam's guest bedroom and crawled into the comfortable bed, shoving one of the decorative throw pillows between my knees for maximum comfort, I couldn't help but feel a small spark of relief within the undeniable feelings of hurt.

Sure, Noah and I had made plans. But now as I lay here, forced to reflect on how I ended up with all of my belongings on the floor of my brother's guest bedroom, I wondered if my heart was ever *really* in it, or if it had all just come down to convenience? If I really allowed myself to be honest, I could confidently say that I'd never felt that gut-wrenching, all-consuming, falling-from-a-sky-scraper feeling with him.

No—*that* feeling—it had been years since I'd felt anything like that. Like I had been launched into the stratosphere without wings, eventually losing momentum and falling into the deep, black abyss. Down, down, down . . .

WHEN I AWOKE, the room felt stuffy and my skin was damp. After a disorienting minute of hazy self-awareness, I threw the thick comforter off of my body and sat up, looking around and re-absorbing my current reality.

I was at Adam's apartment. In his guest room. My things were laid in piles all over the floor. A total, disorganized mess.

I groaned. It wasn't like I had a lot. A small part of my overall frustration at life right now was that moving in with Noah had meant that I'd sold most of my big things because he already had a fully furnished house. Now I'd have to start over with everything except for clothes, books, and a few boxes of sentimental items.

With the holidays fast approaching, I'd have plenty to focus on in the next few weeks to get me through any post-breakup despair. Although, I didn't really feel any of that yet. I just needed to make sure that I kept focus on apartment hunting throughout the upcoming holiday festivities so that I didn't end up at Adam's for longer than necessary. I loved my brother, but living with him again—especially with his new girlfriend around—was not something that I wanted to do long-term.

Throwing my legs over the side of the bed, I pressed my bare feet to the cool hardwood floor and blew out a breath. I needed to get started on organizing this chaos. I got up and moved toward the tall black dresser that stood in the corner of the room. It was modern in style with sharp edges and sleek metal handles, undoubtedly more expensive than anything I'd ever owned. Pulling out a few drawers, I saw that they were empty. *Perfect.*

Next, I moved to slide open the large, mirrored closet doors and saw a beautiful arrangement of built-in shelving next to an expansive clothing rack. All empty. So much space. *Score.*

For the next hour, I went through all of my haphazardly packed items and reorganized them with the use of the ample storage space that the bedroom provided. My clothes didn't even fill a quarter of the closet, and the rest of the boxes stacked neatly within the shelving units. I was a small mouse moving into a mansion, feeling slightly overwhelmed by the amount of things that I would eventually need to shop for.

I made a mental note to look for a *very* small apartment.

After finishing off my organizational efforts by placing the last box—my now decently repacked box of books—up on the top shelf of the closet, I'd decided to jump on my laptop to catch up on work emails and to check the internet for local rental opportunities. I clicked open my email window and read through the few emails that had come in from my newest client, Bite of Life Dental Office. My contact was the office manager, Debbie, and she wanted to meet with me before the long weekend to identify next steps for our contract.

Looking at the time, I saw that it was just past four—too late to organize something for today. I sent a quick reply offering availability in the morning for a call, and then read through a few marketing newsletters before closing down my email window and opening up the internet browser to begin my search for a new apartment.

I thought for a moment about what neighborhoods I wanted to live in. With the flexibility of remote work, I could really live anywhere I wanted to. Being near the city was preferred so that I could easily get to some occasional in-person client meetings, but there were a lot of charming suburban areas that surrounded the city limits.

I tried searching through a few neighborhoods near Adam's place, but didn't find many affordable options—Adam lived in an affluent area of the city. I made note of a couple smaller condos that were somewhat competitively priced, and then moved on to look at availability a little more outside of the city.

After reading through what felt like thirty rental advertisements, I'd built a decent-sized list of potential places. I would make it a priority to call them all soon to find out more about the leasing terms and opportunities for tours. For now, though, I needed a break. And I was hungry.

I shut my laptop closed and placed it neatly on the night-stand before padding over to the bedroom door. As soon as I twisted the doorknob, the delicious smell of Indian food wafted through my nostrils. I opened the door and saw Adam in the kitchen setting down a bag of takeout on the counter. It looked like he'd just come in the front door, but I hadn't heard anything from inside the room. Damn, these fancy walls were thick.

"Smells good," I said, smiling at him.

"Of course, food always brings you out from the shadows," Adam replied with a playful grin.

"Okay, that's rude. I haven't eaten anything since dinner last night!"

Adam shook his head. "I'm just messing with you. I picked up your favorites—I knew you'd probably be hungry."

"Wow," I replied, eyeing the aloo paratha and lamb biryani. "That was thoughtful. Thanks!" My mouth watered. Adam handed me a plate and I shoveled the glorious food onto it.

"Sleep okay?" he asked.

"Yeah, I didn't mean to sleep that long. I'm probably going to be up all night again."

"I have work tonight. I'll head out in about an hour. Help yourself to whatever you want. The TV is set up with all the streaming apps, and there's some beer in the fridge. I don't have a lot of food, but"—he nodded toward the cartons of Indian food on the counter—"this should be enough until tomorrow. There's also some ice cream in the freezer, I think."

"Wow. You are an *excellent* host." I smiled. "Thank you. For all of it."

"Of course," he said, eyeing me seriously. "I'm glad you came here." He kept looking at me for a beat or two and then sighed. "It all works out perfectly anyway, since we head out to Breckenridge tomorrow."

Oh yeah, I'd almost forgotten again. "What time are we leaving?"

"I'll be home from work in the morning, and then I'll need to sleep for a few hours. Logan and Rachel know to be here by about two, and we'll head out soon after that."

I felt the hairs on the back of my neck stand up, and my heart skipped a beat or two in my chest. "Logan? He's coming? With . . . us?"

Adam looked confused. "Yeah, why?"

"Oh, I just haven't seen him in awhile. He didn't come last year . . . and . . . I guess I just didn't know he was coming this year."

"Well, last year he had to stay back because of work, but yeah, I talked to him a couple of days ago and he said he was coming. I told him to just hop in with us." He shrugged.

My face was burning. It was as if I had just opened the door to hell and was greeted by its never-ending fiery depths, scorching off my skin in seconds. "That makes sense."

Adam's look of confusion only deepened. "Why do you look like that?"

"Like what?"

"Like you just found out your grandmother turned into a zombie and ate your cat."

"Uh . . . okay, wow. That's oddly specific," I muttered as I took a step backward, almost dropping my plate. "I'm okay, I think I'm still just a little tired? I'm going to put on a movie. Mind if I eat on the couch?" I turned around and walked away from him and toward the living room.

"You're so weird," was all he said before I heard him retreat into his bedroom. As I sat down on the couch, being careful not to spill any of the contents of my plate.

*Shit.*

I suddenly felt light-headed. I hadn't seen Logan much in the last three years. Not since . . . Well, not since things got complicated. I should have known to expect him at my parents' for Thanksgiving this week, but I'd done a decent job of not thinking about him unless absolutely necessary, which wasn't often. Even hearing Adam speak his name just now sent my body reeling.

I groaned as I put a forkful of biryani in my mouth. While the flavor was incredible, I no longer felt hungry. My anxiety was in overdrive.

Well, I couldn't just sit here and stress all night. I placed the plate of food on the coffee table and got up to head back into the kitchen. I opened the fridge and saw that it was mostly empty in its sparkling glory except for a case of beer and some random condiments. I grabbed a beer and went back to the couch, plopping myself down as I opened the can and took a big gulp.

*Much better.* I took a deep breath, holding it in as was habit for me in moments like this. I felt my heart rate slow back to a normal level. Honestly, I knew I was being a bit silly. It might be nice to see Logan again. It *had* been a long time, and a big part of me missed having him around.

Adam and Logan had been inseparable growing up after meeting each other in kindergarten, spending as much of their time together as possible—and almost always at our house. Which meant that I, too, spent a lot of time with Logan. He was practically like another older brother.

Except for when he wasn't.

My mind quickly tumbled through a series of memories that I'd had every intention of keeping a very tight lid on. Quickly distracting myself, I turned on the TV and found a movie that I'd been wanting to watch—a romantic comedy with an assured happily ever after. I clicked it on and grabbed my plate back from the coffee table, tearing off a big piece of the aloo paratha and stuffing it into my mouth. I washed it down with another sip of my beer and settled in on the couch.

Eventually, Adam reappeared from his room, freshly showered and shaved and ready for work. He gave me a swift kiss on the top of my head before heading out the door, reminding me that he'd be back in the morning and to pack a bag for Breckenridge.

Later, when the movie reached its emotionally enthralling and incredibly romantic end, I wiped away my inevitable tears and cleaned up any trace of my existence from the living room before heading back to my temporary bedroom. I took a quick shower in the en suite bathroom—spending a little extra time letting the hot, scalding water cascade down my back—and then climbed into the big, soft bed.

As if to torment me, my mind immediately flooded back to visions of Logan. Knowing that I'd be seeing him tomorrow set alight a flame inside of me that I thought had been extinguished for good, and I wasn't sure how that could even be possible after everything we'd been through. It dawned on me that I was more emotionally tormented by the mere anticipation of seeing Logan again than I had been this morning leaving Noah's, my boyfriend of almost three years.

What was *wrong* with me?

So what if Logan was coming with us tomorrow? So what if I was going to be trapped in a car with him for the almost two hours it would take to drive to my parents' house in Breckenridge? And so *what* if we'd be sleeping under the same roof tomorrow night, so that we could all spend Thanksgiving together as a family?

My heart throttled on that last word—family.

It was true. Regardless of the past, Logan *was* family. And I needed to make sure I got myself in line before seeing him tomorrow.

Despite the long nap I'd gotten earlier, the beer and hot shower had made me sleepy again. I pulled the covers up over my head, thinking about how my own happily ever afters always felt just out of reach, and eventually drifted off to sleep.

# Chapter Three

SEVENTEEN YEARS AGO (AGE 8)

PUMPING MY LEGS AS HARD AS I COULD, I SOARED higher and higher on the swing. The cool morning air tickled my face as my feet reached for the big sky above me. I loved swinging, especially when my body reached its peak into the sky and I froze mid-air, right before I started to fall. It never mattered how many times I did it, my stomach almost always felt woozy in the moments before the chains snapped tight and I knew that everything would be okay.

It was amazing, the rush of it.

The swings to the left and right of me were busy with other kids having their turn. I'd been at the park for an hour already after begging Adam and Logan to take me before the usual Saturday morning rush. I loved the park near our house. It had the biggest playground I'd ever seen—way bigger than the one at school. There were three different slides, monkey bars that were pretty high up, a huge merry-go-round, and a whole big row of swings.

As more and more kids arrived, the crowd around the swings grew bigger. This was exactly why I wanted to get here early—I *hated* waiting in line and I wanted to have one all to myself while I could. Luckily, Adam and Logan didn't usually mind bringing me here. There was a skate park next to the playground, and both boys had been focused on practicing their skateboarding skills this summer.

It wasn't long before I realized that a line had formed in front of my swing, but I tried not to let it bother me.

Now, I knew the rules. Once someone was in line for your swing, he or she had to count to a hundred. Only after the first person in line counted to a hundred would the swinger have to stop and give it up.

Some kids could be a bit annoying about counting really fast so that the swinger only had less than a minute or so, but most of the time, we all understood the give and take and to do the right thing so that the next person in line would be fair when our turn came. To be the *most* fair, counting Mississippily was your best bet. I didn't make up the rules—I just followed them.

And sometimes, I enforced them.

The taller, dark-haired boy who stood in front of my swing was not interested in being fair, and started loudly *speed*-counting. Heads turned in his direction as his voice got bigger, and annoyance shot through me like a fierce, flaming arrow.

Not half a minute later, he reached one hundred. Other than the squeaking of the swings around me, everything was quiet as the other kids continued to stare.

I let my swing slow down, taking my sweet time as I kept eye contact with him. His dark pupils held firm, and we found ourselves in a bit of a standoff. As my swing continued to lightly rock back and forth, I refused to put my feet onto the ground for another whole minute.

When my swing stopped moving, I gave it an *extra* ten seconds—Mississippi seconds—before I finally let my pink, Converse high-tops drop to the sand below me. As calmly as possible, I stood up and headed back toward the skate park to watch Adam and Logan until it was time for us to head back home. Just as I reached the outer edge of the sand pit, I heard a boy's voice call out from behind me, "Bitch!"

I stopped in my tracks. The blood in my body immediately ran cold with all of the rage that I could possibly muster. I turned back to look at the boy and found him still standing in front of the swing. His face was red with frustration, and everyone else around him was frozen and staring back at me to see how I would react.

I might have been eight, but I was mighty as I shouted back to him, "Look, I'm sorry your mother doesn't love you"—an insult I'd picked up from Adam—"but I can't help you feel better about it, okay? You have to work that out for yourself." I turned back around and stepped up onto the sidewalk, just as I noticed that Adam and Logan were walking toward me from the skate park, probably ready to go back home. From the distance I could see that Adam was animatedly showing Logan a new scratch on the bottom of his board, likely recreating whatever "killer" trick he'd just landed.

It was when I heard the heavy thuds of footsteps landing in the sand behind me that I quickly turned around to see the dark-haired boy running at me, eyes full of anger. I noted that, as he stepped up right in front of my face, he was a whole two heads taller than me. He peered down at me with a level of intensity that shot fear through my spine. "What did you say to me, you little bitch?" I could feel the spray of his hot saliva on my forehead. *Disgusting*.

"Hey!" I heard Adam roar behind me, and we both turned in his direction. Adam and Logan were running now, both of them dropping their skateboards on the cement. They reached us and my brother grabbed my shoulders to pull me back as Logan catapulted himself in front of both of us, pushing the boy back with his chest. I was immediately surrounded by the safety of their bodies and felt relief flow through me.

"What the hell are you doing, Bobby, running up on a girl like that?" Logan's voice was full of a venom that I'd never heard before. *Bobby*. Logan knew this kid, which meant Adam probably did, too.

He was old enough to be in middle school, and still bullying kids on the playground. Figures.

I couldn't see Bobby on the other side of Logan, but the silence told me that Bobby was likely on the verge of going number two in his jeans. In my smug attempt to try and peak over Logan's shoulder, I noticed a deep purple bruise on Logan's arm, mostly hidden by the sleeve of his T-shirt.

My eyes caught on the discoloration. Something about it made me pause. Logan and Adam were twelve-year-old boys, so bruises were pretty common. But this one looked extra mean. I wondered if he'd been in some sort of skating accident.

Logan pulled me out of my thoughts then when he turned to asked me, "What happened?" His face was full of concern. Despite his anger, his voice was soft when he spoke to me.

"He called me a b-i-t-c-h," I said, feeling instantly embarrassed that I spelled out the bad word. I made myself look at Bobby and saw the fear mixed with anger now. "Twice."

At this, Adam whirled me behind him and moved toward Bobby to try and rush him, but Logan was already swinging his fist, moving quicker than lightning. The smacking sound of skin on skin as his fist connected with Bobby's cheek would have made it to the swing set, where I heard the audience of other kids begin to yell "Fight! Fight! Fight!" as they ran over to swarm around us.

It was chaos. Logan kept raining down punches on Bobby's face, knocking him down into the sand. Kids from all over the playground were surrounding us, trapping us into a tighter and tighter circle. Adam, who'd been about to push Bobby around himself, looked shocked as he realized the hell that Logan was pouring into this kid and quickly moved to pull Logan off of him. "Dude, stop. Stop! You're going to get us in trouble! He's down, Logan, he's down!"

After what felt like days of being frozen in fear as adrenaline began coursing through my body, Adam finally pushed Logan far enough off of Bobby to step in between them. He kept pushing Logan back toward me, telling both of us it was time to go. "We need to run, *now!*"

Logan looked back at me, and it was like I was looking at someone I didn't recognize. His face was full of so much anger that he almost looked like a wild animal, cornered and about to be caught. As our eyes made contact, I could see him searching me, *within me,* for some sort of assurance. "I'm okay," I said, my voice small, my thoughts panicked.

At this, I saw his face shift. It was as if he was brought back into reality. "Shit!" he yelled, and started running—Adam and I close on his heels.

We ran the entire way home, never once looking back.

THAT NIGHT, as Mom was cooking dinner in the kitchen, I overheard her talking to my dad in a hushed voice. She sounded upset, and I wondered if she knew what had happened that morning at the park.

When Adam, Logan and I returned home, they'd gone straight to Adam's room. Heart racing from adrenaline and running the entire way home, I plopped myself down on the couch next to Dad, who'd been watching college football.

"You kids have fun out there?" he asked, keeping his eyes on the television screen. Although he wasn't a big fan of watching sports, college football was always an exception.

"Yeah, you could say that," I responded, quickly checking his face to make sure I hadn't revealed too much. He was zoned into whatever game was on, and I moved to rest my head on his lap, letting a sigh loose from my lungs.

Now, hours later, I was back in our living room standing just outside the kitchen's doorway, frozen in place after realizing I was about to walk in on their conversation.

Their low tones made it seem like they were talking about a secret, something only for grown-ups, and I realized with relief that it wasn't about this morning at all.

My relief didn't last long.

"Richard, I saw more bruises on his arm today. We can't just sit back and pretend like something isn't going on . . ." Her voice was only a whisper, just audible over the sound of boiling water. I could hear the fear in her voice.

I felt the panic in my bones rise up, remembering the bruise

I saw on Logan's arm as I heard my father sigh. It was heavy, like all the oxygen in his body left in that quick moment. "I agree. I think it's time. Quite frankly, I have a professional obligation to report something like this, Elizabeth, and as much as we've hoped that this isn't true . . ."

"I know, dear. I know. I just can't believe that poor boy is dealing with something so awful." *Logan?* Is that who they were talking about? It had to be . . . who else's bruise would my mother have seen? It couldn't have been a coincidence. "We need to do whatever we can to protect him," I heard her say.

"We need to be prepared," my father replied, keeping his voice so low that I almost couldn't hear him. "Once the proper authorities get involved, things can, and likely will, happen very quickly. Given the circumstances, I have no doubt that he'll be removed from his home and placed into the system. At least until they can figure out where it's best for him to be. I'm not sure if there's any other family around."

When my mother spoke again, I could tell that she was crying. I'd never heard my mother cry before, and the sound of it made my skin erupt in chills.

"Richard, what if we have him here, with us? He's such a sweet boy, and it would help for him to have Adam . . ."

"Oh Liz . . ." My father sighed again. "We can try. It won't be easy, and nothing would be guaranteed. But we can try."

I quietly ran to my room and shut the door behind me. I could hear Adam and Logan in the bedroom next to mine, laughing as they played video games.

Logan. That's who my parents had been talking about, I was sure of it. I thought about the bruise I saw on his arm this morning at the park and wondered what it all meant. *I have no doubt that he'll be removed from his home and placed into the system.* Removed from his home? What could be so bad that Logan would need to be removed from his home? And how did he get that bruise? My stomach soured as I tried to figure it out.

At dinner, we all sat around the kitchen table and ate my mom's lasagna. Logan took his usual seat to the left of my brother, and I couldn't help staring at him as he ate.

I wasn't the only one acting different. My mom, who was normally asking all of us a zillion questions about our day— about school, about friends, about anything she could think of —stayed quiet. Her eyes kept flicking to Logan while she ate. And my father, who was always quiet during meals, simply watched Mom with the stirrings of a storm in his eyes.

The sudden clank of Adam's butter knife falling to the ground sent Logan flying backward in his chair, and my heart cracked into a million pieces as I saw the terrified look in his eyes. I realized with awful clarity that it was the same wild look he'd had this morning, when Adam pushed him away from Bobby. Why was he so scared? What was going on?

"Dude, it was just my knife," Adam said, incredulously. My brother might have been Logan's best friend, but he was the only one in the room who didn't know that something was terribly wrong. *How long has Logan been in danger, neither of us noticing?*

"Oh honey," my mother gasped. My father cleared his throat, as if to gently warn my mother to keep herself together.

Logan studied the knife on the floor for ages before he sat up straight in his chair. Avoiding eye contact with everyone, he scooted himself forward, back toward the table, and picked up his fork again.

We were quiet for the rest of the meal.

MUCH LATER, when the house had long been dark and quiet except for the sounds of an end-of-summer rain storm, I woke up from the sound of Adam's bedroom door lightly cracking open. I could hear muffled footsteps from the hallway outside my room, making a slow pace across the hallway and down the stairs. I listened for several minutes, and swore I heard the back patio door open and softly close again.

Throwing the covers off of my body, I rose, gently placing my feet on the ground as I felt a chill across my skin. I grabbed a coat and put it on before I, too, quietly made my way down the stairs and toward the back patio door.

Through the window of the door, I saw Logan sitting on a patio chair as he stared into the dark backyard. His wavy brown hair had grown out past his ears, and he was in nothing but the same T-shirt and shorts he'd worn all day. *He must not like wearing coats*, I realized as I tugged mine tighter around me. *Or maybe he just didn't have one.*

The possibility of that made me sad.

I opened the door to step out into the cold air, sticky with the rain that was coming down around the patio's awning. Without a word, I pulled up a chair next to Logan's and shrugged off my coat, wrapping it around his shoulders. It was much too small for him, but he let me rest it on him without a fight.

I sat down and gently placed my head on his shoulder. I didn't know exactly what was happening, or the words that would help him. I didn't know what I could even say to make him feel better. So I just let my body relax around his, hoping he understood what it meant.

I was here. And I always would be.

After a few minutes, Logan reached his arm around my shoulders and pulled me in closer to his body. The warmth from him, under my coat, was the most comfortable thing I'd ever felt.

# Chapter Four

I woke up just as the sun was rising, spreading its gloriously golden rays into the apartment through the half-open shutters. Thoroughly rested, I decided to set up a bit of a workstation in the living room, wanting to prepare for my meeting with Bite of Life. Debbie had responded to my email with a meeting request for eleven o'clock that morning, so I spent a few hours working on a presentation that identified ideal marketing channels to help the dental office bring in more customers.

Adam came home at about eight thirty with a coffee and a small white paper bag in hand. "I stopped at the place on the corner," he'd said, holding out the to-go cup and bag. I took both items from him and looked inside the bag to find a freshly baked and perfectly toasted bagel smeared with cream cheese. It smelled amazing.

"Wow," I replied, "I just might never leave this apartment if you keep feeding me like this."

Adam smiled, faint lines appearing around his eyes. He looked exhausted. "I'm going to hit the sack. I was in surgery all night and officially can't feel my feet."

"Okay, get some rest. I'll keep it quiet out here. I have a call with a client at eleven, but I noticed your walls don't let a lot of sound through so hopefully you don't hear a thing."

Adam chuckled. "I'm glad you approve of my walls."

"It really is quite impressive."

Still laughing, Adam shook his head and disappeared into his bedroom.

I grabbed a plate from the kitchen and enjoyed the delicious bagel before I refocused on my work, finishing up the rest of the presentation. I checked out a few more apartment listings and organized my list to highlight the apartments that I would call to inquire on after the holiday weekend, and then decided to spend time getting some fresh air out on the expansive patio that wrapped around the corner of Adam's apartment. I needed to call my mother, anyway.

Taking my coffee and my phone with me, I quietly opened the heavy sliding glass door and stepped outside. The air was brisk and chilly—it wouldn't be long before the first fall of snow here in the city, and I couldn't *wait* for it. The magic of the changing seasons was one of my favorite things about living near the Colorado mountains.

Sitting down in the plush cushions of a cute patio chair—obviously another touch from Rachel—I set my coffee on the matching end table and dialed Mom's number.

"Good morning, honey!" My mother's voice was bright and cheerful.

"Hey Mom, how are you?" I wrapped my arms around myself, using my oversized sweatshirt to keep warm.

"I'm great, sweetheart. How about you? We're excited to see you kids tonight."

"I'm okay," I said, hesitating for a second. "I actually have a bit of an update about the trip—Noah isn't coming. We broke up."

I heard my mother gasp on the other side of the line. "Oh, Amelia , what happened?"

"It's really not that big of a deal and I promise I'm okay, but . . . I caught him cheating on me. So, I left." I kept my voice even and controlled, which was surprisingly easy to do. Since I'd left Noah's house yesterday morning, I'd been anticipating the wave of emotion and sadness that was *certain* to come. But the only thing I'd really felt so far was relief.

"That son of a bitch."

I couldn't help the smile that tugged at my mouth. My mother was the sweetest woman I'd ever known, but she could turn lethal against anyone who messed with her family. "Really, mom, I'm doing just fine. I'm at Adam's—he's letting me stay here for a little while until I can find a place for myself. I feel good about it all. I'm surprisingly not that upset."

"Well, I have to tell you, honey, it never really felt like you were all that crazy about him. But that in *no* way gives him the right to disrespect you like that. I'm so sorry."

"You have nothing to be sorry for," I assured her. "Like I said, I'm fine. And I'm excited to get out there and see you and Dad."

"We'll have a nice time, for sure. I have all of your rooms ready for you." She paused. "You know, Logan isn't bringing anyone either. He can keep you company."

I stared at a small leaf that had fallen on the top of my sock before flicking it away. "Mom, I don't need Logan to keep me company . . ."

"Oh, you know what I mean. With Adam bringing his new girlfriend, I just meant that not everyone is coupled up. I don't want you feeling uncomfortable, honey. What time are you guys heading out this way?"

I didn't miss the subject change. "I'm not sure. Adam worked last night, so he's sleeping right now. Logan and Rachel will be here later this afternoon, and I suppose we'll head out once Adam's up and we're all ready to go."

"Right, well text me when you leave and make sure you guys drive carefully. It's supposed to snow out here tomorrow and I'm hoping the storm doesn't come early."

"I will, I promise. We'll see you soon, okay?"

"Alright, darling. I love you. Drive safe."

"Love you, too," I said, and then hung up the phone. Picking up my warm coffee, I took a long sip and leaned back into the comfortable chair.

*Logan isn't bringing anyone either. He can keep you company.*

Had my mother meant something with that statement? Surely not, Logan was like another son to her. I shook my head and shivered as a cold breeze kicked up. It was getting colder by the minute. I looked out to the horizon—Adam had an incredible view from his patio, displaying the downtown Denver skyline as it sparkled against the silhouette of the majestic Rocky Mountains. It was simply beautiful.

The Breckenridge house was gorgeous too, nestled snugly in the foothills of the forested land that surrounded it. Knowing it was forecasted to snow tomorrow filled me with nostalgic excitement. I made a quick mental note to remember to pack extra warm clothes.

I took in one more deep breath of the cold morning air, feeling it flood down into my lungs, and then got up to head back inside where it was warm. My meeting with Debbie was only forty-five minutes away, and I still needed to shower and make sure that I had time for one last quick review of all of my notes.

Once the meeting was over, I could fully lean into the fast-approaching holiday and all that it brought with it.

Two hours later, I smiled brightly at the lovely woman's face that spread across my laptop screen. "So, just to recap," she said while looking down at what I presumed to be her own notes, "I'll send you the credentials to all of our social media accounts as well as set you up with website access. You'll start working on developing stronger brand guidelines for us, and then we'll jump into some new deliverables in the first week of December?"

I nodded my head encouragingly. "You got it! Once we have firmer parameters around Bite of Life's look and feel, I can start developing new digital content that will bring traffic to the holiday promos that you mentioned."

Debbie sighed. "I'm so glad we hired you. We need this. Thank you, Amelia!"

I chuckled lightly and said, "Don't worry, Debbie, I've got you covered. I'll have a first look at updated brand guidelines over to you to review next week. Enjoy your Thanksgiving!"

"You too!"

I clicked out of the meeting and looked at my own notes,

taken haphazardly on an envelope I found on the coffee table. I'd realized as Debbie was greeting me that, while I was prepared with my favorite purple pen, I hadn't thought of grabbing anything to write on.

I transferred my action items to the project planner I worked out of on my computer before shutting it down and putting it back into my purse, and then headed back into my temporary bedroom. It was just after twelve and I probably had a few hours to kill before Adam woke up and drove us—*all of us,* I reminded myself with a slight shudder—east to Breckenridge. I still needed to pack and more importantly, prepare myself to see Logan again.

It wasn't that I was scared to see him. Okay, maybe I was. A little. But it was more that I didn't know what to prepare myself *for*. Over the many, many years that I'd known him—essentially my entire life—we'd definitely had our ups and downs, and the recent downs were nothing short of brutal.

Flashes of a long ago humid night on a beautiful Mexican beach flooded into my mind, and I quickly shut the memory down. *No time for that.*

Twenty minutes later, I was pressing my small travel bag of toiletries into my faithful duffle bag when I heard a light knock on the door. I glanced at my phone and saw that it was just past twelve thirty and realized, although perhaps a little early, it was an acceptable time for either Rachel or Logan to arrive. This was unfortunate because Adam was still sleeping, and I would have to be responsible for less-than-desired small talk with either one of them.

I was still deciding who I'd rather see when I walked toward the front door. Rachel seemed like a nice woman, and I was certainly looking forward to getting to know my brother's new girlfriend more over the Thanksgiving holiday. But with all of the anxiety that I was feeling about seeing Logan, I knew I was sure to be an awkward-at-best, bitchy-at-worst host right now. And if it was Logan at the door—well, I would just have to face that when it was time.

Turned out, it was time.

I swung open the front door and felt my body go still. Logan was standing in front of me, his large body filling out most of the door frame. He had on fitted jeans and a black T-shirt that stretched across a very firm chest. A khaki, canvas duffle was slung from his shoulders. I was hesitant to look into his eyes, but then my eyeballs outright betrayed me when I glanced up and caught myself locked in his honey-colored stare. His hair was cropped shorter, no longer the long wavy brown locks that had once flowed between my fingers.

*Knock it off, Amelia.*

I realized after a full minute or two of us simply staring at each other that we hadn't said anything. I also realized that I seemed to have forgotten how to breathe. The air inside of my lungs, intent on moving back out of my body—just didn't.

I held on to it. Just in case.

It was a truly wild sensation, being in this big, fancy apartment with the sturdy, soundproof walls and endless storage space. Even still, Logan's mere presence was so overwhelming and everywhere, it just didn't feel like there was enough air for both of us to breathe. So, I held in what I could and prayed like hell that I wouldn't suffocate.

It appeared that I may not have been the only one struggling during this total dive bomb of a greeting. Logan's eyes looked . . . panicked? Definitely panicked. And his face was contorted into a display of utter discomfort. If I didn't know him as well as I did, his expressions would have been entirely too subtle to be seen for what they were. But, I did know him —very well, in fact—and it was undeniably obvious to me that Logan was experiencing a very similar fight or flight response to seeing me.

I felt a swift bubble of irritation pop inside my mind at this. Enough to decide that the air around us *was* worth breathing. He can suffocate, for all I care.

"Hey," I said, with just a touch of hostility.

"Hi, Amelia." His wide eyes still bore into my own. "I didn't realize you would be here."

I did my best to ignore the fact that his voice felt like soft velvet against my skin. "Well, here I am." My attempt at a chuckle sounded forced and dry.

He nodded. "Can I come in?"

"Oh . . ." I quickly moved out of his way, remembering we were still standing at the front entrance. "Of course, come in." He walked into the apartment, pausing just inside to turn back and look at me. His tall frame was slightly dizzying. "Adam's still asleep, he had a shift last night. But he should be up soon. You can"—I waved toward the couch in the living room— "take a seat. Make yourself comfortable. I'll just be a few minutes."

He nodded again and dropped his bag down onto the hardwood floor before ambling toward the couch. I watched as his long body folded as he sat, sinking deep into the cushions.

Forcing my gaze back in the direction of my bedroom, I shuffled inside and closed the door behind me.

Okay, that wasn't so bad. Was I awkward? Most definitely. Was Logan thrilled to see me? Didn't seem like it. But if I were really honest with myself, I could admit that I didn't like where things were between us. Logan had been in my life—in all of our lives—since I was practically born. Despite everything that had occurred between us, we were family. He was always going to be Adam's best friend—they'd been thick as thieves since kindergarten.

And, truthfully, I *missed* him.

This upcoming Thanksgiving holiday in Breckenridge gave me an opportunity to right some wrongs, to admit to Logan that I'd been really naive and impulsive all those years ago. It gave me an opportunity to apologize. And maybe . . . maybe things could go back to the way they once were. All of us together.

I may not have Logan the way I'd once dreamt of but I'd moved on from that a long time ago, and not having him in my life at all was too painful.

So, it was simple. I wouldn't let that happen. Not anymore.

Deciding I couldn't hide in my room like this for too long, I finished packing the few remaining pieces of clothing that I'd laid out on my bed, and then zipped my duffle shut. I grabbed a warm coat and a pair of boots from the closet and made my way back out.

Logan was still sitting on the couch, facing forward and seemingly lost in his own thoughts. I took a long look at the back of his head before I put my bag and boots down next to his and laid my coat on the top of my bag. "So, how have you been?" I asked as I joined him in the living room. I felt him watching me as soon as I was in his field of vision, and suddenly remembered what it was like to carry his attention. The spark of electric energy that always seemed to make me so hyperaware of his eyes on me.

"Good, actually. Thank you." His deep voice purred at my

senses. "I've been good, really focused on the business." I sat down on a stiff armchair opposite of the couch and looked up at him, noticing that the sunlight from the wide window had turned his eyes into a molten, burning amber. "How are you, Amelia?"

I almost shuddered at hearing my name on his lips again. "I've been . . . well—" *My boyfriend cheated on me, I don't have a place to live, and I'm feeling incredibly self-conscious with you right now.* "I've been okay."

A flash of concern overtook his face before he regained control of his features, settling back to a relaxed expression of . . . disinterest? Boredom? "Just okay?"

I gave him my best, noncommittal shrug. "How's the shop?" Logan opened his own auto body shop over a year ago. For as much as he worked on cars as a teenager—which was practically every weekend—it was fitting to know that he was making a career out of it with his own business.

Logan let out a breath. "It's good, thanks for asking. It's really good. We're slowing down a little bit because of the holidays, but it's been a damn good year."

I couldn't help but notice the pride in his expression, and I felt a warmth spread through my stomach in response. "I'm so happy for you, Logan." I smiled at him. "I would love to come see it."

There was a subtle pull at the right side of his mouth. "Nothing would make me happier."

*Oh.*

I felt the flash of a flame thrum along my veins as Logan continued to pierce me with his gaze. Silence hung in the air around us.

*Nothing would make me happier.*

"Logan!" I heard my brother's voice bound out from the hallway behind me. "You're here. I hope you haven't been waiting long?"

Logan's eyes shifted past me to Adam as his mouth grew into one of his untamed smiles that almost knocked me out of my chair. "Hey, Adam. No, not at all . . . I've only been here for a few minutes." His eyes skirted back to me. "Millie was a gracious host and kept me company. We were just catching up."

"So I'm guessing she told you about what that prick, Noah, did to her?" Adam growled.

Logan's eyes shifted back into concern and question as I felt heat rise to my cheeks. "Um—" I started, but was interrupted by another knock at the door.

"That's probably Rachel," Adam said as he moved toward the front of the apartment.

I kept my eyes on Logan, who was looking at me with such intensity that I could feel him piercing into my mind. "What happened?" he asked, voice low enough for only me to hear.

"It's really not a big deal . . ." I smiled, knowing my cheeks were likely flushed by now. "Come on, let's greet Rachel." I stood up and turned away from him, thankful that Rachel's arrival had provided me with an excuse to avoid this conversation. For now.

# Chapter Five



S ITTING IN THE BACKSEAT OF MY BROTHER'S BMW, I watched as the quaint, brick boutiques and bustling coffee shops flew by through the window. Adam was driving, softly murmuring to Rachel who sat next to him in the front passenger's seat. Their hands were clasped together on top of the center console.

As we'd all made our way toward the car in the parking garage, Logan had graciously insisted Rachel take the coveted shotgun spot as he opened the car door to the backseat for himself. Climbing in on the other side, I couldn't help feeling engrossed by the *closeness* of Logan's large body seated next to mine. I briefly wondered if he'd done this on purpose, to sit with me in the backseat—before shutting down the thought.

In the ten or so minutes that we'd been on the road, I'd done my best to keep my focus on the world outside the car, but every inch of my body still jolted awake at the seating arrangement.

I snuck a quick glance at Logan, trying to get a handle on what might have been going through his head. His back was ramrod straight, hands resting on his knees, and he looked like he was ready to bail out of the car at any moment and roll right on out to the highway.

Okay . . . maybe he hadn't done this on purpose.

"So, how do you and Adam know each other, Logan?" Rachel asked from the front. Odd question—surely Adam had told her all about his best friend? Maybe she was just trying to find an excuse to fill the air with some small talk.

Logan cleared his throat. "Same kindergarten class. We've been best friends for practically our whole lives."

"Ohhhh, that's a long time!" she responded excitedly.

"How did *you* and my brother meet?" I chimed in.

Adam and Rachel briefly looked at each other and smiled before Adam returned his focus to the road. "Well, we first met at CSU in our pre-med program . . ." Rachel started to say.

"You're a doctor too?" I interrupted. For some reason, I hadn't seen that coming. She was too . . . stylish. Too chic.

"No, I'm actually a biomedical engineer."

I stared at the back of Rachel's headrest, at a loss for words. I definitely hadn't seen *that* coming. "A biomedical engineer? Wow. That sounds intense."

Rachel giggled. "The title sounds fancier than it really is."

Logan jumped in, the expression on his face equally as surprised. "What does that even mean?"

"I help create and design medical devices. Right now I'm working on developing mock-ups for a new line of artificial limbs."

Logan and I both looked at each other wide-eyed, momentarily forgetting about our current proximity to each other.

"Wow," I said. "That's way cooler than Adam being a neurosurgeon."

Adam chuckled. "No doubt. She's way cooler than me." I watched as he looked at Rachel again, like he couldn't repress the need to get his eyes back on her. And even in such a fleeting moment, it was obvious that he was positively beaming.

My heart flipped inside of my chest. Adam was clearly in love with this girl. The realization reaffirmed that I needed to get to know her as much as I could during this visit to Breckenridge, because something told me she was going to be around for a long time.

Settling back into my seat, I watched the bright yellow foliage of the Aspen trees whirl by. It wouldn't be long now until everything glittered underneath a layer of snow.

It was such a romantic time of year, when the season changed from the soft, warm glow of autumn to a snowy winter wonderland. Seeing Adam so obviously swept up in the throes of his own love story was beautiful to witness, but it also left me feeling like I was swirling inside of a big, gaping hole within my own life—the empty space where love should have been. Completely hollowed out like a Halloween pumpkin.

As much as I'd tried, I could never quite uncover my own happily ever after. I'd spent *so* much time with Noah—almost three whole years that now felt utterly wasted. And the worst part was that I knew deep down I couldn't fully blame him. Sure, his infidelity was the nail on the coffin of our relationship, but I'd also contributed to being back at square one in the love department. My complacency had ultimately been just as problematic as his cheating.

I should have ended things with Noah awhile ago. Our relationship had always been pleasant enough, like a comfortable routine—but somewhere inside of me was always the small reality that I was settling. I knew that I deserved more. That I deserved to *feel* more.

I'd been lying to myself before I'd ever even met Noah. For so long, I lived within the chaos of my feelings for another man. Feelings that I'd refused to admit to until the night that ruined us, shredding us apart like tissue paper in a hurricane. Feelings that I'd since spent a lot of time overcoming and putting to rest deep, deep down inside of my heart. But *had* I actually overcome them? Or was I still here today, continuing to lie to myself?

I glanced back at Logan now, who was still sitting awkwardly, and let my mind wander.

At twenty-nine years old, he was all man now. The boy I'd once known was long gone, and in his place was this breathtaking, dazzling presence of a man. The realization hit me like a tidal wave. The boy had been one of my closest allies, my most precious confidant. Somewhere along the way of him being my brother's best friend, he had also become my *person*. He'd been a safe space for me in times of trouble, and had never made me feel inferior despite our four-year age difference.

Whispers of past memories flitted through my mind, where, somewhere along the way, my feelings for him blossomed into something different. Something more. I wasn't even sure exactly when it happened, if it was within a single moment or a hundred moments over the years—but it'd happened. And it changed me completely before that night.

Now, looking at the man sitting next to me, I wasn't sure who he was anymore. Was he still the Logan I'd loved long ago, or had life changed him into someone else? Did he still reserve his raw smiles for only those closest to him? Did he still favor plain white T-shirts and worn jeans? Was he still quick to explode if someone that he loved was hurt or taken advantage of?

His hair was different. It had once been long and unruly under his go-to Rockies baseball hat. Now, it was cropped shorter and styled with some sort of product—although, I still saw the way it naturally waved, begging to break free, reminiscent of the days it hung wild over his eyes.

I didn't want to let myself wonder whether he was single. Logan was every woman's dream. He was careful and focused, unwavering in his support for those he cared about, and could make you feel like you were the only other person in the world with just a look. And my *god*, he was gloriously handsome. There was no way somebody hadn't snatched him up.

Here we were in the backseat of this car, two adults who no longer knew the intimate details of each other's lives, but who were forever entwined because of our past. Would the kids we once were recognize who we'd become? The thought made me unhappy as I leaned my head against the window and closed my eyes.

AFTER BEING on the road for an hour and a half, we finally made it to my parents' place. As we drove up the long, winding driveway, I couldn't help but hold my breath as the big house came into view. It was one of the most beautiful houses I'd ever seen, and even after a few years of them owning the property, I still felt a giddy surge of excitement about being here.

My parents told us that they bought this home for moments like this, for the whole family to comfortably come together during the holidays or just whenever we all wanted to be together. There was even plenty of room for their future grandchildren, they'd said. They still owned our house in Denver as well, wanting to keep the home that we grew up in, but as my father neared retirement I was certain that my parents would eventually end up in Breckenridge full time.

The house was grandiose as it sat proudly upon a small hill. Two gorgeous, stone pillars flanked the large front door, and I could tell my mother had been planting recently because beautiful splashes of white, purple and orange mums bordered along the front of the house. Large evergreen trees grew scattered around the property, making everything feel safe and secluded. It was simply serene, a magical chateau tucked snugly within the snowcapped Rocky Mountains.

As Adam parked the car at the end of the driveway, Rachel let out a soft, "Wow."

I opened my door to step out, swiftly fastening the top button of my coat. There hadn't been any fresh snowfall here in the mountains in almost three weeks, but a heavy storm was forecasted for the next couple days and a cold breeze had set in as if in warning. Adam retrieved his and Rachel's bags from the trunk of the car, and before I could protest, Logan grabbed mine along with his to carry into the house. When I went to reach for it, he gave me a look that sent a shiver through me—a shiver that had nothing to do with the cold air.

My father waited for us on the front porch with a huge smile on his face. "You made it!"

"Hi Dad," Adam said, reaching forward to give him a hug. When he stepped back, he turned his body toward Rachel and smiled. "Dad, this is my girlfriend, Rachel."

Rachel stepped forward with her hand out in front of her to shake my father's hand, but he ignored it and pulled her in for a hug as well. "Rachel, Liz and I are so happy to meet you. Thank you for coming out here for the holiday."

"Thank you for having me, Mr. Campbell," she said into his shoulder.

"Oh that's not necessary," he chastised, pulling away from her to look her in the eye. "Please, call me Richard."

Rachel smiled back at him and stepped back toward Adam, who put his arm around her. I took the opportunity to step forward and wrap my arms around my father, who was warm and soft in a comfortable, black sweater. "Hi, Dad."

"It's so good to see you, sweetheart." He released me with a quick peck on the cheek just as Logan came up from behind me to give him a hug, too. It was hard not to notice how tightly Logan held my father during their embrace. Moments like this always felt like a gentle reminder of how much he truly *was* a part of this family.

We all made our way inside and I once again felt enraptured by the beauty of this house. The high ceilings seemed to soar above us as large, dark beams hung in formation all throughout the space. The walls opened up through the floor-to-ceiling windows, providing incredible views of the property all around us. An enormous, cobblestone fireplace stood as the focal point in the front living room, burning with a fire that radiated a heavy warmth.

My mother came skipping in from the kitchen around the corner, an apron tied around her waist. "You're here, you're here!" One by one she handed out hugs, giving special attention to Rachel. "Oh, my goodness, you're beautiful, darling!" The guys had set our bags down, abandoning them for later, and we all moseyed into the kitchen where my nose picked up the nostalgic combination of cinnamon and cloves.

"Mom"—I nudged her gently on the arm—"you're not supposed to be cooking. It's pizza night!" For as long as I could remember, our family always ordered pizza the night before Thanksgiving. We'd all sit around the table, eating way too many boxes of mediocre pizza as we played games all night and drank festive cocktails. It had started out of some long ago desire to save all cooking energy for the next day, but it had transformed into a lasting tradition that I couldn't imagine us not carrying out.

"We are, dear," my mother assured me. "I just thought I would make us a little treat for later." She gave me a quick wink and playfully nudged me back.

My father decided to give Rachel a tour, and we all followed along as if this were also our first time seeing the house. Logan hadn't been here in quite some time either. He'd missed out on the holidays last year because he was focused on his newly opened business, so he was just as focused and curious as Rachel was while my father led us through the various rooms.

I was excited to learn—after we were all led down the staircase that brought us to the house's massive basement—that my parents had finished renovating the space earlier this year. Before, the basement had existed as a dark and dreary storage dungeon underneath the structure of the house. Now, it had been transformed into a charming game room, complete with a foosball and pool table on one side, and a circular poker table with eight chairs on the other side. There was even a small kitchenette with a sink and fridge, and a built-in tap to pull beer from a keg.

"Damn, Dad," Adam exclaimed as he plunged himself

down into one of the heavily cushioned poker chairs. "This is amazing!"

When we made our way back up the stairs and to the second level of the house, my father pointed out the bedrooms that my mother had prepared for everyone earlier in the day. I was slightly on edge to learn that Logan had been placed in the bedroom directly across from mine at one end of the hallway. Adam and Rachel were sleeping in a room on the other end, and my parents would be in the primary suite on the other side of the house.

After the tour, we all scattered to collect our bags and bring them up into our respective rooms. Once again, Logan grabbed mine and carried it with his up the stairs as I followed behind him with a lump in my throat. As we reached our end of the hallway, he turned to look back at me, holding out my bag.

"Here you go," he said quietly.

I reached out to grab it and sling it over my shoulder. "Thank you."

He nodded his head once before disappearing into his room, shutting the door softly behind him. Once inside my own room, I dropped my bag onto the floor and flung myself onto the soft, queen bed.

# Chapter Six

## THIRTEEN YEARS AGO (AGE 12)

CONCENTRATING ON KEEPING MY HANDS FROM shaking, I worked the small brush to paint each of my toe nails as I sat in the front lawn of our house. The bright, neon pink polish that I'd just gotten from the drugstore that morning on an errand with my mom was the perfect shade for summer. It would look *so* good with my pink bathing suit, and I was already trying to figure out how I could get Adam and Logan to take me swimming at our community-shared pool.

The sun was blaring down with particular strength on this hot July day, and I could feel sweat dripping down my back through my tank top while I squinted at my toes. This summer break from school had honestly been . . . well, *boring*. Adam was in a collegiate-level online summer program despite the fact that he was only about to be a junior in high school. I swear, he was such a nerd. And Logan had been busy either working one of his two jobs as a busboy at a couple of restaurants in town, or working on fixing up his car.

That damned car.

He'd bought the 1970 Chevelle SS from an older man two streets over who couldn't look after it anymore. Dad had seen it sitting on the street with a for sale sign during one of his night-time strolls through the neighborhood and had brought Logan over to look at it, knowing he was working hard to save money to buy his own car. He'd always been good to Logan in that way. He treated him like a second son, without fail. Where Adam was bookish and brainy, Logan was street smart and good with his hands, and my dad had figured out over the years how to be the father that both of them needed.

It was important to all of us that Logan felt like a member of this family, never an outsider. Besides us, he really only had his grandmother, who'd taken him in after all of his dad's ugly secrets had come to light.

His dad had been—to summarize it in a few words—a *very* angry drunk. He'd become even angrier after Logan's mother passed away when he was only five years old, which was around the time he'd met Adam in their kindergarten class. For so many years, Logan had been living in absolute hell in that house.

After Dad sent word about my parents' suspicions to child services, Logan had been pulled from his house and was kept away for a couple of weeks while the authorities worked to figure out what to do with him. My parents had volunteered to be his guardians, but his grandmother was blood-related and, for reasons unknown to me, was given the first opportunity at having Logan. She'd accepted, although she really didn't have the resources to care for him either, seeing as how she was older, basically immobile, and only making an income through her social security checks. Even still, the state said it was an acceptable placement, and so Logan was dropped off at her house.

While my parents were careful to only show us kids their positivity about the outcome, I knew that they were somewhat bitter. Logan deserved more than the bare minimum, and they'd wanted to give him so much more. Luckily, Logan's grandmother also lived in town (on the other side, but still . . .) and so he was still at our house practically every day and most weekend nights with Adam.

So, last year when Dad showed Logan the old muscle car down the road, his excitement had been super obvious, and they'd gone up to knock on the car owner's door together. Logan paid the twenty-five hundred dollar asking price for the car, even though he was only fifteen and couldn't actually drive it yet. My parents let him keep the car in our garage while he worked to restore it, which he'd been obsessive about all summer when he had spare time. He'd finally gotten his driver's license last week on his sixteenth birthday, and now was even more preoccupied driving that thing all around town.

And I . . . was bored.

As if in answer to my prayers, I heard the loud rumble of the Chevelle as it rounded the corner up the street. The glossy, black frame of the car glistened brightly under the sun as Logan drove the car toward the house and turned into the driveway. I watched as he rolled the windows up before he shut off the ignition and opened the car door.

He stepped out onto the driveway, his long and lean body looking more like it should belong to a man in his twenties rather than a newly sixteen-year-old boy. He wore a white T-shirt and fitted black jeans, looking—as usual—like a classic teenage heartthrob. As he began to move toward the front door, he spotted me sitting in the grass. "Hey, Mills," he called out, using a nickname that only he used. I couldn't help but notice the way his brown hair blew back from underneath his backward hat as a warm gust of wind curled around him.

"Hey," I said, nonchalantly. "When are you going to take me for a ride in that?" I asked, nodding toward the car in the driveway.

Logan paused his stride and smirked. "You want a ride in the Chevelle?" I didn't miss the small air of haughtiness that expelled out from him.

"Why wouldn't I?"

Logan continued to smile at me. "Okay, Millie. Sure. I'm here to make some plans with Adam for tonight, but I'll take you out soon, okay?"

I nodded. "What are you guys doing tonight?"

Logan took a subtle glance at the front door before looking back my way. He let out a quick breath before stepping into the grass, coming over to where I was sitting. "Your parents are going out of town," he said once he reached me, keeping his voice quiet.

I'd known this already. Dad was giving a keynote presentation at a surgical conference downtown in the morning, and he and my mom had planned to spend the night at a ritzy hotel in the city. "So?"

Logan chuckled, and I felt the low sound rumble within my own belly. "*So . . .* we might have some people over. Nothing major, just a casual hangout."

"Like a party?" I asked, suddenly excited. A party would be a *fantastic* way to break this summer boredom tour.

"No no—just a few people hanging out. Nothing big at all. Your parents would kill us if they found out."

That was true. My parents were fairly trusting—enough to leave Adam and I home alone tonight—but if they caught wind that Adam had anyone over to the house besides Logan without their prior approval, I have no doubt that he'd be totally grounded. They would probably even try grounding Logan for it. "Can I hang out, too?"

Logan narrowed his eyes. "You're twelve. You shouldn't be hanging out with a bunch of high schoolers."

"Logan, I'm *bored.* I'm not just going to stay in my room while you guys throw a party!"

"Shhh," he said, panicking as he glanced back over his shoulder, as if my father could hear him all the way from inside his home office. "I already told you, it's not a party, Mills."

"Fine, but I still want to be included. You guys have practically ignored me all summer." I scoffed.

Logan sighed. "Okay, look, you can hang out for a couple hours, max. But you're also still just a kid, so when we say it's time to scram, you need to listen. Deal?"

I rolled my eyes. "I'm *not* just a kid, I'm practically a teenager!"

"Millie." Logan's voice was full of warning. "Deal or no deal?"

I made it a point to start painting my toenails again before I answered him. "Fine."

"Good," he said stiffly, and turned around to go back into the house. When I knew he wouldn't catch me, I stole a glance in his direction to watch him slip inside of the front door. His hair was getting longer, practically reaching his shoulders. It looked nice, and I wondered if I should tell him that.

. . .

My parents left the house around four-thirty that night, leaving some cash on the table that they said we could use to order pizza. Logan, who had left about an hour after he got here earlier so that he could work a quick shift at the diner, had just gotten back to the house and was wielding a case of beer.

"Logan! Are you *insane*?!" I sneered when I found him in the kitchen with the large blue box. "My dad is going to murder you, you know that right?"

Logan grinned, only half of his mouth rising up. "Mills, are you going to be cool or do we need to cancel your party pass?"

I crossed my arms over my chest in defiance. "You can't cancel me, we have a deal. And of course I'm going to be cool, but my *dad* isn't going to be cool when he catches you."

Adam came barreling into the kitchen, likely having heard the sound of Logan's car. His eyes grew wide at the box that Logan was loading into the refrigerator. "How did you score that?"

Logan looked up toward Adam and winked. "Mara got it from her older brother. She gave it to me at work."

"Dude, your girlfriend is clutch," Adam replied as he swatted Logan on the shoulder.

*Girlfriend.* I felt my body bristle in reaction to this foreign word. A word that surely had no place in any conversation that involved Logan or my brother. "Wait, you have a girlfriend?" I asked incredulously.

Logan's honey-colored eyes flicked to mine. "Yeah, so what?"

"Since when?"

His gaze on me held steadfast. "I don't know . . . a few weeks ago."

"Huh." I couldn't come up with anything better, as I was

trying to disguise the overwhelming feeling of jealousy that was suddenly spreading throughout my body like wildfire. "Is she nice?"

Adam rolled his eyes at me. "Amelia, mind your own business!"

Logan chuckled softly, keeping his eyes on me. "*Yes,* Millie. She's nice. You can meet her tonight, actually. She's coming over."

I felt my eyes widen in response. I looked down at my outfit —an old lavender tank top with small, white daisies printed all over and cut-off denim shorts that had a marker stain near the hem—before spinning on my heels and racing up the stairs to change. I probably looked like a total idiot to the guys, but I didn't care. This would be my first experience hanging out with teenagers who weren't my brother and his best friend, and I'd be damned if I looked like a ratty little kid.

*Especially* in front of Logan's new girlfriend.

Ugh, the mere thought of her existence in his life seriously bummed me out. Why was I feeling so jealous about this? It wasn't like I liked Logan—he was practically my brother. Honestly though, I'd hardly seen Logan or Adam at all this summer and knowing that *girls* were in the picture now meant I would see them even less. *That* was why I felt upset. It had to be.

I tore through my closet, looking for something more "mature" to wear, when I found a pink T-shirt dress in the back. I had only worn it once for picture day at school, and it was just the right amount of casual-yet-sophisticated. Plus, I could easily dress it up a little with some jewelry.

I changed into it, realizing as I pulled it down that it was a little bit smaller on me than it had been last fall when I wore it to school. Checking myself in the mirror, I confirmed it looked tighter and didn't quite reach the top of my knees like it used to, but it still worked. If anything, it was accomplishing what I was going for in my attempt to look a little older.

Keeping my steps light, I hurriedly snuck into my parents' bathroom to use some of Mom's mascara. I pulled the wand over my lashes a few times and decided that a swipe of a neutral lipstick wouldn't hurt either. Perfect.

Back in my room, I spritzed myself lightly with some of my strawberry perfume and put on gold hoop earrings and a dainty gold bracelet to match.

Looking at myself in the mirror again, I felt elated. I didn't look half bad, and I could definitely pass for at least fourteen. My boobs might not have been those of a fourteen-year-old's, but all things considered—I looked good. I gave myself an air kiss before I left my bedroom.

I found Adam and Logan still in the kitchen. Adam was holding the wireless house phone between his ear and shoulder as he ordered pizzas to the house, distractedly doodling on the white board meant for messages that hung on the wall.

I found Logan at the breakfast table by the big bay window. He saw me as soon as I came around the corner, and the look on his face was *not* a happy one.

"What the hell, Millie," he said, looking me up and down, "is that makeup on your face?"

I was hoping it wouldn't be *that* obvious. "Hardly." I shrugged. "It's nothing major. Definitely nothing for you to freak out about," I stated matter-of-factly.

He scoffed in response. "Go wash that shit off of your face right now."

I rolled my eyes. "Why?"

Adam, now off the phone, had walked over to assess me himself and took the opportunity to butt in. "Amelia, why do you look like that?"

"Like what?" I said, losing my patience.

"Like . . . *that.* Why is your dress so short? Why do you even have a dress that short?"

Logan pinched the bridge of his nose, looking just like my dad.

The sound of knocking came from the front door, and Adam made to go and answer it. On his way out of the kitchen, he turned back to Logan and said, "If she wants to look like a fool, let her."

I felt my heart shrivel a little bit at his words. I knew they were probably just trying to look out for me, but they were acting like I'd dressed scandalously. It was just a pink dress with a little mascara and lipstick. What was the big deal?

The anticipation of seeing who'd arrived came over me as I followed Adam to the front of the house. He opened the door to a crowd of five people gathered on our doorstep; three girls and two guys. I felt Logan standing behind me for a minute before he moved to greet their friends. I watched as he reached the blonde girl in the middle and gave her a hug.

She must have been Mara.

I stared at the girl, memorizing every detail that I possibly could. She was tall and skinny with tanned skin and plump, rosy lips. Her blonde hair was obviously natural and not dyed, and it cascaded down below her elbows. She wore a simple, white slip dress with thin straps that hugged her chest along her collarbones, and the glint of a thin, gold chain adorned her neck.

She was a goddess. Of *course* Logan had a girlfriend that looked like that.

Adam gave me the courtesy of making introductions to everyone as they walked in, and most of them just waved or said "hi" as they passed by me. Mara, however, took hold of my arm and sweetly purred, "Hi Amelia, I've heard so much about you. I'm so glad you're here!"

I smiled back at her in response. "Thanks. But, where else would I be?"

Mara giggled, and it sounded like fairy bells. She grabbed Logan's hand and pulled him into the family room where everyone else was gathering, leaving me alone where I stood.

Taking a deep breath, I pushed down a flare of nerves. Despite my best efforts in getting ready, I was still feeling like a little kid next to Adam and Logan's friends and *especially* compared to Mara. I would just have to make sure that I didn't act like a twelve-year-old.

Suddenly, a brilliant idea came to me. Heading to the kitchen's pantry where my parents kept a large, plastic bin for our recyclables, I found an empty wine bottle and pulled it out. I took it to the kitchen sink and did my best to wash out any sticky wine residue before I dried the empty bottle off with a paper towel.

In the family room, everyone was gathered together, either sitting on our sofa or on the floor, most of them already holding a beer in their hand. They were positioned in a semblance of a circle, which was perfect for what I had planned. Adam was in the middle of telling a joke—always needing to be the center of attention in social situations—and when everyone laughed at the punch line, I took my opportunity.

"Anyone up for a little game of spin the bottle?" I tried to sound as casual as I could, moving into the room to sit on the floor between a beautiful dark-skinned girl with curly hair and a redheaded boy with acne. Carefully avoiding Adam or Logan's eyes, I looked around at the stunned faces of everyone else.

"Amelia, what are you doing?" I heard Adam say, but I pretended like I didn't. Turning to the girl next to me, I offered her the bottle. "Do you want to go first?"

She smiled at me, reluctantly taking the bottle from my hands. "Um, okay. Sure." I watched as she set the bottle down on the carpet, laying it on its side in the middle of everyone. Her long fingers gripped around the label as gave it a spin.

The bottle moved around in two rotations—the fibers of the carpet eventually slowing it down—before it stopped its movement to point at Adam.

Adam flushed, the tips of his ears growing red. He chuckled nervously as the girl got on all fours and crawled over to where he sat on the far end of the couch. When she reached him, she got up onto her knees, placed her hands on either side of his legs and quickly pecked him on the lips. She flashed him a smile before making her way back to her spot on the carpet.

Her confidence was mesmerizing.

Everyone kept their eyes on Adam, who began rubbing the back of his neck as his own smile grew wide on his face. He seemed to have forgotten that I was the one who set this game in motion, and that suited me just fine.

I stole a glance at Logan, who still didn't look amused. Mara, however, looked delighted. "Adam, it's your turn to spin!"

Adam glanced around at everyone, likely considering every

possible outcome, before he scooted forward on the couch to reach the bottle on the ground in front of him. With a firm twist of his hand, the bottle started to spin.

This time when it stopped, the open end pointed right at me. Adam's face sunk. "I'm not kissing my sister."

Feeling a strike of embarrassment, I shot back at him, "I wouldn't want to kiss you, anyway."

Mara, somehow becoming the leader of this whole game, determined that we didn't need to kiss each other. "We'll just consider it a wash."

I nodded and realized that meant it was my turn to spin. I took a look at everyone around me, the fact that they were all so much older than me swiftly sinking in. Besides Mara and the girl to my right who had spun first, there was another quiet, brunette girl who sat on the couch between Adam and Logan. I had a total of three chances to land on a girl. Otherwise, I would either land back on Adam, on Logan (my heart did a summersault at the thought), the pimply redheaded boy who sat to my right, or the guy on his other side with black hair and matching black nail polish.

I sent up a quick wish to the ceiling before grabbing the bottle. I watched for what felt like endless seconds until it finally landed on the black-haired kid.

He snapped his head in my direction and locked eyes with me, the hint of a devilish grin spreading across his face.

Instantly, I felt a heavy dread crawl through my limbs. Something about the way the kid was looking at me gave me the heebie jeebies. How old was he, anyway? He looked older than sixteen.

"You coming over here or should I go over there?" he asked, his smile wicked.

"You're not kissing my sister." Adam's tone was firm.

The kid glanced up to where Adam sat on the couch. "Why wouldn't I? It's the game. It was her idea anyway."

I felt Logan's posture straighten. "Seth, knock it off."

The boy—Seth—feigned a wounded look. "What's with all of the hostility? Let her kiss me."

Logan looked at me, eyes flaring with anger. "Amelia, I'm calling it. Time to scram."

"But *Logan*," I whined.

"Amelia, I swear to God I will throw you over my shoulder and drag you up those stairs myself." His amber eyes were full of hot fury.

The tension in the room was palpable. I felt hot tears stinging in the corners of my eyes as I stood up from my spot on the floor.

"You're such a jerk!" I yelled, before running out of the room and up the stairs, slamming my bedroom door shut behind me.

# Chapter Seven

After unpacking and hanging the few outfits I'd brought up into the closet so that they wouldn't wrinkle, I left my room and went downstairs to find Adam making cocktails while Rachel organized a beautiful charcuterie board with cheese, salami, fruit and crackers.

"Yum." I smiled at them as I approached the large kitchen island. "What can I do to help?"

Adam looked up at me as he expertly poured bourbon into a mixer cup. "Can you grab the club soda out of the fridge for me, please?"

"Sure," I replied. "Rachel, do you need anything?"

She looked over at me, smiling sweetly. "No, thank you!"

I grabbed the large bottle of club soda out of the fridge and set it down on the counter next to Adam. "What are you making?" I asked, peeking inside the mixer.

"Old fashions. Want one?"

"Oh, definitely." I nodded eagerly. "Thanks. Where's Mom and Dad?"

"Mom went upstairs to change, and Dad is out on the back patio with Logan." He tilted his head toward the back door. I glanced through the windows at the back of the house to where they were sitting together at the patio table, both smiling, seemingly lost in conversation. It was heartwarming, seeing them together like that. I knew it was long overdue.

I turned my attention back to the kitchen and moved around Adam to grab six lowball glasses out of the cabinet behind him, setting them down on the counter. "Thanks," he said. "We have a couple of hours to kill before dinner. I was thinking we could play a little game of bocce ball out in the backyard."

"Sounds fun." He and my dad loved to play. Although more of a summer game, our family had started playing it in the snow a few years back. Depending on how much snow was on the ground, the balls didn't usually do a whole lot of rolling, so the aim on the throw had to be much more exact. The game was undoubtedly a lot harder and usually kicked our competitiveness into high gear. "I'm just going to run upstairs and grab my coat."

Adam was pouring the mixed cocktail into the six glasses. "Okay, see you out there."

Back up in my room, I grabbed my coat from a hanger in the closet then looked at myself in the mirror above the dresser. I frowned at my reflection, noting that I looked windswept and tired and definitely *not* cute. Not that looking cute was necessarily important—I was just with my family.

*And Logan.*

Frowning even more, I pulled my long, dark hair out of its

ponytail and finger-combed through it until it looked smoother. I pulled it back up and tied it into a fresh ponytail, and then decided to take it a step further and twist it into a bun, tucking the end back through the elastic. At least the wind wouldn't completely obliterate it now. I pinched my cheeks for good measure, hoping to simulate a natural blush, then headed back down stairs to join everyone.

As I opened the back door from the kitchen, I noticed that Adam, Rachel, and my mother had joined Logan and my father out on the patio. Rachel was setting out her cheese board while Adam handed out old fashions from a tray. Logan had gotten to his feet to give my mother another hug, and my father was beaming from the head of the table, watching us all come together.

I grabbed a drink from Adam and took a sip, feeling the burn of the bourbon as it slid down my throat. At least the liquor would help warm us up against the chill in the air. "Alright, what are the teams?" I asked.

"Rachel and I against you and Logan."

Just then I felt a warm hand cover my shoulder as a voice whispered in my ear. "We're going to kick their asses."

Goosebumps manifested all over my body as I shivered. I turned to look at Logan who was smiling down at me. All evidence of his previous discomfort with me seemed to have been forgotten, or at least he'd stuffed it deep down inside as a courtesy.

The smile he gave me now was almost paralyzing.

I did my best to return a joyful expression. "I wouldn't expect anything less." I held my glass out to clink against his in cheers as a test of the waters, and was delighted when he lifted his as well.

Adam announced that we'd play first to twelve, and then picked up the black bocce ball bag as the four of us made our way out to the snow-covered lawn, leaving my parents to spectate. Adam and Rachel took the set of dark red balls while Logan and I took the dark green ones. Rachel, who'd never played before, got first dibs at tossing the tiny pink ball, landing it about twenty feet away from where we stood.

There was about three inches of snow on the ground from the last snowfall a few weeks ago—a heavy storm that had only hit the high country—so the only mark we had was the hole the ball had made.

Logan handed me two of the heavy green balls, giving me the first turn. "Show her how it's done, Mills," he murmured. If that weren't enough to send a burst of electricity through my body, the wink he threw me certainly was.

*Mills.* I hadn't heard him call me that in a long, long time. And it felt so good to hear it. Heat rose to my face as I smiled back at him, suddenly feeling enraptured by his gaze. His black shirt made the glow of his honey eyes brighter in the bending sunlight. He was still so beautiful.

It took everything I could muster to tear my eyes away, knowing that Adam and Rachel were waiting for me to throw my turn. I turned to where Rachel had thrown the jack and tossed the first ball, landing about six inches in front of where it lay. Only the round peak of the top of the ball was showing through the snow.

"Nice," Logan encouraged from behind me, and I felt a thrill from his praise.

When I tossed my second ball and got about an inch closer, I couldn't help looking back at Logan. What I saw was something that resembled appreciation in his smile. "Your turn."

He nodded his head and stepped up to throw. With near perfect aim, he tossed both of his balls into each of mine, a soft "clink" sounding as they each made impact, pushing them closer to the jack. I would bet actual money that he'd pushed my balls against the jack in the snow, which would earn us extra points as long as Adam and Rachel weren't able to knock them all away.

"Wow," Adam said, shaking his head lightly. "Lucky first turn for both of you." He handed Rachel two of the red balls, signaling for her to throw first.

She stepped forward to throw each turn, coming up about a foot short each time. "Okay," she said, giggling. "I'm obviously not going to be good at this." She turned to look at Adam and pointed a finger in his direction. "You picked the wrong partner, babe."

Adam smiled back at her. "Oh no, you could throw your balls in the opposite direction of where we're playing and I would still pick you as my partner." She blushed at that.

He leaned down to give her a quick kiss before he stepped up to take his turn. His first ball smacked the side of one of Logan's balls, pushing it further into mine. "Damn," he let out.

"Maybe if you weren't so busy flirting, you'd be more successful," Logan chimed from where he leaned against a tree, a smirk on his face. "Then again"—he flicked his eyes to me—"Millie has us in a strong position to win. I'm not sure you'll be able to change that now."

My heart did a somersault in my chest.

"Shut up, Logan," Adam replied as he concentrated on his next throw. He swung his arm underhand and threw his second ball up into the air . . . and it landed about four inches to the left of ours. He threw his hands up in the air in defeat. "Alright, you guys had a lucky first round."

All four of us made our way over to assess, and found that Logan had indeed pushed both of my balls against the jack, earning us one extra point each. "If I have my math right, Adam, we already have six points." Logan's smug expression was contagious as I felt myself smile in response. As he passed me, whispered, "It's you and me, Mills," sending a chill along my neck where his words lingered.

I just about fainted on the spot.

As it turned out, Logan and I won the game in just four rounds. Adam and Rachel scored points in the third, but we ultimately prevailed.

It was a rush, the thrill of it. The forgetting of the past. The falling right back into place. Within hours of being here, Breckenridge had transformed the way Logan looked at me from discomfort and indifference to familiar joy and appreciation, and I could almost kiss the ground in thanks. Maybe there was hope for our friendship, after all.

My parents had ordered pizza from town, and we all gathered around the new poker table in the basement as we ate way too many slices and drank way too many cocktails. We played Texas Hold'em, blackjack, hearts, and then before I knew it my mother had pulled out the box of Cards Against Humanity.

The woodburning stove in the corner of the room—along with the continued pouring of bourbon—kept us all warm and comfortable as we spent much-needed time together as a family, often laughing so hard that we cried. Adam had even snorted his cocktail out of his nose, causing Rachel to choke on hers.

I felt more at ease than I had in months. I was in my most favorite place in the world with the people who mattered most to me, and it was all too easy to forget about life's problems. So what if I was single again, starting over with love? So what if I had to find a place to live by myself, and work through ensuring that I could manage all of the bills on my own? I had more than enough all around me, and starting over was an opportunity to create a life for myself that felt more like *this*.

We all stayed gathered in the basement together until everyone was properly drunk and exhausted from so much laughter. Adam, who'd come off of a night shift at the hospital the night before, could barely keep his eyes open as he finally stood up to say goodnight with Rachel trailing behind him. Shortly after, Logan excused himself, too.

I helped my mom clean up and put the leftover pizza away while my father added more wood to the stove, making sure the house stayed warm for us all throughout the night.

At some point, while we were all in the basement, the snow had begun falling outside. I'd noticed a flurry of white glistening through the kitchen window as I tucked the leftover food into the fridge, and immediately felt a surge of delight. Tomorrow morning we'd all wake up together under one roof just like old times, and outside would be a snowy wonderland —a perfect setting for our Thanksgiving holiday.

After kissing my parents goodnight, I headed up the stairs to my room. I grabbed my warm pajamas from the dresser and changed before heading to the bathroom with my small bag of toiletries. When I opened the bedroom door to cross the hallway to the bathroom, I noticed that Logan's door was also ajar. I could have sworn that it was closed a few minutes ago when I got up here, but I brushed off the thought as I entered the bathroom and shut the door behind me.

I washed my face and thoroughly brushed my teeth twice, not wanting to wake up in the morning with the taste of stale alcohol on my tongue. After downing a large glass of water, I headed back to my room.

The door to Logan's room was still open, and I noticed how dark it was inside. Was he asleep in there? Doubtful—I couldn't imagine him choosing to sleep with his door open. Was he somewhere else in the house?

The pull of curiosity was too strong to ignore. If he was downstairs somewhere, perhaps I could catch him alone so that I could apologize. We'd had such a great day today, and I wanted to put in the effort to keep it going. After all, what happened all those years ago wasn't his fault. I knew I needed to take responsibility and finally clear the air.

I went back into my room to grab my coat in case I found him outside. I had a feeling he'd be out there, somewhat reminiscent of how I used to find him in the middle of the night when we were younger.

I kept the lights off when I reached the bottom of the stairs and as I peered out through the glass panel of the backdoor in the kitchen, I could see Logan's dark silhouette from the same chair he'd been in earlier when he was talking with my father. The snow fell lazily around him as he sat unmoving in the night, right in front of me but also miles away.

The sight of him out there—the familiarity of it—hit me deep in my bones. He was always so carefully rooted within himself as he worked through things in his mind. He kept most of his thoughts and feelings close, only sharing what was at the surface with those around him. I yearned to go back in time, when things were so much easier between us, to be the person that he opened up to. Someone that he shared his biggest dreams and his deepest fears with.

I felt a swell in my chest, a feeling of hope that we could get close to that place again.

I walked out the back door and turned the handle before I let myself chicken out. Immediately, the cold air sent a wave of goosebumps over my skin. The heavy winds from earlier had calmed down some, but the lasting breeze was near freezing as it curled around me. I put my arms through my coat and zipped it up, grateful for the warmth it gave.

Logan didn't move as I made my way toward him. It was possible he didn't hear me come out, but more likely it was that he'd somehow known it was me, just like old times. I sat down in the chair beside him, feeling the déjà vu of a past life.

I turned to study his stoic profile; his eyes were locked on some tree or hill in the distance as snow collected in his hair. My eyes caught on a snowflake as it landed on a long eyelash. I took a deep breath before I found my voice. "Thank you."

I saw his eyebrows furrow mere millimeters as he kept his eyes focused on whatever he was looking at, keeping himself guarded. "For what?" he asked.

"For today. It was a really great day."

His eyebrows furrowed even deeper. "I didn't do anything."

I rolled my eyes. "Yes you did. You treated me . . . *normal*. I'm not sure that I deserved that, but I'm grateful for it. It was nice to feel back in that place with you."

At this, he looked at me. His face was swirled in confusion. "Why wouldn't you deserve for me to be normal around you?"

"Because . . ." I took a deep breath in pause, nervously looking down at the ground. This was my chance. My chance to come clean and make things right. "Because, I messed things up between us a long time ago. And I . . . I deeply regret it." Logan continued watching me but he didn't say anything in response. "Look, I never should have been so naive to assume I knew what your feelings were toward me back then. You're family, Logan. And I *threatened* that for you. For all of us."

This time, it was Logan who let out a long breath. "Amelia, I don't blame you for anything. I never have. You have nothing to apologize for." His amber eyes watched me carefully. Insistently.

I shook my head. "Look, I'm the reason we haven't been friends in years. I'm the reason you've been so distant. And I get it! I was reckless with my feelings and I blamed you for the inadequacy that I felt as a result. I was selfish and destructive and you never deserved any of it from me."

"Stop." Logan's command was firm, even as he kept his voice soft. "If anyone was reckless with their feelings, it was me. If anyone was selfish or destructive, Amelia, I assure you that it was me. So don't you for a *second* burden yourself with the blame of where we are now. It's not your burden to bear, I promise you that."

I stared at him for what felt like endless seconds, completely baffled by his words. Why was he trying to take responsibility for what happened? I was the one who let my feelings get in the way of our friendship. Unless . . . "Wait. Are you saying that you *did* have feelings for me back then?"

Logan turned his eyes back toward the distance. His neutral expression had changed into something more raw, but I didn't know what to make of it. I leaned back into my chair, taking all of this in. Had I actually been right all those years ago?

After so much silence that I was sure the conversation was over, I heard Logan quietly ask, "What happened between you and Noah?"

I looked back at him, seeing the firm set of his jaw as he waited for my answer. *No reason not to be honest about it*, I thought. "I came home early from a work dinner and found him cheating on me," I responded, working to keep any emotion from my tone.

His jaw flexed in response, and I could see a flash of anger in his eyes before he settled himself back into his mask of neutrality. "Hm. I never liked him."

I couldn't help but chuckle in response. "If I'm being really honest with you, I don't think I did either. Not as much as I thought I did, at least."

I saw the slightest tilt of his mouth at that before he got up out of his chair. "It's late, Mills. We should get some rest." He pressed his hand briefly to my shoulder as he turned back toward the house, and my skin immediately ignited at his touch. I heard the back door open and close as Logan retreated inside, headed off to his bed just across the hall from mine.

It was late, but there was no way I'd be getting to sleep anytime soon after that conversation. There was so much to unpack. So instead, I shifted in my chair to get more comfortable and invited the cold air to numb my wild heart.

# Chapter Eight

By ten o'clock next morning, the house was bustling with activity. We awoke to a layer of soft snow surrounding the house as the sun shone brightly through the trees and scattered clouds. Not even our moderate hangovers could dampen the mood. The weather forecast promised a substantial snow storm later in the day, due to start brewing in the early evening—although, it was hard to imagine that any sort of storm was coming with how serene the landscape looked now.

In the kitchen, my mother was putting Rachel and I to work prepping various food items that would be needed for dinner tonight while music softly played through the house's built-in surround sound speakers. My father had Adam and Logan out in the backyard helping him chop more wood to prepare for the storm later, ensuring that we'd have enough to stay warm for as long as we'd need to hunker down.

The house had a central heating and cooling system, of

course, but the wood burning stove in the basement was just as proficient in providing heat throughout the house, and in the event that the main system froze during the storm, we'd be safe.

As I worked to peel what felt like an endless amount of potatoes, I couldn't help but think about my conversation with Logan from the night before. I was thankful for the opportunity to apologize and clear the air, but I didn't anticipate him taking any sort of responsibility for what'd happened between us. It left me feeling confused.

*If anyone was selfish or destructive, Amelia, I assure you that it was me.*

My mind replayed his words over and over again, still trying to make sense of them.

"Oh my gosh," I heard Rachel mumble behind me, and when I turned to look back at her I saw that she was peering intently out of the kitchen window with her mouth hanging open.

"What is it?" I asked curiously, stepping toward her so that I could see over her shoulder. When I looked out the window, my own mouth dropped open. Logan and Adam were out there, both of them yielding axes and both of them—despite the current low-fifties temperature—without shirts on. I watched as Logan approached a log that was propped up on the knee-high wooden platform my father had built, and before I knew it he was vigorously swinging the axe above his head and slamming it down, instantly splitting it into three pieces that fell onto the ground at his feet.

*My god.*

My brother then took a turn stepping up to the platform, setting another one up on top of it to be split. He, too, swung his axe down in a very lumberjack-like way, splitting the log with ease.

"Wow," Rachel whispered, eyes locked on my brother.

Logan, again, took his turn—and I couldn't help staring at his body, at the muscles that danced within his back and chest as he moved, at the pulsing cords of his broad arms as he swung the axe down. It was unlike anything I'd ever seen.

Rachel and I both stood there at the kitchen sink, completely still and utterly transfixed, looking out the window for a solid ten minutes until I heard my mother clear her throat from behind us.

We both whipped around in mild terror. My mother stood on the other side of the island with a ruffled, pastel yellow apron on. She'd been digging for her mixer in the garage shelving and must have come back in without us realizing. We'd been completely locked under hypnosis from the lumberjack games occurring in the backyard. "Everything okay?" she asked, smiling brightly. Knowingly.

Obviously I wasn't watching my brother, so she'd definitely just caught me checking out Logan. There was no excuse that I could possibly come up with. "Yep," I answered quickly, my face feeling hot. "All good here!" I hastened back to my pile of potatoes and began fervently peeling. Rachel jumped back into place on the other side of the kitchen, chopping celery and carrots with the force of a jackhammer.

A moment later, I heard my mother open the fridge behind me. "So, Rachel," she started merrily, "how long have you been seeing Adam?"

"Oh . . . um, almost six months? We've been friends for a few years though—I met him at CSU during our pre-med program."

"You didn't date at all back then?" my mother inquired.

"No—" She paused. "I was actually seeing someone else at the time." My ears perked up slightly at this.

"Oh, to be a young girl in college," my mother mused. She'd married my father right out of high school and never had the single-girl college experience.

Rachel giggled. "I honestly wish I would have ditched who I was dating back then and gotten together with Adam a lot sooner."

"You do?"

"Absolutely. Adam is literally my dream man," she stated, "and the guy I was dating back then was a total bummer. I just, unfortunately, didn't really see it at the time."

"Amelia just broke up with a total bummer!"

I stopped peeling the potato in my hand and turned around to face them both. Rachel looked at me with a hint of sadness in her eyes. "Adam told me," she said quietly. "I'm so sorry—you definitely didn't deserve what that guy did to you."

I smiled in response. "Thanks, but I'm actually not that upset. I think it needed to happen."

Rachel nodded. "Yeah, I know what that's like. That's how I felt about my ex. I probably would have stayed with him for a long time if he hadn't broken up with me first. I don't even know why I stayed so long—he wasn't exactly the nicest guy."

I shrugged. "For me, I feel like it was comfort, more than anything. Not exactly in Noah himself, but in our routine." I looked down at the counter on the island, tracing the lines of the marble with my eyes. "Looking back, it's easier to see it for what it was. But until I'd caught him cheating, I don't know . . . I guess I felt like it was all good enough."

In the corner of the kitchen, my mother clicked her tongue.

"Good enough isn't *good enough*, sweetheart. Real love is bigger than that. You deserve a whole lot more than just 'good enough.'"

"I know, Mom," I said, hesitating. "I just thought that maybe it was me. Like, maybe I'm incapable of feeling love in a bigger way, more than what our relationship was."

My mother's features turned to concern. "Why on earth would you think that, Amelia?"

"I don't know. I've dated, I've had fun, but I've never felt all the things you read about in romance novels." *Except maybe with the shirtless lumberjack outside. But I can't have him, can I?* "Maybe it's just not in the cards for me."

Shaking her head, my mother dismissed the thought. "Nonsense. You just haven't found the right man, yet." She grabbed flour and baking powder out of the pantry. "Once you do, I assure you that you'll know. And it will feel much better than *good enough*."

"She's right, you know," Rachel said. "I know it's kind of early in our relationship, and I just met you guys so I'm sorry if this is a bit forward, but the way I feel about Adam . . . it's just like what your mom is describing. It's unreal. You'll know." She gave me a small smile and turned back to the vegetables on her area of the counter.

I caught my mother's eyes with a grin and we exchanged a knowing look. It seemed that she and my brother were definitely in love with each other.

As my mother began mixing the ingredients for a homemade pie crust, I took the chance to peek back out of the window. Logan and Adam were still out there, goofing off with each other as they laughed at something I couldn't make out. I noticed my father in the far corner of the backyard with a bundle of thick tree branches in his arms. He must have been out beyond the tree line looking for more wood while the guys chopped the bigger logs that were already collected.

I looked on as my father watched Adam and Logan with pride in his eyes, likely reminiscent of the two young boys they once were. Both of them had grown up to become kind, responsible, hard working men.

AN HOUR LATER, my brother came into the kitchen from the back door, sweaty and dirty and holding a beer. I shot him a look of feigned disdain. "Gross."

He smiled in response, and then turned his attention to Rachel. "How's everything going in here?"

Rachel blushed as she looked at his naked torso and I internally vomited. "It's going!" She smiled at him.

"Oh, shit!" my mother suddenly exclaimed.

Immediately, I turned around to find her bent at the waist as she rummaged through a pantry shelf. It wasn't like her to curse. "What is it, Mom?"

She sighed heavily as she stood up, shaking her head. "I swear I had more sugar in here. We still have so many desserts to make and I'm out of sugar!" She looked panicked.

"It's okay, Mom," Adam's baritone voice bounded from behind me. "One of us can go pick some up."

Just then, Logan opened the back door to come inside. He had his white T-shirt back on, but his face was flushed and glistening from the exertion. He took in my mother's flustered look and concern swept over his face. "What's wrong?"

Adam answered for us all. "Mom ran out of sugar, we need to go pick some up."

I saw Logan's eyes flick down to the beer in Adam's hand, no doubt calculating how many he'd already had during their outdoor activities. "I can go get some."

My heart whirred at his desire to quietly take control of the situation.

"I can go with you!" I heard the words come out of my mouth before I even realized I was saying them. As if my brain completely lapsed and my body acted out on its own.

Logan eyed me. "Sure. Okay."

I grabbed my phone from the counter to look for the nearest grocery store on my map app, finding the closest one that was open, and then went to grab my purse off the entry table near the front door. Returning back to the kitchen, I saw that Logan had put on his jacket and was taking the car keys from Adam.

"Would you mind grabbing more beer, too?" Adam asked.

Logan nodded. "Yeah, sure. Anything else?" He looked at my mother.

She shook her head as she beamed up at him. "No thank you, sweetheart. Thank you so much for doing this. I swore I had more sugar . . ." Her eyebrows drew tight as she looked back toward the pantry, no doubt contemplating how she could have been wrong.

He smiled back at her and the sight of it stirred something deep in my belly. "It's no problem at all." His golden eyes found mine. "Ready?"

I nodded, pulling my purse onto my shoulder.

"Be careful out there," my mother warned. "That storm will come in quick."

"Yes, ma'am," Logan answered.

I walked through the front door and was struck by the mild

warmth of the sun and the brisk, chilly breeze. I realized distantly that I'd forgotten my coat on the hook by the back door, but the effort to go back and get it didn't seem important. Not when Logan was stretching his arm out in front of me to open the passenger side door of Adam's BMW, looking down at me with amusement in his eyes as I got in and sat down.

He shut the door after I was fully in, and then rounded the front of the car to let himself in on the other side.

I pulled up my map app again, confirming the route to the store. "It looks like it's just about two miles down the main road in town."

Logan nodded and shifted the car into gear.

The first four minutes of the ride were silent as Logan kept his focus on the road. I was attempting to hide the fact that I was cold, bouncing my legs up and down to both create some movement in my body for warmth as well as to alleviate some of the mild anxiety I was feeling about being alone in the car with him.

"So," I said, cutting through the silence, "turns out you're a bit of a lumberjack." I kept my eyes on the windshield but felt his focus shift to me.

"You saw that?"

I turned to him, smirking. "Yes, I definitely saw that."

He looked back at the road, a hint of a smile on his lips. "Your father had us out there earning our Thanksgiving meal tonight."

"And did you?"

Logan's smile grew. "What do you think, Mills? Did I?"

I felt my heart pound wildly, but I kept my face controlled. "I'd say so."

A flash of white teeth and crinkling eyes, it felt like the first genuine smile I'd been able to pull out of him in . . . *years*.

At the store, Logan told me to hang tight before getting out of the car and jogging back to my side to open the door for me.

"And they say chivalry is dead," I teased.

He rolled his eyes at that.

We walked through the automatic doors of the store where cold air blasted from the ceiling, and a shiver rattled through me.

"Are you cold?" Logan eyed the goosebumps on my arms and was already taking off his jacket.

"I'm okay," I responded, but it was useless. He was holding open his jacket for me to put on, the decision to give it to me already made, so I reached my arms through the sleeves and relished in the warmth from his body heat.

And the smell of him. All over me, now.

"Thank you."

He took lead as we walked through the store, looking for the baking aisle where sugar would be. Something about his confidence as he navigated through a grocery store, like he wasn't a man above such an activity, had me feeling like I was walking on the thinnest edge of a tightrope.

We eyed the sugar options for a moment before I grabbed a couple bags of the generic brand. "This should be fine."

Logan nodded once. "Looks good to me." He took the bags out of my hands to carry them himself before moving to the line of fridges in the back of the store where the beer was. I trailed closely behind him, and as we approached the fridge that held Adam's favorite brand, Logan casually stacked both bags of sugar into his left hand and then used his right hand to open the glass door and grab the cardboard handle of a full case.

"I can help carry something," I said, reaching out to take the sugar back.

Logan steered the sugar away from my reach and shook his head. "Nah." He winked, and then effortlessly pulled a case of beer out of the fridge, as if it were as light as a pillow.

"Show off," I muttered. I heard his low chuckle deep in my chest.

We took our items to a cashier in the front of the store to pay—Logan somehow pulling his wallet out faster than me despite my hands being empty—before we walked back out into the cold. The wind had picked up considerably in the ten or so minutes that we'd been inside, and what was left of the leaves on the trees around the parking lot cascaded down to the ground in angry flurries.

Logan again opened my door for me and waited for me to get situated in my seat, shutting the door behind me and jamming the groceries in the trunk before getting in on the other side. "Good thing we got to the store when we did. The clouds are looking pretty damn angry over there—" He pointed to where the sky was dark and ominous to the north of us, a total juxtaposition from the bright, blue sky directly above us.

I pulled Logan's jacket tighter around me. "Good thing we weren't planning on leaving Breckenridge tonight."

Logan nodded in agreement.

"And also," I added, because I was clearly already on a roll, "please consider me eternally grateful for your morning lumberjack games. The fire in the stove tonight will be stocked solid."

He shot a look my way before shaking his head. "You are such a wise ass, you know that?" he said, putting the car into gear.

I smiled brightly as I kicked my feet up onto the dash.

After a few moments, Logan cleared his throat and I looked over to find him watching me. "This is nice, you know," he said, quickly looking back at the road before finding my eyes again. "I've missed you, Mills."

And just like that, my heart was soaring.

# Chapter Nine



THE SMELL OF BURGERS AND BACON FROM THE GRILL wafted into the house along with the fresh chill of autumn as my father came in through the back door. He was wearing a black apron with the words "Kiss the Chef!" emblazoned across the front in bold, white lettering. Ironic, since he was the one who kissed the top of my mother's head as he passed us all sitting in the family room.

It was Labor Day weekend, and Adam was home from campus where he'd been living in his own studio apartment. Logan, who'd earned his Associate's degree in business at the local community college and was taking a break from school to commit to a full-time job at a mechanic shop, had taken the long weekend off to spend time at the house while Adam was in town. Both boys were lounging on the large sectional, watching the first week of college football games.

Since graduating high school a couple of years ago, they'd

developed lives beyond the ties of this family and little town outside of Denver. Adam was taking pre-med college courses at CSU's main campus an hour north of here, and Logan had been working hard on his dreams of owning his own shop. In the last two years, I'd begun to feel the loss of them as they'd made new friends, dated various girls, and spent more and more time away from here.

Without fail, though, they'd always made it a priority to come back home, usually coinciding their visits with each other so that we could all be together as family. This holiday weekend was no exception, and it felt so good to see them both sprawled out on the couch.

I missed them.

My mother and I sat on the opposite side of the large sectional with my laptop, looking through an online catalog of semi-formal dresses that I could potentially wear to my homecoming dance.

"Oh honey, this one is beautiful," she said, pointing to a sleeveless pink dress with a sweetheart neckline. The hem of the dress was above the knee in the front and cascaded down to the floor in the back.

"It's a little . . . *girly*." I winced. A little too princess, which I certainly was not.

"Okay, what about this one," she asked, pointing to a slinkier dark purple dress that was less frilly and more sophisticated. "Better, for sure. But still not convinced it's the one."

"Who are you going with to that thing, anyway?" Adam asked, keeping his eyes on the game.

"Paul," I responded casually.

I felt Logan glance at me. "Who's Paul?"

I looked up to meet his gaze. "Just a guy I've been kind of

seeing." He frowned, keeping his eyes on mine for a long moment before he turned his attention back to the television.

Adam chimed back in, "You're a little young, aren't you?"

"I'm sixteen! You guys were dating girls at my age."

"Yeah but it's . . . not the same," Adam retorted.

"How is it possibly not the same?" I asked incredulously. If either one of them said it was because I was a girl I was going to sucker punch them both in the gut. Adam didn't respond, and Logan kept his eyes locked on the game. I didn't miss the clench of his jaw.

I rolled my eyes as I stood up, closing my laptop. "I'm going to go see if Dad needs any help," I announced as I made my way toward the kitchen. I found him standing at the sink, washing the platter that he'd used to carry the raw burgers out to the grill. "Hey Dad, need any help with dinner?"

He glanced over at me, eyes always full of warmth. "Thanks, sweetheart," he replied. "Trying to spend some time with your old man?" He threw me a sly grin.

"Yeah, that," I responded, "and the boys are being asshats."

My father chuckled. "Well, in that case, I could use an extra hand to prepare the lettuce and tomatoes for the burgers."

"Done!" I moved to the refrigerator and grabbed everything out from the drawer. My dad handed me a long knife and a cutting board, and I got to work on slicing the tomatoes.

"So," my dad started, "what earned Adam and Logan the prestigious title of 'asshats'?"

I sighed. "Adam asked who I was going to homecoming with, and they didn't seem to like the fact that I have a date. But both of them had plenty of girlfriends in high school . . . and Paul isn't even technically my boyfriend."

"He's not?" My father's eyes were genuinely curious.

"No, he's just a friend. Mackenzie is dating Paul's best friend, so it made sense for us to pair up and go together with them to the dance. We've all hung out as a group a few times, and I could see it maybe turning into something more, but . . ." I trailed off.

The truth was that I felt completely unsure of myself in the arena of dating. My best friend, Mackenzie, had been dating Eric since the end of sophomore year. I'd been a firsthand witness to their relationship as it naturally and effortlessly blossomed from friendship, to liking each other, to deciding that they were exclusive by the end of summer break. Mackenzie wanted to make sure that when junior year started, everyone knew that Eric was hers. Eric didn't seem to mind—it was obvious that he was really into her, too.

The ease of their relationship perplexed me. I didn't understand how they fell so easily into coupledom, when I still felt like boys were a foreign language. I asked Mackenzie one night during a sleepover at her house, as we lay wide awake together in her room.

"How did you know that you really liked Eric?" I asked.

Even in the darkness, I could feel the smile that grew on her face. "He brought me a first edition of Alice and Wonderland."

I scrunched my eyebrows. "What?"

"During English class last year, we were discussing our favorite childhood stories, and I said that mine was Alice in Wonderland. Something about the story felt so . . . freeing. Like you can go anywhere you want to, experience legitimate magic, and all you have to do is go to sleep and dream. I've always loved that idea.

"Anyway, Eric was in that class and must have remembered,

because at the beginning of summer break he showed up at my house with a first edition for me. We'd only been dating for a few weeks. His mother owns a used bookstore, and I guess he found it there. And he remembered. And it just felt like . . . like a good thing. You know?"

Silence wrapped around us as I contemplated that. The idea that maybe love wasn't some big, giant trust dive off of a cliff. Maybe it was rooted inside of a collection of smaller moments. A culmination of meaningful encounters and thoughtful experiences that created the foundation for something more.

I'd eventually met Paul through Eric, and the four of us went out on a couple of group outings like to the bowling alley, the arcade, and once we'd even caught a double-feature night at the drive-ins. That had been fairly awkward, as Mackenzie and Eric made out on Eric's tailgate while Paul and I sat in folding chairs six feet away, pretending not to notice.

I wanted to like Paul. I even felt like I *could* like Paul. He was the first boy I ever considered for something like that. But I kept waiting for the moment that Mackenzie said she felt with Eric . . . when it felt like a good thing. When I felt something truly meaningful.

And that's where I was now. Still waiting. Sixteen years old, and I've never so much as held someone's hand. Never been kissed.

As I moved the sliced tomatoes to a plate, I heard my dad take a deep breath behind me. "Amelia, you're growing up right before our very eyes. And you're a smart, beautiful, tenacious young lady. Don't rush into the world of boys if you don't have a good reason to. Take your time, and make sure that any boy you do decide to let into your heart is worth the effort.

"Adam and Logan know from their own experiences that most boys your age don't have the best of intentions. Hell, they didn't always have the best of intentions themselves when they were your age. And I know they just want to protect you."

Just as my dad finished talking, Logan walked into the kitchen. He paused when he saw us, likely realizing he'd interrupted something. "Sorry, I was just seeing if there was anything I could help with . . ." He looked back and forth between my father and I.

"Sure, son. Let's go check on those burgers." He picked up a pack of sliced cheese off the counter and joined Logan at the back door.

I watched him and Logan through the kitchen window, poking and prodding at the burgers and bacon on the grill, working together to get dinner ready for all of us, as I contemplated my father's words.

A HALF HOUR LATER, we were all seated around our dining room table. As we ate our delicious bacon cheeseburgers, I kept catching Logan looking at me with an odd expression. I thought that maybe I had something on my face or a piece of bacon lodged between my teeth, but after excusing myself to use the restroom, I couldn't find anything amiss.

When I returned to the table, I again felt his eyes on me from across the table. Glancing up at him, our eyes locked on each other before Logan broke the connection, reverting his eyes back to the plate in front of him as he took a big bite out of his food.

Adam didn't seem to notice how quiet he'd been all night, and as he went on and on with stories about his life at college, I could tell that Logan wasn't listening to a single word.

During a rare break from my brother's yapping, my mom took an opportunity to bring Logan into the conversation. "What about you, Logan? How are things going for you? Are you still seeing Stephanie?"

I had to forcibly stop myself from rolling my eyes at her name. Logan had met Stephanie in one of his classes and had been dating her for the last six months or so. I'd met her a couple of times when he'd brought her to the house, and even did my best to be welcoming after realizing that it must have been serious if she was meeting our family.

It wasn't easy though. From the get-go, I knew Stephanie was everything *not* to like about college girls. She was vain, selfish, and didn't seem to have a grasp on the complexities of real life. It was as if she were incapable of doing anything for herself that didn't involve posting to Instagram, and I didn't like how Logan enabled her helplessness by doing everything for her.

He'd made her plate at dinner ("only a little bit, please — I need to lose, like, five pounds before the pool party next week"), refilled the diet soda that she kept slurping down through a pink straw that she'd pulled out of her purse ("soda is, like, *so* terrible for your teeth and makes them turn yellow, so I *only* drink it with a straw"), and helped my parents clean up after dinner while she sat on the couch and scrolled through her social media feed.

Needless to say, I didn't understand what he possibly saw in her.

"Uh, no, actually," Logan responded. "We broke up about three weeks ago."

"Oh, goodness!" My mother put her cheeseburger down and rested her wrists against the table, giving him her full attention. "I'm so sorry, Logan."

Logan shrugged. "It's okay. It's really not that big of a deal."

Adam studied Logan, a perplexed look on his face. "You didn't tell me that you guys broke up."

Logan looked back at him. "You didn't ask."

Adam's eyebrows scrunched.

Logan's eyes landed back on me. A look passed over his face, one that I didn't recognize. Like he was waiting for something. Something from *me*.

"You deserve better, anyway," I said softly. "You deserve much better." I noted the slight tilt of Logan's head at my words. As if he was considering them, flipping them around in his mind to explore them from every direction.

I kept my eyes on his, willing him to understand that he deserved the best type of girl. Someone who really knew how to see him. And who didn't take advantage of his kindness.

Suddenly, my mind was transported back in time to the young boy that he'd once been, when I'd found him out in the cold in the middle of the night. That boy—he deserved to know real, true, aching love.

My father cleared his throat, snapping my focus back to the table. I looked around at everyone's plates and saw they'd been basically licked clean. Standing up, I began collecting all of the dishes, feeling a strong need to distance myself from the moment and the memories inside of my head.

As I turned the faucet on at the sink and poured soap onto the sponge, I sensed someone walk into the kitchen behind me. Judging from the overt awareness that prickled throughout my body, I knew who it was before he even spoke.

"Mind if I help you?" Logan's voice was low.

I turned to look at him over my shoulder. I heard Adam roll into another college story from the dining room, still having an audience at the table with my parents. "Sure," I responded, turning back to the dishes in front of me.

I began washing the plates, using the sponge to scrub away any remaining food, and then handed them to Logan who rinsed them on the other side of the sink and then set them into the drying rack. We worked together silently, yet comfortably—catching an easy groove together.

"How do you figure?" Logan abruptly asked, taking a plate full of soapy suds out of my hands and holding it under the running water.

I looked up at him, taking in the glow of his profile in the light of the kitchen window. The sun was setting outside, its dusty rays showering warm light upon us. "What do you mean?" I asked, not understanding the question.

"That I deserve better. How do you figure?"

"Oh." I looked back down at the soapy water on my side of the sink, reaching down and wrapping my fingers around a fork. I took in a breath before answering. "Stephanie was . . . selfish. She didn't seem to care about anything but herself. And you . . . you deserve someone who really cares about *you*. Someone who sees how good you are, and who makes you feel something meaningful."

I felt Logan's eyes on me, but I kept my focus on the sink in front of me, suddenly feeling embarrassed. Logan stayed still next to me, seemingly frozen in place, for what felt like an eternity. I finally looked back up at him, finding his honey-colored eyes. "What?" I asked, feeling my face growing red from blushing.

A large smile bloomed on his face, and I felt something small ignite in my chest. A whisper of a spark. The quick surge of a current. It was a rare, unfiltered expression of emotion—something Logan did so rarely. He was always rather guarded in sharing his feelings, preferring to keep interactions with people as light and airy as possible. But this smile— It was raw. Genuine. And it suited him.

"Is that how you feel about . . . Paul, is it?" He looked back down at the running water.

I hesitated for a moment before answering. "Yes, his name is Paul. But . . . no. I haven't felt anything meaningful . . . not yet." I found myself needing to quickly add, "With Paul, anyway."

"Mm . . ." Logan hummed.

He stayed quiet after that, finishing with the dishes that I handed over to him until everything was cleared out and cleaned up. He even went as far as wiping down the kitchen counters with meticulous scrutiny. As I leaned against the fridge and watched him, I realized—whether he knew it or not—that he was doing what he could to extend this moment, not wanting either of us to leave the bubble we'd inadvertently created inside of the kitchen.

I found myself needing to say something else, to get it out before we weren't alone anymore.

"You know I'm still always here for you, right?" I asked.

I watched as his hands froze in front of him as he rinsed the sponge before he turned the faucet off, grabbed the towel that was hanging from the stove handle, and then turned to face me as he dried himself off.

He grinned, although I could tell he was back to his more controlled mask of indifference.

"I know, Mills," he stated, as if nothing else was ever considered. And then he winked at me before heading back into the dining room to rejoin the others. Leaving me to grapple with the churning inside of my heart.

# Chapter Ten

As was tradition in our family, my mother showcased the beautiful, roasted turkey in the middle of the kitchen island as the whole family gathered around to watch my father carve it, turning the chore into quite the production. Rachel and I had been helping my mother in the kitchen, and I was positively starving after being around the aromatic food all day.

The second that my father made the first cut into the juicy, roasted turkey, the family erupted into joyful cheers and clinked our various glasses of whiskey, wine, and in my brother's case, a newly opened can of beer. I felt my cheeks strain as I smiled widely, feeling incredibly content in this moment.

It was still very early in the evening, but the house was darker than usual from the heavy clouds that came in about an hour ago, making it feel much later than it was. We could hear the house creak and moan as the wind outside gained speed, promising the arrival of a very active storm.

Rachel tucked herself beside Adam, wrapping her small arm around his waist, and I saw them briefly look at each other with so much tender appreciation. I found my mother watching Dad with adoration in her eyes as he cut through the turkey she'd worked so hard on.

My eyes flitted to Logan next, standing there across the island, and for what felt like the hundredth time today, I saw that he was watching me. I didn't miss the way his eyes all but lit up, like a golden spark flashing within those rich, amber hues.

I felt a burst of longing ignite inside of me, suddenly desperate to move closer to him, to tuck myself into him as Rachel did with Adam. But I held my position, knowing that our recent truce could only exist if I stayed firm in the boundaries that I'd foolishly disregarded so long ago. Since being in Breckenridge, I could feel the budding possibility of a genuine friendship again, and I couldn't—wouldn't—do anything to risk that.

I tore my eyes away from him and focused back on the beautiful turkey. When my father had finished cutting the meat and expertly presenting it on a platter, we all grabbed plates and began loading them with the feast before us.

Logan came around the island on the hunt for the loaded mashed potatoes that were in front of me, and I felt his arm brush against mine as he reached for them. The deep stirring in my belly at the feeling of him so near me was a glaring indication that I needed to reestablish my own internal boundaries.

*Rule number one, keep at least three feet between us at all times.*

I took a few steps away from him, busying myself with adding creamed corn and glazed ham to my plate, when I felt him coming near me again. I moved swiftly down the island, building my plate full of food, before I grabbed my glass of wine and headed into the dining room.

My father followed behind me, settling in his seat at the head of the table to my left. "You must be hungry, Amelia. I've never seen you move so quickly to sit down!"

I gulped down a large sip of wine in response. My mother walked in a moment later and placed herself at the opposite end of the table from my father, smiling appreciatively at our full plates of food. Adam and Rachel moseyed in not long after, sitting next to each other across from me, which meant . . .

Logan came around the corner, eyeing the open chair next to me. *So much for three feet.*

He pulled his chair out and sat down, and I swore I heard him hum in approval before my father cleared his throat to get everyone's attention.

"It has been some time since the whole family was here together," he started, looking toward Logan with a twinkle in his eye, "and I feel overwhelmingly grateful to have you all at this table."

"Oh, Richard," my mother whispered to herself, already dapping her napkin to her eye.

"I know this isn't something we normally do, but I would like to borrow the Thanksgiving tradition of going around the table to give thanks for something meaningful to you. Adam, you start."

Adam dipped his head before he looked at Rachel. "I'm thankful for her," he said. And that was it. He didn't say anything else, and I felt such joy for my brother at that moment.

Rachel, who was positively beaming as she looked back at him, spoke next. "I'm so thankful to be here with you all, now having met Adam's wonderful family. He's such a good man, and I can see where he gets it from," she said.

My mother dabbed at her eyes again. "Oh goodness, you kids. It simply means the world to us that we can keep getting together like this. I'm so proud of you all, and so thankful that you are all such strong, happy adults." She looked at Logan as she finished speaking, smiling brightly at him.

Logan looked around the room at everyone before he started speaking. "I know I've been really busy these last couple of years, and I regret not being around last year. But please know that I am thankful every *single* day for all of you." He cleared his throat. "I'm not sure I would be here today if it weren't for your continuous love and support. So, thank you."

"Oh, Logan!" My mother burst into tears as she grabbed his hand. "You are such a blessing to us."

I felt my own eyes burn with the tears that were forming, but I quickly shoved the emotion down just as everyone turned in my direction for my turn to give thanks. "Um," I started, looking down at my napkin as a swirling mix of nerves came over me. I looked at Adam. "I'm thankful for my family who lets me mildly fall apart so that I can build myself back up." I quickly glanced at Logan before looking back down at my napkin. "And . . . I'm thankful for new beginnings."

I heard my father clap his hands together, prompting me to look back up. "That was very inspired. Thank you everyone." He looked down at his plate. "Now, let's eat!" The clinking of utensils on plates took up space as we all quieted to shovel the amazing food into our mouths. Besides the occasional hum of appreciation, no one spoke again for several minutes.

Eventually, my father began asking Rachel questions about her work with medical device modeling, which led to further discussion about hospital-related qualms. Next to me, Logan was talking to my mother about his auto shop and the hurdles he'd had to overcome over the last year as a new business owner. As I listened in, something that he said caught my attention.

"I have a really strong team and we do great work. I'm so proud of all the business that we've continued to bring in. But I do sometimes worry about the future and making sure that I can keep us all consistently busy. I'm trying to figure out how to get a website built, but I'm not very techy so I keep putting it off."

"I can help with that," I heard myself chime in. For the second time today my mouth acted completely on its own, as if disconnected from my brain, to volunteer myself up to Logan.

Logan turned his head and in some fleeting surge of magic, the sun broke out through the clouds at a near-perfect angle, casting a warm ray of light through the window and over his face. In the glow, his eyes became a pure gold fantasy, and for a moment I was completely transfixed.

*Rule number two, don't look him directly in the eye for more than a quick, sheepish second.*

"I . . . um . . ." I continued, "I can build websites. And I can help with any other general marketing things you might need, like social media, or email campaigns . . ."

"That's right," Logan interjected with a slight smile. "I forgot you were at a marketing firm."

"Actually," I corrected, "I left the firm almost a year ago and started my own business as a freelance marketing consultant." I could see Logan's smile growing. "I specifically work to help smaller businesses get their digital foundations built—so I could help you." I felt a twinge of embarrassment. "If you want me to, that is," I amended.

Logan nodded, still smiling wide. "Absolutely, Millie. That would be amazing. I would love your help. Thank you."

"Cool," I said, before refocusing on the plate in front of me. God, why was I *so* awkward?

*Rule number three, just be quiet.*

AFTER OUR PLATES were empty and our bellies full, my mother disappeared into the kitchen to grab the assortment of desserts she'd made. There was a decadent pumpkin cheesecake, a pecan pie, and a large bowl of bread pudding.

We all dove into the desserts, unable to resist my mother's famous recipes. Cheesecake was one of my most favorite things in the entire world and I wasn't ashamed to admit that I ate the majority of what was now missing from the dish.

After dessert, we all busied ourselves with cleaning up. My father and Adam went to check on the stove in the basement to see if it needed more wood. The storm was now fully upon us with snow coming down in heavy clumps. Rachel and my mother transferred food into containers to put into the fridge, and I began working at the kitchen sink. After a few moments, Logan saddled up beside me, pushing his sleeves up along his corded arms.

"Mind if I help you, here?"

"Sure," I answered, giving him a small smile. "Just like old times, huh?"

His returning grin held a hint of surprise, as if he too were thinking of the same memory but didn't expect me to remember. "Yeah." His voice was deep and low. "We have a lot of those, Mills."

The kitchen suddenly felt too warm. I pulled at the neck of my sweater, spreading a stream of soap along my neck.

"Are you okay?" Logan asked as he followed the movement of my hand.

"Yeah, just a little hot."

I watched as his grin grew.

*Great.* Probably not the safest choice of words. Feeling self-conscious, I picked up a dirty plate and began scrubbing, ignoring the flush that I felt in my cheeks. As I cleaned each dish, I handed them over to Logan to rinse and dry, unintentionally noticing the many calluses that riddled his fingers. It made sense that he would have them knowing he worked with his hands at the auto shop.

I felt myself blush again as I thought of what else he could do with his hands, before I was completely startled from my brother's booming voice behind us.

"Dude, they have you in here washing dishes?"

I turned and threw my brother a pointed look. "No one asked him. He's *actually* helpful in the kitchen—unlike you."

I heard Logan chuckle beside me as Rachel giggled from the other side of the kitchen's island where she was packing up the turkey meat. "She has a point, babe."

Adam swiftly smiled in her direction. "Alright, alright. Do you need help with anything, love?"

I looked at Logan and rolled my eyes, making him chuckle again.

"He is so whipped," Logan whispered playfully.

Now it was me who was giggling as I gently pushed my hip into his in response. I felt him look down at me, but I kept my focus on the large glass bowl in my hands that was slippery with suds. It was the last of the dirty dishes, and it was heavy. I was scared I was going to drop it, so I kept holding it with both hands as I handed it over to Logan.

He reached over to take it from me, his hands wrapping around mine over the bowl.

I gasped, quietly enough that Adam and Rachel didn't notice, thank god. Logan's face held an expression of thoughtful intrigue, and for a long moment, I was helplessly locked within his burning stare.

We both looked away, busying ourselves with mundane tasks and working silently side by side for a few more minutes.

"I should probably call and check in on my dog," Logan announced rather loudly as he felt for his phone in his pocket, "my neighbor has him right now. Won't take long."

"You have a dog?" I asked, surprised.

"Yep."

"Since when?"

"Since a year ago, when I rescued him," he explained, his voice full of pride.

"Oh, that's very sweet, Logan," my mother said as she put the leftover pie into the fridge.

"Hook is, like, the coolest dog I've ever met," Adam interjected from where he stood next to Rachel.

*Hook.* That was an odd name. "I'll be right back," Logan said before walking toward the formal living room to make his phone call.

As I watched him leave, I let my mind wander. I had no doubts that we'd just shared another unspoken moment, an old and familiar spark that, until last night, I assumed was something I'd possibly fabricated. But now, if Logan's words last night were true, that spark was something that we *both* felt.

Another thought prickled my mind—hearing that Logan had a dog was a stark reminder that there was so much about his current life that I didn't know about. Adam had known, which was proof that it wasn't something Logan had kept private from the family.

It was such a small thing for my mind to be this stuck on, but it still somehow felt monumental. I wanted to reconnect with Logan, to rebuild our friendship and get back to a place where I was more involved in his life. But . . . What if we were meant for more? I couldn't help thinking that maybe we actually *did* have a chance at this back then, and in my chaos I'd ripped that away from us, too. Was it all too late?

# Chapter Eleven

The storm was in the peak of its fury, dumping snow in turbulent gusts all around the house. The walls whined against the high winds that raged against everything in its path, causing creaks and thumps from all directions. Everyone had gone up to their respective bedrooms for the night a few hours ago, drunk and merry and full of the incredible food we'd continued to graze on all night.

Despite the late night hour and the darkness that covered the house like a warm blanket, I couldn't seem to get my brain to quiet. I felt restless, incapable of keeping myself still. Since arriving in Breckenridge yesterday afternoon, it had felt like I'd been thrown right back into Logan's magnetic orbit—I was struggling with the influx of old emotions and feelings that it entailed, like reopened wounds that were never left alone long enough in the first place to fully heal.

As I sat in the dark kitchen on the island bench, sipping on a glass of red wine, my mind whirled with the flashes of replayed scenes from the last couple of days. Logan's wickedly engulfing smirk during the bocce ball game. His eagerness to take responsibility during my fumbled apology. The way I caught his eyes on me today, feeling *seen* by him again. The feel of his skin against me as his hand brushed mine at the kitchen sink.

I was admittedly in a dangerous headspace that resembled the turmoil of a younger Amelia. I wasn't even sure why I allowed myself to be surprised by these feelings. This was the way it was between us, and it had been for as long as I could remember. I would forever be ensnared by Logan's smile, forever enslaved to his eyes of honey, like a gnat trapped within the sticky, sweet nectar.

Sometime tomorrow, Adam would drive us back to the city where we'd resume our normal lives. Logan would no doubt slip back into the version of himself that pretended this thing between us didn't exist, and I'd slip back into nagging self-doubt and desperation for more of him. I'd already felt the scarred edges of my heart begin to flare in anticipation of the let down, knowing that it was all inevitable.

His words from last night continued to replay in my mind as I took another large gulp of wine. I needed to get ahead of the disappointment. I wasn't that young, naive girl anymore. Knowing the quiet rejection was coming should count for something, right? It was a cycle that I was all-too familiar with.

I felt something drip on my arm, and when I looked down I realized that I was crying. Hot tears slid down my face as my head tilted, and more tears fell into my lap.

*Get a grip, Amelia.*

I picked the wine glass up off the counter and downed the rest of the cabernet before I stood, grabbed my coat from the hook on the wall near the back door and opened the door to slip outside.

Within seconds, the freezing cold air numbed my face. My hair whipped around and thrashed at me, but I welcomed the external chaos as a distraction from the chaos simultaneously occurring within my heart. I had hoped the raging snow storm would help to numb me enough that I could get some sleep, but the wild beauty of it so accurately mirrored the way that I was feeling that it became even harder to escape.

The truth of it all felt like a ticking time bomb. I was in love with Logan, and if I was being honest with myself, I could admit that I'd been in love with him for a very long time.

I'd spent so much time and effort attempting to shove that love down. Over the years, he'd made it clear that even if he shared my feelings, it wasn't enough for him to pursue it. And rightfully so—Logan was *family,* and I could never, ever allow my feelings for him to jeopardize his place here with us. It was a dangerous line to cross and I fully respected his hesitation, if my suspicions were right and that was what it had been about. He didn't have anyone else apart from us.

Or maybe he did. It had been years since I was close to him. Perhaps there was a girl at home that was important to him that I simply didn't know about. He never shared the details of his dating life with me, but I'd figured that was out of respect. Or maybe pity. Either way, he would have thought he was doing the right thing by keeping me out of the loop. God knew he didn't owe me an explanation. Besides a few stolen glances and our hands brushing against each other, it wasn't like he'd led me on.

I felt my mind get stuck there. Because as much as I tried to convince myself that he didn't contribute to the way he made me feel, my heart flared up in response as if to scream at me: *YES, AMELIA—YES HE DOES!*

*If anyone was selfish or destructive, Amelia, I assure you that it was me.*

My god, what did that actually mean? Therein lied the worst part of this whole love-me, love-me-not catastrophe forever brewing within my heart. The not knowing. The hidden meanings. The answers that weren't ever quite there. The obscurity of trying to see the truth so delicately hidden in the shadows of the night.

I felt more tears slide down my cheeks as I shook my head. My hands were frozen and I could no longer feel my fingers. This was ridiculous—I was standing outside in the middle of a blizzard having a complete breakdown over a man's potential (or lack of) feelings for me. A breakdown that I'd had before, for the same damn man. So many times.

I took a deep, cleansing breath, knowing that I needed to get myself together. Tomorrow, we'd head back to the city and I could focus my energy on finding a new apartment. I could throw myself back into work and my clients, and do what I'd learned how to do best.

Forget Logan Davis.

I turned on my heels back toward the house and almost jumped out of my now frozen skin when I saw Logan standing at the door, staring at me. I must not have heard him come outside through the whipping of the wind. He was wearing a T-shirt and sweatpants and didn't have a coat on. He didn't even have shoes on.

I saw that his hands were clenched into fists at his sides as he looked at me so intently, so earnestly, that I felt my mouth fall open in response. I paused to wait for whatever it was that he'd come out here to say because it looked like it was going to burst out of him.

We stood there like that, staring at each other across the back patio, for what felt like forever before he finally made a move, taking a hesitant step my way. And then he took another one. Our eyes remained locked on each other as he continued to move his feet to where I stood.

When he finally reached me, his tall frame towering over me as he peered down at my face—his eyes flitting from my eyes, my cheeks, my mouth, and back to my eyes again—he lifted his hand to wipe a tear away from my cheek with his thumb as his palm cupped my jaw. His hand was full of warmth that my skin so desperately craved and as the snow blew around us and the wind tore in between our bodies, we both stood still within the madness. I held my breath in beautiful anguish beneath his touch.

The look on his face spoke the affirmations and declarations that his mouth seemingly could not, and I saw *everything*. It confirmed what I'd been searching for, everything I'd been missing from him for so long.

This was real.

I sighed, leaning my face further into his palm, feeling the weight of impending heartbreak dissipate like steam. Logan reached his other hand up to tuck a strand of wild, wind-blown hair behind my ear, and then he held my gaze as if I were the only other person to ever exist in the world before his mouth *finally* found mine.

At first, the kiss was deliciously slow. Our mouths opened easily as we breathed each other in. I slid my hands around his waist, tucking my arms beneath his as he continued to hold my face in his hands. His lips tasted like cinnamon and whiskey as they pressed against mine.

I felt his right hand lightly slide from my face to the back of my head, his fingers intertwining with my hair as his tongue pressed past my lips and explored the inside of my mouth. I couldn't help the small moan that escaped me.

The sound of it seemed to ignite Logan as he pressed my face against his, deepening the kiss, while his other hand slid down my back and pressed me firmly into him, leaving no space between our bodies.

Goosebumps exploded over every inch of my skin, and I knew with certainty that it wasn't from the cold. His touch fanned the flames of my fire in a heated fury. I wrapped my arms around his neck and pressed my tongue against his, feeling his breath catch.

His broad arms reached down as his hands slid around the backs of my thighs and before I knew it, he was hoisting me up. My legs wrapped around his waist as he held me to him and I relished the angles that this new height gave me.

I wrapped my fingers through his hair as I became aware that we were now inside the kitchen, my empty wine glass left abandoned on the counter. Still, I couldn't focus on anything except for his mouth on mine. He set me down on the nearest surface and his hands immediately roamed my body, something I could barely feel through my thick coat.

I gently pushed against his chest to separate our mouths, feeling the torturous loss of his lips against mine. I quickly unzipped my coat and threw it on the floor, not taking any notice of where it landed.

"Amelia," he breathed, looking at my mouth. Like he simply needed to get back to it or he would die. The hunger that poured out of him unlocked something feral inside of me.

Using my legs still wrapped around him to pull him back against me, I curled my arms around his neck as his lips came crashing back down on mine. I felt him lightly thrust his hips, pressing his groin against me while his tongue flicked against my own.

His breathing became rapid and I could tell that he was beginning to lose control. We became nothing more than mouths and limbs and need and lust as we pressed against each other with fury, but it wasn't enough to satisfy the deep hunger that had been left unclaimed for far too long. My body was pure flame beneath his touch, as if he were the sun and I was burning against him. Burning for him.

Suddenly, we were moving again. Logan was carefully carrying me up the stairs, maintaining our fervent kiss as his mouth took control of mine. When we reached the top of the stairs, he pressed my back against the wall in the hallway and again thrust his hips into mine, more urgently this time. The low grunt that came out of him sent tingles down my spine.

Another moan escaped from within me, and Logan bit my lip to shush me. His mouth moved across my jaw and down my neck as he thrust the large bulge of his groin against me once more before moving us down the hall. When we reached the end of the hallway, he pushed open the door to his bedroom and used one hand to close it behind us.

He set me back down onto my feet and I was immediately reaching to pull his T-shirt over his head.

I took a step backward, wanting to see all of him in the frame of my vision. The sharp corner of his jaw as it rolled. The way his collar bone tilted from his erratic breathing. The jutting lines beneath his stomach, disappearing into the hemline of his jeans that hung low on his hips. I'd seen him without a shirt on before, of course, but never like this.

He was the most beautiful man I'd ever seen. I relished in the tortured intimacy of it. The way he swallowed, twice, as I unfastened the top button of my pajama shirt. The way he straightened when he realized that I wasn't wearing any sort of bra beneath it. The way his eyes were hazy pupils focused on my fingers as I opened the last button of my shirt and slid the fabric off my shoulders and down my arms, letting it fall to the floor behind me.

His mouth parted as he watched me push down my pajama pants, stepping out of them to stand in front of him in nothing but a simple, white thong. Presenting myself like an offering. I watched as his eyes swept up my entire body, like he was memorizing every feature, filing away every possible detail so that he could revisit and reflect upon it later. "My god, Amelia." His voice was hoarse. I should have felt embarrassed, baring myself to him like this, but I didn't. I wanted him to see me—*all* of me.

Something inside of my chest thrummed wildly as I watched him take an eager step toward me. It was his turn to take back control of this moment, and I felt a damp aching between my thighs in anticipation. He studied my breasts, eyes glazed, seemingly distracted from anything else but the way that my nipples pebbled as he approached.

His hand reached out to cup my breast, and the feel of his warm hand encircling me, fingers reaching to knead not-so-gently around my nipple, sending an electric shock directly to my core. I felt myself clench there, but it was hollow. Wanting. Needing.

Logan bent down, setting one knee to the floor, and gently pressed his soft lips to the sensitive skin underneath the breast he still held in his hand, skating over my rib bone with his tongue. I arched myself against his mouth, desperate for more of him, more of this. As he nibbled and sucked, he simultaneously pinched my nipple and I gasped, having to press both of my hands against his shoulders to hold myself upright.

His mouth moved across to explore along my rib cage, traveling lower, and I felt the pressure of his teeth as they grazed along my hip bone just above my panty line.

His other hand, the one not currently working my breast into a delightfully blinding fury, pressed against my spine at the small of my back, forcing my hips forward against his face. His nose brushed against the inner lining of my thong, along my thigh, and I felt an intense throbbing from the sensitive point at the center of my panties, so close to where his mouth was. I pressed my thighs together, squeezing my muscles in an attempt to create pressure, but it wasn't enough.

As I tilted further into him, needing his mouth to find my center, I heard a guttural groan escape from the back of his throat. He knew what I wanted but was making me wait for it, teasing me into oblivion as his mouth descended even lower, moving to another sensitive point inside my thigh.

I felt myself involuntarily buck my hips into the air above him, and he hummed his approval as his tongue and teeth skated back up my leg. The hand that had been on my breast traveled lower, and I saw as he watched his own thumb glide gently along the center of my panties, where the fabric was now damp. The warm hand he had on my back pressed into my spine again, pushing me further against his thumb, and I saw stars. The pressure of his thumb, *there*, was almost more than I could take.

Except I was wrong. Because that very thumb gently pushed my panties to the side, revealing my glistening skin underneath, and Logan moved his head to lightly kiss me where I throbbed, and I almost exploded into a fury of fire on the spot.

"My *god*, Amelia," he said again, his voice hushed and raspy, his eyes locked in on my center, "you taste incredible." I could feel his hot breath on my skin, and I felt my hips buck again, desperately seeking the friction of his mouth against me. He smiled as he looked up at me, his eyes full of longing, full of outright appreciation and shimmering mischief, and I watched with amazement as he covered my core with his mouth.

My knees buckled, but Logan held my hips up with his strong hands, keeping me from falling over as his mouth began a silent assault, licking and sucking and nibbling. My head lolled back, eyes closed, as I surrendered my entire body over to his touch.

A gasp escaped me as his right hand curled around my left thigh and carefully forced my legs open wider to give his mouth better reach. I felt his tongue slide lazily along my seam, as if he had all the time in the world to explore every inch of me.

Maybe he did. God, the thought of it sent chills up my spine as I clutched my fingers into his shoulders. I was distantly aware of some echo of resounding joy within my heart at the fact that I was here, practically naked in Logan's bedroom, his hands and mouth on me. But the way his tongue slid against me, the way he gently nipped and grazed, it took all of my focus away from anything else.

In this moment, I was his. I felt myself submitting to him

wholly, wanting nothing more than . . . *more.* I didn't have room in my brain to think about what this meant, what we were risking. I was only acutely aware of the fact that we weren't alone in this house. And only enough to know that we needed to keep quiet.

I could feel the crest of something building within me, something low in my belly thrumming and edging closer and closer to the brink of oblivion. Logan could feel me tense, could feel the way my legs squeezed around his face, and his tongue began darting against me with more pressure. I felt his hands reaching behind me to cup my ass as my legs began to tremble, and I felt a mild flush of embarrassment at my inability to control myself. Trying to hide how affected I was, I lifted one leg and hung it over his shoulder, using the opportunity of the new angle to squeeze myself against him, desperately creating more friction as the cresting inside of me reached a new height. I was close . . . so *close.*

"Don't stop," I heard myself beg, panting as I began bucking myself against him, sliding myself up and down his face as his tongue curled around every crevice of my pleasure. White hot pressure mounted, and suddenly Logan was sucking on my throbbing point of pleasure, sending me into blinding ecstasy.

I was no longer in my body. The high that overcame me was unlike anything I'd ever felt, more than I'd ever thought was possible. It took everything I could possibly muster to refrain from screaming his name, vaguely aware that my brother was sleeping just down the hallway.

After several minutes, as I came down from the high, my chest heaving and legs weak, Logan's mouth roamed again to my hip, grazing up my ribcage, nibbling at my breast as he stood up, and then his mouth found mine again and I could taste my own pleasure on his tongue.

It was by far the hottest, most erotic experience I'd ever had.

Logan smiled as he looked at me with an intensity that told me this was far from over. There was also something desperate and urgent in his eyes . . . *need* in its rawest form. As if he'd been wanting this for as long as I had.

"What took you so long?" I whispered, reaching up to cup his jaw.

Logan let out a breath, shaking his head and wrapping his arms around me as he bent down to nuzzle his nose into my neck. I felt him breathe me in before lifting his head back up to look into my eyes. "I don't want to fuck this up, Amelia." His voice was barely audible, riddled with vulnerability and unmistakable fear.

I slid my hands down his chest. "You won't."

And then I slipped my hand into his jeans, softly cupping him over his boxers. I watched his face change, felt his sharp intake of breath as his eyes glazed over again. He was so . . . so *hard*. Impossibly hard. I felt him pulse beneath my hand.

And then Logan was lifting me up again, furiously kissing me as he moved to lay me down onto his bed.

# Chapter Twelve

## EIGHT YEARS AGO (AGE 17)

I'D BEEN IN A DEEP, BLISSFUL SLUMBER—SO DEEP, that unexpectedly coming out of it felt like being hit by a freight train.

I jumped up in my bed, feeling drool dripping down my chin. With eyes only half open, I used the neckline of my T-shirt to wipe my chin as I looked around my room. It was still very dark, and it took a full sixty seconds for my still asleep brain to realize that my phone was vibrating on my nightstand. *What the hell?* I had no idea who would be calling me in the middle of the night.

I picked up my phone just as I missed the call. Actually, according to my notifications, I'd missed six calls. All from Logan.

Panic crept into my mind as I pressed the button to call him back, taking a quick mental note that it was one-thirty in the morning. Why would Logan be calling me this late unless something was wrong?

I heard the phone line connect before I heard a sigh. "Millie?" His deep voice penetrated my spine.

"Logan? What's wrong?"

"I'm so sorry for calling," he slurred.

The worry I felt was suddenly laced with irritation. "It's okay. Um. Are you drunk?"

"Yes."

I waited for a beat, but when he didn't say anything else, I pressed further. "Are you okay?"

"No. Mills. I'm not." He sounded small and defeated in a way that I'd never heard before, and it cracked something open inside of me. The irritation that had flared up a moment ago was gone, leaving me instead with fear bubbling up in my stomach. "Can you come and get me?"

"Yeah, yeah. Of course. Where are you?" I got out of bed and started looking for my purse.

"Jackson's."

Jackson's was a dive bar downtown. I knew this because Adam celebrated his twenty-first birthday there a couple of months ago. It was at least twenty miles away. "Okay. I'm on my way. It's going to take me a bit to get down there." I found my purse on my dresser and made my way downstairs.

"I know. I'm so sorry, Millie." Was he crying?

My adrenaline spiked. "Logan, it's okay," I whispered, not wanting to wake my parents. "I'm glad you called. I'll be there as soon as I can."

I hung up the phone and grabbed the keys to our family SUV from the kitchen counter. I knew it would be parked in the driveway and not in the garage like my father's car was, and I didn't want to risk any unnecessary noise by opening the garage door.

As quietly as I could, I unlocked the sliding glass door to the backyard and slipped outside into the cool night air. I went through the side gate, out to the front of the house, and got into the car.

I didn't turn the headlights on until I was about five houses down the street, and then I floored it.

It took me twenty-three endless minutes of driving before I saw the neon sign for Jackson's. It was almost two in the morning, and the bars on the busy, downtown strip were no doubt about to close up for the night. I needed to find Logan before the street became crowded with foot traffic from the night's patrons as they headed home.

I slowed the car down to a crawl and searched the shadows along the sidewalk, assuming he would be outside waiting for me—but I didn't see him anywhere. I decided to pull over so that I could check inside the bar, and had just parallel parked into an empty spot along the sidewalk when I noticed a figure ahead of me, illuminated by the SUV's headlights. A man was sitting on the ground against the brick building with his head between his knees.

Logan.

I jumped out and walked over to where he was sitting. He didn't look up at me until I was standing at his feet.

His face was filthy. There was dirt smeared under his nose and across his right cheek. "Millie?"

"Hey, Logan. Let's get you home, okay?" I held out my hand to him to help pull him up, but his attention was caught somewhere along my thighs. Looking down, I realized I'd left the house in nothing but one of my brother's old, oversized T-shirts—the hem of which fell about four inches above my knees.

But worse . . . I wasn't wearing any pants.

I felt the flush of embarrassment as Logan's gaze raked over the shirt before they rose and met mine. He looked so sad, and yet . . . there was something almost predatory that flashed in his eyes.

"Come on, Logan. It's late." My hand still hung in the air between us. His eyes flitted back to my hemline, caught on the fabric's edges for a few seconds before he reached up to wrap his fingers around my wrist as I pulled him up into a standing position.

I was tall for my age, taller than most of the girls I knew at school, but Logan stood at least six inches taller than me. He peered down at me in the darkness of the night, swaying a little, and smiled. His teeth were a flash of white in the dark. "Thank you for coming for me, Mills."

I rolled my eyes in mock annoyance, a smile forming wide on my own face. "Of course I came to get you, dork. Come on, let's get you to the car."

His hand was still attached to my wrist, so I used my other arm to steer him toward the SUV.

After I got him into the passenger's seat, I moved to the other side of the car and got in. With the dome lights on, I took another look at Logan and was horrified to find that the dirt smeared on his face was actually dried blood. I could also now see that his left eye was swollen, and a bruise was forming around it. I couldn't stop myself from gasping.

"Logan, what the hell happened to you?"

His face fell. He turned his head and looked straight out of the windshield. "Just drive."

My heart started thumping in my chest as I stared at his profile. Something bad was happening. Or had it already happened? Either way, I could feel adrenaline sliding through my veins like ice.

"Okay," I replied, mostly to myself. I put the key back into the ignition and pulled out of the parking spot just as a crowd of people burst out of Jackson's.

We drove for fifteen minutes in silence. Logan stayed focused on the road ahead, but I could tell he was lost in thought. The *not*-knowing what happened was killing me, but I knew that pressing him about it wasn't going to work. "So, where am I taking you?" I kept my voice light.

I could feel his gaze shift over in my direction. He didn't answer, but he didn't look away, either.

"My dad's dead." It was almost a whisper.

I turned to look at him, meeting his eyes. They were full of so many emotions, and he was giving me every single one of them. Anger, hurt, guilt, disappointment. He was letting me see it all. I'd never talked to Logan about his dad before—not directly. But I'd known enough. "How?"

His gaze stayed locked on me. "Drank himself to death. His liver gave out. He was dead for a week before anyone even found him."

"*Oh.*" I released a breath, not knowing the right thing to say. An apology or condolences seemed natural, but his relationship with his father was anything but. "Are you okay?"

"I don't know, Amelia." His lips were tight as his eyes bore into mine. "Am I?" His voice cracked.

He was genuinely asking me. I felt my heart break wide open for him, shattering into tiny pieces as it became so clear to me that he *wasn't* okay. He was hanging on by a thread.

Desperate for hope. And I realized altogether that he had been for a long time.

All those years ago, my father made a phone call that likely saved his life. A phone call that got Logan out of *his* father's custody so that he wouldn't be hurt anymore. I'd always assumed that he was happy after that, but now looking into his eyes, filled with so much pain, I started to realize how absolutely naive I'd been.

Logan never really had a relationship with his mother, and his father's abhorrent behavior in raising him was something he'd had to endure alone for twelve years. But his pain didn't just stop there. He'd had to carry all of it—the horrors of his past and his likely fears for the future—every single day of his life.

"Logan. Of *course* you're okay," I declared, with every ounce of confidence and assurance that I had. I felt hot tears stinging in the corners of my eyes but I blinked them away, refusing to show him any weakness when what he needed from me in this moment was my strength. "You're one of the fucking good ones, Logan. One of the very best. And I have no doubt that you're going to be one of the greatest men that this world has ever seen. You're not him, and that is *not* your future."

I could feel my knuckles tightening around the steering wheel, praying like hell that I could be enough for him in this moment. That I could give him what he needed. What he deserved from the second he was born on this earth. Unconditional love. Understanding. Faith. Belief.

Silence enveloped us again in the darkness of the car, the visual pulse of street lights beating against us as we approached our sleepy neighborhood. I was about to make the turn to bring him to the house, thinking he'd want to sleep the night off in Adam's room, but as if he could read my thoughts, he quietly said: "I'll go back to my house, if that's okay."

I nodded. "Yeah, of course." I turned the car in the other direction, to the street that his grandma lived on instead.

Two minutes later, I parked in front of the small, Victorian style house that looked like the before photo of a home renovation. I opened my door and hopped out of the SUV, making my way over to join Logan on the other side where he'd also gotten out and was leaning against the passenger door, arms hanging loosely at his sides. He seemed much more sober than just a half hour ago when I'd picked him up.

"Hey," I said, meeting his tired eyes with my own. "You're okay." I nodded my head, attempting to double down in convincing him that he *was* okay.

He gave me a small smile in return, one that didn't quite reach his eyes—but it was enough to make me breathe again. I hadn't even realized I'd been holding my breath. "Thank you, Millie." He looked down at his feet, kicking a rock on the gravel. "Could you maybe, not, tell Adam about this?"

"Sure," I replied, keeping my voice casual. But I was surprised at his request. I'd assumed that Logan only called me and not my brother tonight because Adam was away at school. He was staying on campus at CSU, which was an hour north in Fort Collins. I had been the much closer option for a ride home.

Would Logan have still called me, even if Adam *was* around? Had he really been looking for *me* to be there for him tonight?

Suddenly, unexpectedly, Logan reached his hand for my waist, watching his own fingers as they pinched a piece of fabric from the old shirt I was wearing. He held the material between his fingers, as if exploring the feeling of cotton for the very first time. "I'd give anything to see you in one of mine," he murmured, his voice low.

I froze. Air fully stopped entering my body, and the hairs on the back of my neck stood up. I watched as his eyebrows furrowed.

His eyes flicked up to mine, his honey irises now darkened. His gaze was dangerous. It was a moment that stopped time, as we hung suspended in each other's eyes. I could feel my heart pounding so ferociously within my chest that it had to have been audible to him. The fingers that were clutching my shirt loosened, and I felt Logan's hand open as his palm pressed lightly against my hip before it slowly slid to the small of my back. My skin burned in its wake, engulfed in fire beneath the shirt.

He was suddenly closer, towering above me as he no longer leaned against the car. He looked down at me with a curious intensity that left me reeling. His expression held a question as he pulled me closer, giving me the opportunity to stop him, until I saw his pupils dilate as his gaze traveled down to my lips half a second before his pressed down against them.

It was like a bomb detonated inside of me.

I was suddenly more awake and alive than I had ever felt my entire life. I'd never been kissed before, and for Logan to be my first was more than I could have ever dreamed of. My body absolutely lit up at his touch, moving where he moved, meeting him with fire. The kiss was hungry. Wild. Desperate.

Our lips fit together perfectly, two halves from the same whole. As if we were made for this. As if we should have been doing this all along. We shared the same hot air, giving each other life as we breathed together. His nose grazed over mine to deepen the kiss, slipping his tongue inside of my mouth, exploring. He tasted like whiskey and something sweet. Honey? The shock of feeling his tongue inside of my mouth sent a jolt of electricity through me, a delicious tension growing low in my belly.

The hand on my back lightly traced up my spine until it was tangled in my hair. His other hand grazed up my thigh, slipping under my shirt and over my butt, which was covered only by a pair of black bikini underwear.

He moaned into my mouth at his discovery, and I felt myself become engulfed by roaring flames at the sound. I wanted to shine so brightly for him, so brightly that I could chase all of his shadows away. In this moment, I wanted to give him everything, every piece of me. To trade my vulnerability for his so I could flush out his pain and banish it with my touch.

His mouth separated from mine as it moved down along my jaw to my neck and I relished the feeling of his tongue on my skin, licking and sucking as his hands continued to roam. It was intoxicating. The delicious rush of a first-time high. Needing more, I whispered his name, a desperate plea, "Logan . . ."

As if I'd flipped a switch inside of him with my voice, it was over in an instant. I felt him go rigid against my body, his shaking hands coming to a stop. His breaths were wild on my neck, the hot air from his mouth snaking down my skin.

He took a swift step backward, clumsily hitting the heel of his shoe against the fender of the SUV. I ached at the loss of him, my body still burning for more. More of him. More of his touch. I felt the urge to get him back, but the look I found in his eyes gave me pause. He was fighting for control, fighting against his obvious desire to simply devour me. I watched as the need in his eyes was slowly replaced by guilt. Replaced by something that looked a lot like shame. No, no, *no* . . .

It was like a sucker punch to the stomach, knocking the wind out of me. I couldn't bear for him to look at me like that. Like this was a mistake. An accident. My mind swirled as I felt dizzy. I reached for him, but he maneuvered his shoulders to dodge my touch, as if I really *had* burned him. "Logan, what's—"

"I'm so sorry," he whispered, before he moved around me —so careful not to touch me—and walked, head slung low, in the direction of his house. He reached the entrance and let himself in, the door shutting behind him with finality.

He never even looked back.

FIFTEEN MINUTES LATER, I was back in my own bedroom. I threw my purse down on my dresser and kicked off my shoes before throwing myself back into my bed.

It was three in the morning at this point, but I was wide awake.

My whole body hummed with the aftershocks of being touched so desperately. My lips were sore and swollen as I traced them with my fingers, staring wide-eyed at the ceiling above me.

Logan Davis had *kissed* me. And not just kissed me. That was like the grand finale at the end of a fireworks show. Dangerous, manic, *filthy*.

I had been clay in the palm of his hands, molding myself to his every move, soothing his every lick of pain, covering every wound with a gentle kiss. I felt a resounding shift inside of my body, inside of my soul. His kiss was enough to claim me forever. And I'd happily obliged, entranced like a moth to a flame.

*I'd give anything to see you in one of mine.*

But it hadn't been enough. He could probably tell how young and inexperienced I was. How I'd fumbled in my reciprocation of his touch. Too innocent to match his need for a more mature obscenity. Too boring. Too— I felt the hot sting of tears in the corners of my eyes as panic pooled inside of my stomach.

I'd failed him.

# Chapter Thirteen

I was still coming down from the high of Logan's mouth between my legs and he was already winding me back up again. His lips were skating lazily along my collarbone, his knee pressing into the bed between mine as he kept himself propped up over me, his fingers teasing me as they grazed my stomach.

"Logan," I breathed, arching toward him.

He was distracted again, focused now on kissing my jaw. His movements were sporadic, almost clumsy, like he didn't know which need to yield to first.

"Hmm?" he hummed into my ear.

I closed my eyes as he bent down to slide his tongue over my nipple. "I want to feel you," I whispered.

I heard a low grunt from the back of his throat as his teeth nibbled my hip. God, why did that feel so good? "Do you feel this?" he asked as he slid his finger over the center of my panties, over that deliciously throbbing point of pleasure.

I gasped, and then he was kissing my mouth again, as if wanting to taste my reaction to his touch. He nipped at my lower lip before his mouth was back on my neck.

"Yes, but . . ." I gulped, trying to focus. "But that's not what I meant."

His hand slid underneath me, cupping my ass and squeezing as he easily lifted my hips off the bed and then set me back down. "What do you mean, then?" He kissed my mouth. "Tell me, Amelia. I'll give you anything you want."

His eyes—normally a bright, honey brown—were now dark and dangerous as he regarded me. My body buzzed beneath him. "I want to feel you," I repeated. "Inside of me."

Logan stilled. His eyes were opaque. Frosted and glassy. But a maddening hint of concern traced along his forehead.

"I don't . . ." He hesitated, looking down at my mouth before snapping his eyes back up to mine. "We don't have to do anything more." His restraint, I could tell, was already disintegrating. But still, he tried. "I have no expectations, Amelia."

"I don't think you do," I assured him. "But Logan—" I paused, looking him in the eye. "I *need* to feel you. Please."

I watched his throat bob. "Amelia." My name was ecstasy on his tongue.

Reaching my arms out to his waist, I started to unfasten the button of his jeans. He watched my fingers work with intense focus as I tugged his zipper down before slipping my hand beneath the elastic of his boxers. I curled my fingers around the base of him and he thrust himself into my hand, a guttural moan escaping from somewhere deep in his chest.

His breathing became completely erratic as he moved to push his jeans all the way off, and then he was pushing off his boxers, and I couldn't help but stare at him.

He was . . . big.

"Amelia." His voice was velvet and uneven. "I don't have anything . . ."

I had to focus on his words for a moment before I realized what he meant. *Oh.* "It's okay. I'm on birth control."

He nodded once, as if still unsure. His eyes raked over my body as I lay before him. And then he gently hooked his index fingers into the straps of my panties, pulling the fabric slowly down my legs and off of my body.

"You are so perfect," he said, his eyes wild, caught between my legs. Utter admiration and awe poured from him.

"Come here," I commanded, my own voice raspy.

His eyes flicked to mine as he leaned over me, pushing my legs open with his as he looked down at me with that dedicated focus. His nose grazed mine. "Amelia." He said my name like a prayer. "Are you sure?"

I curled my fingers into his hair and nipped his chin with my teeth. "Yes, Logan. I've never been more sure of anything in my entire life. Please. Let me feel you."

It was enough to satisfy his concern. Enough, even, for him to realize that concern was a waste of time. And then he was slowly, delicately, carefully pushing into me.

Closing his eyes, he rested his forehead on mine as he bottomed out inside of me. "Oh my god, Amelia." I felt . . . so full. Almost to the point of pain, and yet . . . It was incredible. I felt my walls clamp down around him, as if wanting to hold him in. To never let him go.

He groaned, kissing me. And then he lifted his head and peered down at my face as he pulled himself back out, only to slam back inside of me again.

I cried out, but Logan swiftly covered my mouth with his

hand. His eyes went completely black as he studied my face. "Amelia, you have to be quiet."

And then he slammed into me again with such force, and I swear I saw stars glittering around the dark room.

I gasped, desperate to release some of the deliciously painful ecstasy that he filled me with. I could feel my body squirm beneath his as he somehow found the ability to exercise a precise amount of control.

"Amelia," he murmured as he thrusted again, "do you know how long I've wanted this?"

His eyes were feral, watching my mouth before he bent down to tug on my bottom lip with his teeth. I felt him thrust into me again, and I could do nothing but whimper.

His breath caught at the sound.

"Do you know," he continued, "how often I've dreamt of this?" He nibbled at the base of my neck. "You have consumed my mind for as long as I can remember."

His words broke my heart open. It was as if an ever-winding vise had finally relinquished its excruciating hold on the muscle that pounded inside of my chest. The torment and anguish that I'd been feeling around Logan for years could finally be let go. The way he was holding me, touching me—it was unlike anything I'd ever experienced in my entire life. It felt so good, so right.

He wanted this—seemingly *needed* this—just as badly as I had. Where we were supposed to go from here, I had no idea. But at least in this moment, for this one night, we were finally together. We were finally vulnerable and honest with each other, validating this burning flame that existed inside of both of us.

Logan kissed my mouth and it was the embodiment of passion. He was pouring so much of himself into me, lighting me up as he came undone. His thrusts became unruly as he was consumed by my body beneath him. I felt the crest of burning ruin rising up again inside of me, and as I looked into his eyes —so familiar and sure—he whispered my name as if to seal this moment through his lips and the sound of it sent me over the edge, falling into the steep abyss with Logan tumbling right behind me.

And then we soared. Together.

I STIRRED awake sometime later and felt Logan's body behind mine, pressed against me as completely as two people could possibly be. One long, warm arm was hung over me, holding me close to his chest. I could feel him softly tracing his fingers through my hair as the wind howled against the window across the room.

Slowly, I turned my body to face him, resting my head on his arm.

His smile was striking yet lazy. As if we had forever to lie together like this. "You're so beautiful," he whispered.

My heart faltered. "How long have I been asleep?"

"Not long. Twenty minutes, maybe." I felt his hand lightly stroke down my arm, raising goosebumps all over my skin. He noticed them and concern swept over his face. "Are you cold?"

I reached up to press my hand to his cheek, looking intently into his eyes. "No."

His eyes darkened and he lifted his head, leaning forward to kiss me. It was soft and hazy in the aftermath of what we'd just done together, and when he finished kissing me, he pressed another quick kiss to my forehead before settling his head back down on his pillow.

I felt the tug of a memory come to life in my mind. "Do you remember the first time you kissed me?"

Logan looked down at my mouth. "Yes." He sighed. "I was a broken man back then, Amelia. I feel like I still am sometimes. But you . . ." He looked back up into my eyes. "You've always been a bright force for me. It's like you can cast my shadows away just by being you. I remember feeling like I just needed to touch you. To hold you. Like I needed only you to survive in that dark moment of my life."

My hand, still resting lightly on his cheek, moved to graze lightly through his hair. "Then why'd you run away from me?" I felt slightly anxious about what his answer would be, but I needed to know. I'd always held a distant, lingering feeling that I'd done something wrong that night.

"I couldn't bear to drag you down because of my demons." His voice was low as he answered. "I wanted to just be selfish and give in to it all, but I couldn't do that to you."

It was a relief to know it wasn't about me, but I could feel pain searing within the familiar cracks inside of my heart, old fissures that broke open for him so long ago. Reaching my arm around him, I snuggled in closer to his body. "I convinced myself that you didn't feel the same way about me. That maybe I was just too young and inexperienced."

Logan hummed into my ear as he, too, held me tighter. "I'm so sorry, Amelia," he whispered, his breath trailing along my neck as his voice faltered, "I've always tried so damn hard to do the right thing . . . keeping you at arm's length. A safe distance. I'm not what you deserve and I know that. My god, I tried so hard—but I could never figure out how to stop wanting you."

I broke away from him to look up into his eyes again. "What do you mean, you're not what I deserve?"

He hesitated. "You could be with anyone, Amelia. You're . . . so perfect. You could do much better than me. I don't deserve you, and you deserve so much more."

I felt like I was seventeen again, looking into the eyes of a boy whose heart was forever broken by the world. The familiar need to overpower his self-deprivation with giving him an abundance of *more* burst from my chest. "I wish you could see what I see when I look at you, Logan," I said softly, running my hand down his chest, feeling him inhale. "When I look into your eyes, I see strength and power. When I look into your heart, there is nothing but kindness and safety. You are, without a doubt, one of the best men I've ever known. Right behind my father. You're even further up the list than Adam, but if you tell him that I'm going to have to kill you."

Logan chuckled as he wrapped his hand around my waist, but his eyes remained focused as he continued to listen.

"I don't know if you know this, but when you kissed me that night, you changed my entire life. You seared something inside of me that you can't ever take back, something permanent that I haven't been able to ignore. Trust me, I *tried*, Logan. I tried to move on. I tried to date other people, tried to build a life that didn't include you in it . . . not in the way I wanted, at least. But it always felt like living life in black and white, void of all color. Nothing ever felt right, nothing around me had meaning. *You* showed me colors in a way I'd never experienced them before, and it changed me."

I paused, realizing that I'd just revealed so much. I felt

incredibly vulnerable, lying naked in Logan's arms having also just bared my heart to him. But it was worth it—worth it for Logan to hear that he was wanted, to say all of the things that had been on my heart for so many years.

He reached up to brush a strand of hair that had fallen into my face before his eyes settled back on my lips. "I really don't deserve you, Amelia." And then he moved toward my face again, as if the urge to do so was the only thing he could yield to at this moment. His lips brushed against mine and I felt my heart pound against his chest.

The need for Logan to understand how much he meant to me flared up from my bones. The deep, unwavering need to appreciate him, to adore him, to spoil him—anything I could do to fight against his hidden insecurities, against his belief that he was damaged because of a past that he had no control over —consumed me.

This was a part of him that no one else quite understood. To the rest of my family, Logan appeared to be walking through life on solid ground. He was confident, driven, focused—lord knew he was strong. But hidden in the depths of his soul was a man desperate to be truly, fully, deeply loved. A man who was scared to death of becoming his father. Who needed, sometimes, to fall apart. But who felt like at any moment, everything good around him could be ripped away if he was incapable of maintaining the house of cards that he'd created to survive.

*This* was who he'd been showing me since we were kids. The part of himself who needed someone to recognize his vulnerabilities and tell him it was okay. Logan trusted me. And that was, quite frankly, the greatest honor of my life.

It would take time, of course, to successfully break through the walls he'd built so high against the rest of the world. But now knowing that this electric force between us was real, that it wasn't something I'd built up inside of my mind to settle and soothe my own ego . . . I would make it my life's mission to love Logan as hard and as fiercely as I could.

Love. It seemed so fast. So wildly messy. But this love had been slowly brewing under the surface for as long as I could remember.

For now, our bodies were communicating in a way that our hearts and minds couldn't quite articulate through words. It was like a new, foreign language. There was confession in his touch, longing in his shallow breaths, and I mirrored his need with my own.

As Logan kissed the hollow spot of skin beneath my ear, I situated myself over him so that my legs straddled his hips. Bending over his gloriously warm body, I skated my mouth along his neck as I felt him position himself beneath me before he pushed inside of me again.

I sat up straight, my back curving as my head rolled at the exquisite feeling of him. Closing my eyes, I began moving my body in a glorious rhythm against his, feeling his breath catch as he half-mumbled praises of *just like that* and *good girl* and *you're so perfect, Amelia.*

There was no doubt in my mind that, just as his kiss had done eight years ago, this night was going to absolutely wreck me. There was simply no coming back from something like it. I was irrevocably changed, forever branded by Logan's fingerprints. By his lips. He existed so deeply within my heart and bones and soul that I wouldn't be able to disentangle myself from him even if I'd wanted to, and I doubted that I ever would.

This night was about more than just sex. It felt fated, like there was no one else that I should be sharing a bed with. No one else that could ever share my heart with.

# Chapter Fourteen

"Something smells amazing," I said as I turned around the corner to the kitchen. Rachel was standing at the stove with a large ladle in her hand and one of my mother's pastel pink aprons tied around her waist. She was the epitome of a gorgeous, modern housewife, practically glowing in the morning sunlight.

"I'm making pancakes for everyone." Her smile was bright as she pointed out a bowl of batter sitting on the counter next to the stove.

"Wow. After yesterday, I'm surprised you have a desire to be back in the kitchen."

Rachel giggled, tucking her hair behind her ear. I noticed she had a bit of loose flour on her cheek. "I don't mind. I wanted to do something nice for everyone." She used the ladle to pour batter into the pan. "You guys have been so warm and welcoming toward me, and I happen to have a pretty killer cinnamon pancake recipe. I found all the ingredients in the pantry. It's really not a big deal."

"Can I help with anything?" I looked around for an opportunity to jump in.

"I got it! It's easy. We'll eat in, like, twenty minutes."

I nodded. "Sounds great. Where is everyone?"

"Adam and Logan are out shoveling the driveway. We got over a foot of snow last night!" I watched as her eyebrows furrowed thoughtfully. "I haven't seen your parents yet this morning . . . they might still be in bed?"

I looked at the time display on the stove next to Rachel and saw that it was almost nine thirty. It wasn't like my parents to sleep in this late, but we'd stayed up the last few nights—not to mention all the cocktails that had been consumed—so it was good that they were getting their rest.

I decided to go back upstairs and get a start on packing. We'd be heading back to Denver today and I was starting to feel a mild churning of anxiety in my stomach about leaving Breckenridge. This had been, without a doubt, the best few days of my life. Last night with Logan was nothing short of a fairy tale beyond my wildest dreams. But what happens now, after we leave the magical bubble of this house?

Logan and I had a lot to figure out and there were many conversations to be had. I was certainly up for the task, knowing that it could mean finally being with him after all this time . . . but I also knew him. I knew his fears, and I knew that there was a strong chance of him pulling away from me again like he'd done before. Based on his actions in the past, there was a possibility that he'd try to avoid talking about what happened altogether.

I wasn't sure I could survive that. Not again.

I made it back up to my bedroom and shut the door behind me before letting my body fall onto the soft comforter on my bed. I felt utterly exhausted despite the bright, electric humming that still thrummed within my body.

I'd left Logan's room just as the sun began to rise this morning, quietly slipping back across the hallway after spending the early morning hours wrapped up in his arms. I only managed to sleep for a couple of hours in my own bed before the sunlight was blasting through the bedroom window and straight into my face.

I heard my phone vibrate from where it was still charging on the nightstand. Reaching out to grab it, I saw the notification was for a text from my best friend.

MACKENZIE

Hope you had a great Thanksgiving! Let's get lunch this weekend? I haven't seen you in a couple weeks and I have some news!

I felt a small groan escape from my mouth, realizing that I hadn't talked to Mackenzie since last weekend. Which meant that she had no idea how much my entire world had shifted in the last few days between leaving Noah, to now living with Adam, and having just spent an incredible night with Logan.

I'd never outright told Mackenzie about my feelings for Logan growing up, but I wondered if she ever guessed. She'd never pushed the subject, even after that disastrous trip to Mexico. Instead, she found ways to wield a more silent level of support, like finding elaborate ways to pull me out of the depths of my own mind.

She and her long-term boyfriend, Eric, had been together for almost a decade—and I was absolutely thrilled for them.

Besides my parents, Mackenzie and Eric were a real-life example of love, commitment, and the consistent hard work that was necessary for a successful relationship.

They'd started dating in high school, and even through the chaos of college and the turbulent days that came in their early twenties, they'd somehow managed to survive relatively unscathed and stronger than ever.

My thumbs moved swiftly across the phone's screen as I typed out a reply back to her.

> Grateful for you, Mack 🤍 I'm definitely up for lunch. Sunday?

I waited for her reply, which came in not even thirty seconds later.

> MACKENZIE
>
> Sounds perfect. See you then! 😊

I set my phone back down on the nightstand and forced myself up from the bed to start gathering my clothes. I spent the next fifteen minutes folding everything I'd brought and tucking it all neatly away, pausing for a moment with the pajama set I'd worn last night. I brought the shirt to my face and inhaled, smelling Logan's scent within the fabric. I caught myself smiling, despite the small bouts of worry that I was still feeling.

It was all so surreal. Last night had *actually* happened.

Just as I zipped my bag closed, I heard voices coming from downstairs. Rachel's pancakes were probably ready, and I was quite literally starving after all of last night's . . . *exertions.*

I made my way down the stairs, following the notes of cinnamon and vanilla that hung in the air, and rounded back into the kitchen. Rachel was at the sink, cleaning off the pan she'd just been using while a platter full of thick pancakes sat in the center of the island.

My mother was already transferring a stack of them to her plate while my father stood just behind her waiting for his turn. They were both still in their pajamas, hair rumpled, and the sight of them together in such a state was outrageously heartwarming. "Good morning," my mother chirped when she saw me.

"Good morning! Wow, those look delicious," I said, nodding my head at the food.

"I'll say," my father answered, "and they smell incredible, too. Rach, this is truly amazing."

Rachel turned from the sink to look back at him, not even trying to mask the pride in her voice when she said, "Thank you."

I picked up a plate from the stack on the counter and waited until my father finished getting his portion. When I was stabbing into the pancake at the top of the stack, I heard the front door open and shut as footsteps shuffled in. A moment later, Adam and Logan were walking into the kitchen, and my heart skipped a full beat or two at the sight of Logan.

He was bundled in his heavy jacket—the same one he'd let me wear yesterday at the store—and a black beanie. His face was flushed from shoveling snow, and there was a light layer of sweat on his forehead. His warm eyes found me, and I was instantly transported into the very recent memory of his body against mine.

"Good morning," I managed to say.

Logan smiled. "Good morning."

I couldn't help the huge smile that formed on my face. I

had to look back down at the food in front of me to distract myself from the electric buzz that was filling my head.

"This smells amazing, babe!" Adam moved further into the kitchen to wrap his arms around Rachel, who squealed when a few clumps of snow from his coat fell on her shoulder. I headed into the dining room where my parents were already seated, noticing that someone had already set out butter and syrup on the table.

It wasn't long before Adam and Rachel bounded into the room with their plates in hand. Trailing not far behind, Logan soon followed and sat down right next to me. This time, I reveled in the close proximity to him at the table, my body oscillating in excitement. I felt his knee swing over to touch mine under the table, as if in silent acknowledgement that he felt it, too.

All through breakfast, I felt Logan look at me at least a dozen times. I would then feel compelled to glance over at him as often as I could without being too obvious. How many times *was* too obvious? Was I acting normal? I had to admit, the secret that we were sharing, sitting here in front of my family, was downright thrilling.

With each stolen glance, memories from last night infiltrated my mind and it became difficult to focus on the conversations at the table. So difficult, in fact, that I'd completely missed as the topic of discussion turned in my direction.

"Amelia, did you hear me?" My father's curious voice suddenly came into focus.

*Oh shit.* I quickly looked to the head of the table on my left and saw creases in my father's forehead as he watched me, waiting for me to answer. "Sorry, Dad . . . what did you say?"

"When do you have to go back to work?"

"Oh. I don't have any meetings scheduled until next week, but I have some things to work on for a new client that I'll probably start this weekend once we get back." I tried to keep my tone casual, as if I hadn't just been lost inside of my own head.

"Who's the client? Anyone we'd know?" my mother asked.

"It's a dentist office in Denver. Bite of Life."

At this, my father let out a huffing laugh. "Bite of Life. Now *that's* charming. I haven't heard of them."

I smiled. "That's why they hired me. They're struggling to get new customers because they don't have a strong marketing foundation and no one is finding them."

My father beamed. "Have I told you lately how proud we are of you, dear?"

"Thanks, Dad," I responded, feeling just a smidge embarrassed.

Suddenly, Logan's voice came from the seat to my right. "I'm looking forward to Millie helping me with some marketing for the shop."

I saw my father's eyes widen at this. "Oh! That's a lovely idea!"

I turned to look back at Logan, seeing his eyes twinkle as he smiled. His stare was so bright and intense it felt like he was burning a hole right through my head. "Yeah, it's gonna be a great partnership." I felt my breath falter at his words, but did my best to stay composed. Was Logan subtly *flirting* with me in front of everyone?

I gave him my best attempt at a casual smile before focusing on what was left of my pancakes on the plate in front of me.

It wasn't long before we were packing up Adam's car and getting ready for the drive back to the city. My mother handed me a tote bag full of tupperware containing leftovers, assuring us that it would go to waste if we didn't take it. Both of my parents fawned over Rachel as they said their goodbyes. I watched as my father hugged Logan just as fervently as he had when we arrived, and another tear slipped from my mother's eye. A pang of emotion that I couldn't name flared up within me as I watched them—another stark reminder of just how integrated Logan was in our lives.

"Promise to call when you get home?" my mother yelled once we all piled into the car.

"We will!" Adam yelled back.

And then we settled in for the journey home.

Beside me, I noticed that Logan had his phone out and was furiously typing away into it. I wondered who he might be talking to before my own phone vibrated just as he put his down in his lap, looking out his window.

I felt a jolt of excitement as I pulled it out of my coat pocket to see that, sure enough, there was a new text from Logan.

LOGAN

You look really pretty today.

I covered my mouth with my hand to hide the smile on my face, unable to stop it. I snuck a quick glance back toward Logan and saw that he was still looking out his window, like an innocent little sneak. Looking back down at my phone, I sent him a reply.

Thank you. You don't look so bad yourself.

After a moment, Logan looked back down at his phone and immediately began typing again.

LOGAN

When can I see you again?

My heart instantly fluttered in my chest as relief flooded through me. He wasn't going to blow this off—I felt like I could practically burst with joy. I read his text over and over again, letting it sink in, before I realized that he would be waiting for my response. Looking up front, I caught Adam's eyes in the rearview mirror. "Hey Adam, do you work tonight?"

Adam, who was completely aloof to what was going on in the backseat, shook his head as he watched the road in front of him. "No, I'll go back tomorrow night. I'm going to try and stay up tonight so that I can sleep during the day tomorrow. Might watch some movies. Why?"

I kept my face neutral. "No reason, just trying to plan a hot date."

I could feel Logan's eyes snap toward me, but I kept my focus on the rearview.

Adam chuckled. "Hot date, huh?" His tone was sarcastic, as if I couldn't possibly be serious.

I shrugged. "I could have a hot date."

He rolled his eyes, ever the annoying older brother. "Okay, Millie."

Tomorrow night? 😉

This time, it was Logan's smile that made my body sing.

LOGAN

You are so bad.

You think so? Just wait until I get my hands on you again.

Amelia. Behave. You're going to kill me.

Logan was *blushing* on his side of the car, and I felt immense pride in having elicited such a reaction from him.

*We're in the backseat of Adam's car*, I reminded myself. 'Behave' was right.

For the next hour and a half, I did everything I could to ignore the pull of the man sitting beside me. I also did everything I could not to let my mind jump back into anxious thoughts about what all of this meant and the potential likelihood of Logan bailing on the whole thing. He'd asked to see me again, which was promising. Although he hadn't actually agreed to tomorrow night either.

No other man had ever made me feel so unsure of myself or of the future. But, to be fair, no other man had ever made me feel the delicious highs that I felt with Logan either. It was like being ten steps ahead while simultaneously being fifteen steps behind. We were already so close with so much love to give to each other. But we didn't quite know what to do with it when it was right in front of us.

As Adam finally drove the car back into the parking garage beneath his apartment building, the darkness within overcoming us, I prepared myself to say goodbye to Logan. *It'll be okay*, I thought. No matter what—I would be okay.

Logan got to the trunk first and pulled everyone's bags out. "You coming up?" Adam asked.

"Nah, I gotta get home."

Adam nodded. "Okay, sounds good. Let's catch a game next week if you aren't too busy."

"I can do that." He reached his hand out to pull Adam in for a quick side hug. "Thanks for driving." He turned to Rachel and smiled. "It was so nice to meet you, Rachel. I'm sure I'll see you again real soon." Rachel smiled back as she swooped in for a hug.

And then Logan's eyes fell on me. He kept his face neutral, but even in the darkness of the underground lot I could see the mischievous sparkle in his eye. He stepped forward with his arms outstretched and pulled me into a friendly, platonic hug, knowing Adam and Rachel were right next to us and watching.

As he hugged me, he moved his mouth to my ear where the others couldn't see, and I felt him softly breathe me in. "Tomorrow," he whispered, sending goosebumps up my spine.

# Chapter Fifteen



I HAD JUST FINISHED CURLING MY HAIR WHEN MY mom walked into the bathroom, catching my eye through the vanity mirror.

"Oh my—" She gasped, covering her mouth with her hand. "Amelia, you look absolutely beautiful." I could already see the shine of tears threatening to escape.

Looking back at myself, I smiled. "Thanks, Mom." It took me over three hours to get ready for tonight, and I had to admit that I'd done a pretty decent job. I'd kept my makeup light, wanting to go for a more natural, classic look. I'd added a smidge of blush high on my cheeks and a little bit of shimmer to highlight my bone structure.

A pop of purple on my eyelids brought out my green eyes, making them look much brighter than they normally did. Half of my long, dark hair was pinned up in a loose knot while the other half flowed down in a cascade of curls. My black dress was sequined in the bodice, flowing down from a high waistline into a gorgeous, satin skirt that hugged my curves and pooled around my feet at the floor.

It was a backless dress—not exactly ideal for a brisk night in April—but I didn't care. I knew that this was the *perfect* prom dress the moment I'd seen it in the store.

It was worth being cold for.

"Do you want to eat anything before you go?" My mother approached me from behind, making a small adjustment to a piece of hair in the back before she reached for one of the pearl clips I had laid out on the counter. "I could heat up some leftover chicken alfredo?"

"We're going to eat before we head to the venue, but thanks anyway." My mom's physical presence always had a way of calming my jitters. I wasn't exactly nervous for the night ahead, but it was my senior prom. This was a night I would remember for the rest of my life, and there was for sure a little pressure that went along with that.

"What time is Paul picking you up?" She grabbed another clip to pin up a falling strand of hair.

"He said he'd be here at six," I replied, looking at my phone to see the time. "So, in about fifteen minutes."

My mom finished fastening the strand of hair and looked back at me through the mirror. I felt her take in a deep breath as she wrapped her soft, warm hands around my shoulders. "Are you ready?"

"I think so," I replied. "Are you sure I look okay?"

"I have no doubt that you're going to be the most breathtaking girl there." I turned away from the mirror to face her, reaching to embrace her in a warm hug. "Just don't let Paul pressure you into anything you aren't comfortable with. He seems like a nice young man, but I know the kind of expectations that even nice young men can have on prom night."

I closed my eyes and groaned. "Ew, mom. No way. Paul isn't like that."

She pulled away from our hug and looked me in the eye. "We never think they are, sweetie."

For some reason I felt a small knot form within my stomach. "I'll be careful, I promise," I assured her.

My mother nodded and then kissed my cheek. "I'm going to see what your father is up to in the backyard . . . he better not be touching my flowers. Let us know when Paul gets here so that we can take pictures!" She was already down the hallway when she finished talking.

"I will," I called out to her.

I took a moment to steal another glance at myself in the mirror, willing the onset of nerves to simmer down. I'd been officially—although in my opinion, not so seriously—dating Paul for about four months now. After Mackenzie and Eric started dating the summer before junior year, Paul had asked me to go out with him repeatedly for over a year and a half before I finally caved and gave it a shot.

Maybe I was a little naive, but I was a steadfast romantic at heart. I firmly believed in sparks and butterflies and old fashioned chivalry. Paul was always very kind—and he was undoubtedly attractive—but I'd never really felt a very strong chemistry with him.

We hadn't talked about it directly, but I couldn't imagine that Paul would be surprised by my feelings. I'd sort of assumed that maybe this was just something for us both to explore for the time being without any major strings attached. He was the first person that I'd ever dated exclusively, but I still hesitated to actually call him my boyfriend.

If my mother was right about his expectations tonight, he was going to be sorely disappointed. In the few months that we'd been dating, I'd only let him kiss me. Truthfully, I didn't even see our relationship lasting much longer. Graduation was in less than a month and we were heading to different colleges, so it wouldn't really make sense to continue with our relationship anyway.

I was looking forward to the opportunity to start fresh at CU Denver in the fall, where I'd be around new people and could hopefully even find a guy that I had a genuine connection with. I yearned to feel the pull that Mackenzie talked about feeling with Eric. The one that I'd felt that night eight months ago, when I'd picked up Logan from that downtown bar.

Unfortunately, *that* pull didn't actually take me anywhere. Despite our kiss being one of the most amazing experiences of my entire life, Logan seemed to think otherwise and had avoided ever talking about it with me, preferring to act as if it'd never happened. His avoidance hurt, and left me feeling totally mortified about the whole thing.

After a few weeks, we clicked back into our normal routine with each other and got back to the way things were before he kissed me in front of his grandmother's house. I loved him immensely and I knew he loved me, too. But after that night, I felt so much *more*. I felt what we could be, beyond our close friendship, and it was still sometimes really hard for me to pretend like those feelings weren't there.

I checked the time on my phone again and grabbed all of my makeup off of the counter to put away. With only ten minutes left before Paul was meant to get here, I walked out of the bathroom and made my way downstairs.

From the landing, I heard Adam talking to someone in the kitchen. Pausing before I entered, I listened to see who he might be talking to, knowing my parents were outside. As I stood there, I registered the deep voice that I would know anywhere.

Logan was here.

Adam was home from college for the weekend so that he could study for finals. His roommates on campus were a bit rowdy, which made it hard for him to focus on everything he needed to review before he took his last set of finals as an undergrad next week. As long as he passed this semester—which I had no doubt that he would—Adam was going to officially be heading to medical school in the fall.

Knowing how important studying was for him this weekend, I didn't anticipate Logan being here. But hearing him on the other side of the wall sent a jolt of excitement through me. It had been a while since I'd seen him last, and there was a satisfaction in knowing that he would be seeing me all dressed up like this. With as much confidence as I could muster, I took a deep breath and then I breezed my way into the kitchen.

As soon as I entered, Adam and Logan both looked in my direction. Adam threw me a big smile and reached out to give me a hug. "Dang, Millie . . . you clean up nice!"

I wrapped my arms around my brother. "Thank you, Adam." I looked over his shoulder at Logan, who was staring at me with an unreadable expression on his face.

My god, the sight of Logan did things to me that even I didn't understand. At twenty-one years old, he was straight-up dynamite. My mind reverted back to that night last fall—the taste of whiskey that his tongue spread across my lips, the warmth of his hands as they roamed under my shirt.

*I'd give anything to see you in one of mine.*

"Millie?"

I fumbled, realizing that Adam was looking at me, and met his gaze.

"Sorry, what?" I tried to keep my face casual.

"What time's your date getting here? I want to make sure I give him a little brotherly advice."

"Oh . . . uh, I don't think that's necessary, but thanks." I looked back at Logan, who was ripping up a napkin in his hands as he stared at my dress, eyes moving down to my heels.

"Well, I do. He should be here soon, right?"

"Yeah, any minute. But, Adam, *please* don't embarrass me."

Adam rolled his eyes as he moved past me to open the fridge. "I take offense to that—I'm hardly embarrassing." He grabbed a beer and cracked the tab of it open.

I narrowed a look at him. "I thought you had to study."

"Yeah, well, I'd have to seriously screw up these finals for it to have much of a negative effect on my grades"—he smirked in Logan's direction—"and how could I possibly pass up the chance for a night out on the town with my brother?"

I looked back toward Logan, my mind catching on the word "brother," and saw that he was watching me as if waiting for a reaction. Which was fitting, considering the white hot jealousy that rose in my chest at the thought of them going out. "Where are you guys going?" *Who were you seeing?*

To my disappointment and annoyance, a loud knock came from the front door. Adam instantly walked over to it, saying, "I'll answer it!"

I sighed, still looking at Logan. He hadn't said a single

word the whole time I was in the kitchen. After our kiss last fall, we'd both figured out how to be normal around each other without ever talking about it. But this . . . tonight . . . we hadn't done this yet. I was going out with Paul, and he was going off to do god knew what with god knew who. Was he as affected as I was?

I watched as he stood up from the kitchen chair and walked toward the front of the house, keeping his eyes on me all the way. His expression was still unreadable, the sudden anxiety I was feeling wedging itself firmly in my throat.

I followed, only to find that Adam had already let Paul inside of the entryway. He looked objectively amazing in his black tuxedo, and as he saw me coming from around the corner, he quickly swept me up and down. "Wow, Amelia, you look . . ."

"I would strongly recommend that you finish that sentence as respectfully as possible," interrupted Adam.

Paul's eyes snapped to Adam and then back to me. "Beautiful . . . I was going to say you look beautiful."

"Thank you, Paul. You look great, too." I felt Logan bristle next to me, but I ignored it. It didn't hurt to know that he might not like seeing me heading off to my prom night with Paul, but that didn't take away from the uncomfortable reality that Paul and Logan were in the same room. Or that I was feeling completely anxious about where he was going with Adam tonight.

"I brought you this," Paul said, holding out a plastic container with a beautiful, white corsage inside.

"Oh, thank you! Shoot, I have your boutonniere in the kitchen, hold on one second . . ." I turned on my heels and hurried back into the kitchen to get the flower for Paul's lapel from the fridge. When I noticed my parents in the backyard through the kitchen window, I grabbed the boutonniere and quickly opened the back door to call out that Paul was here, and then I made my way back to the front of the house.

I noted the awkward silence in the entryway when I got there. Adam and Logan were both staring down Paul, who was smiling as he looked back and forth between the two of them. I could tell he was uncomfortable despite his best efforts to appear confident. "Here you go," I said brightly at him as I reached over to pin it to his jacket.

After I had it securely fastened, Paul took out the beautiful corsage, made up of eucalyptus leaves and a simple white carnation flower, and pulled it over my hand and onto my wrist just as my parents came around the corner.

"Oh, look at you both," my mother crooned. "Such a good looking couple! Paul, that corsage is gorgeous. Nice job, dear."

Paul dipped his head and smiled. "Thank you, Mrs. Campbell." He then looked at my father and stuck his hand out. "It's a pleasure to meet you, Mr. Campbell."

I watched as my dad shook his hand, a stoic expression on his face. "Thank you, Paul. Glad to meet you as well. So . . . what's the plan for tonight?"

Adam, Logan, and my parents all turned to Paul expectantly, and I felt a twinge of guilt. He probably wasn't expecting my whole family to be here to send me off. If he was nervous, however, he didn't show it. "I'm taking Amelia to dinner with our friends, Eric and Mackenzie. From there, we'll head to the venue for the dance. And then afterward, I'll bring Amelia back home."

"What time does the dance end?" Adam asked. I threw a glare at him.

"I believe it ends at ten thirty," Paul breezily answered. He was really good under pressure.

"I'll be home by midnight," I announced. I didn't miss the quick, confused look that flashed across Paul's face, and I wondered why that would cause a reaction from him. The venue was only twenty minutes away from my house—surely I'd be home within ninety minutes of the dance ending. The confirmation seemed to settle everyone else, though.

"Well, you can't leave until I get a few pictures of you!" I watched as my mother picked up the camera that she had waiting on the entryway table. I moved to stand next to Paul and felt his arm wrap around my waist, tucking me in close to his body. We both looked at the camera and smiled as my mom took pictures. I felt the hard stares of Adam and Logan the whole time.

After a few overwhelmingly awkward minutes of feeling on display while posing with Paul in front of everyone, I decided my mother had taken enough pictures. "Okay, Mom . . . we'd better go!" I smiled wide in an effort to hide my discomfort.

"Oh, yes, you're right. You kids have dinner reservations to get to!" She put her camera back down and stepped forward to give me a hug.

"Thanks, Mom." I gave her a firm squeeze.

"Paul, take care of my daughter," my father directed.

"Yes sir, of course."

"And we'll see you back here at midnight," Adam stated pointedly.

I rolled my eyes, grabbing my clutch off of the table. "Let's go, Paul." I reached my hand inside of his arm and steered us toward the front door. As we stepped out, I turned to look back at my family, finding myself stuck on Logan's face as he watched me walk away with a smoldering look in his eyes.

Paul and I enjoyed dinner with Mackenzie and Eric at a local steakhouse before the dance. The food was delicious, and it was a bit of a relief to be sitting at the table with my best friend. Not that Paul was a disappointing prom date, but I found myself distracted by Logan's silence back at the house and having Mackenzie next to me provided a little reprieve.

Once we got to the dance, however, I lost that comfort as she and Eric hit the dance floor. They spent practically the entire night dancing, lost in a world that only included the two of them. It was sweet, their love for each other, but it meant that I was alone with Paul for most of the night.

Paul entertained dancing with me for a few songs, but then started campaigning for an early exit from the dance altogether. "Let's go somewhere a little more private, Amelia. We have a lot to talk about . . . like our future."

"Now? Is tonight really the best time for that?" I countered. I didn't understand the desire to leave prom to talk about the future. I didn't buy this dress to sit in his car and have a conversation about our relationship. This was supposed to be one of the most memorable nights of my life.

"Come on, Amelia, please? Maybe I could get us a room across the street? Try and score us a bottle of wine?"

"A room?" I scoffed. My mother's warning from earlier this evening prickled in my mind. "Paul, this is our prom. We're supposed to be *at* prom, dancing and enjoying some of these final moments with our friends."

Paul looked slightly irritated, but eventually dropped the subject.

When the dance ended, I found Mackenzie as she and Eric were coming off of the dance floor. "Millie! What are you guys doing after this?"

I could see Paul light up at the open opportunity for more plans. "I was just going to ask Eric where you guys are heading off to," he said.

"Oh." Mackenzie blushed. "Eric got us a room at the hotel across the street."

Paul gave me a look that said, *See.*

"I should probably get home, actually," I threw out casually, "but you guys have fun!" Mackenzie smiled at me and gave me a hug before she grabbed Eric's hand and dragged him out of the ballroom.

"I thought you didn't have to be home until midnight," Paul asked once they were out of earshot.

"Yeah, but the dance is over . . . and I should probably spend some time with my brother while he's in town." *If he was even home.* Sudden visions of him and Logan out at a bar surrounded by beautiful college girls flashed through my mind, souring my stomach.

The drive back to my house was silent. I could tell that Paul wanted more from this night, but I didn't have it in me to extend this any longer. Maybe he could find an after-party or something else fun to do after he dropped me off. It wasn't like I was trying to end *his* night—I just really wanted to go home.

When he pulled the car alongside the curb in front of my house, he surprised me by turning the car off. "Don't move, I'll come and let you out," he said, and I was happy to see him smiling. It made me feel like maybe I wasn't ruining his night.

Paul jumped out of the driver's seat and jogged around the front of the car to the passenger door, grinning as he opened it. He held a hand out for me in a chivalrous gesture, which was actually really nice because the heels I was wearing were killing me. "Such a gentleman," I said appreciatively.

Catching me off guard, Paul shut the car's passenger door and stepped closer to me, lightly pinning my body between the car and himself. "I have to admit, Amelia, I haven't been thinking very gentlemanly thoughts . . ." He traced a finger up the side of my arm before leaning forward to kiss me.

Paul and I had kissed plenty of times over the last few months, but I always found myself pulling away from him. Something about it never felt quite right. It wasn't surprising, if I was being honest with myself . . . not after knowing what it felt like to kiss someone who *was* right.

I humored him with this kiss for a few moments, but eventually turned my face away to break our mouths apart. "Thank you for the great night, Paul . . ." I tried to say, but Paul wasn't letting up. He was aggressively kissing my neck now, pushing me harder against the car with his body. As I felt him begin to suck the skin on the side of my neck, I tried to gently push him backward and off me, and in the process, he tried to hang on by biting into my skin. "Ow, Paul!" I shoved him, finally getting him to take a few steps back. "What the fuck?"

"What do you mean, 'what the fuck?' Amelia?" Irritation flooded through his eyes. "You always do this. You always hold out on me."

"Hold *out* on you? What does that even mean?"

"You never let us get any further than kissing. We've been together for months. It's prom night. When are we going to take some more steps in this relationship?"

I scoffed. I didn't even have the words to respond to that. Did he really think that I should be *putting out* just because we've been dating for a few months? That just because I'd allowed this so-called relationship to continue for so long, I now *owed* him less physical boundaries? I shook my head at him. "You're disgusting."

I shoved passed him and stormed up to the house, not even caring that my new heels were sticking into the grass with every step. I heard him get back into his car and slam his door shut, but I didn't look back. I would be, quite frankly, happy to never see or talk to him again.

I opened the front door of the house and found the entryway dark. It looked like my parents had already gone to bed. I reached down to unbuckle the thin straps of my heels and heard the soft sounds of laughter from a distance. People were in the basement.

I neatly tucked my shoes against the wall on the floor by the door and then padded down the hallway stairs. Taking my time descending down each step, it became obvious that Adam and Logan were home—and they weren't alone. Soft, feminine giggles flitted over the lower tones of Adam's voice.

Turning around the corner at the bottom of the staircase, I saw Adam, Logan and two girls I'd never seen before seated around the small coffee table in front of the sofa playing a card game. One of the girls, a beautiful redhead, was practically sitting in Logan's lap and murmuring into his ear while he studied the cards in his hands. Adam sat on the opposite side of the table with a brunette who was playfully trying to peek at his cards.

I cleared my throat to make myself known, and all four of them swiftly looked over at me. Logan kept his face completely neutral, while Adam smiled and said, "You're home early! Is Paul here?"

I shook my head. "No, he left."

"What happened to your neck?" Finally, Logan's voice. It was like velvet in my ears—but I was suddenly nervous about what he could see.

I reached my hand up to cover my neck, hoping it wasn't obvious. "I'm not sure, I think I scratched it."

Logan lost control of his expression, looking positively dangerous as his eyes burned on the hand that covered my neck. I knew for sure that he didn't believe me, and that he knew Paul had caused the mark. He probably thought that it was a mark of passion, something that I'd wanted.

Little did he know, the only mouth I wanted on my body was his.

The redheaded girl next to him looked at his face, and I could see her confusion in his expression. Adam, however, remained ignorantly unaware. "Do you want to get in on the game? We're playing spades."

I looked down at the table, avoiding Logan's furious gaze. "No thanks, I think I'm just gonna go to bed."

Adam shrugged. "Suit yourself."

I shot Logan a final look, noting the fragile restraint he had over his anger as he tried to collect himself. It did something to me, seeing him so upset. It was proof that he still thought of me, that he still might yearn for me the way I yearned for him. I wished so badly that it was him kissing me tonight.

He looked back down at his cards, no doubt working hard to disentangle himself from the memories of us just as I was, when I turned to walk back up the stairs.

# Chapter Sixteen

I SPENT THE WHOLE NEXT DAY IN A BUBBLE OF excitement and anticipation for my date with Logan. He texted me around noon to let me know that he would pick me up at six, and I was constantly looking at the time on my phone to count down the minutes until he got here. An undercurrent of mild anxiety was also simmering inside of me, but I tried not to focus too much on the fears that I knew were the root of it.

Like, how maybe he'd want to keep this as a friends-with-benefits type situation. Casual sex. Simple with no strings. I honestly wasn't sure if I could be okay with something like that—my feelings for Logan were anything but casual.

Adam had stayed up the entire night before like he said he would, binge-watching *Game of Thrones*. He'd been asleep all morning but I knew he would likely be getting up soon to get ready for work. Once he left for the hospital, I would have about an hour and a half to get ready until Logan got here.

I made a mental checklist of things to do, like shave my legs and put on a face mask before I put on any makeup—my skin had been so dry lately. I also already picked out an outfit and had it laid out on my bed in my room. Until I could start getting ready, though, I sat on the couch and watched trashy reality television in hopes that time would move by faster.

Eventually, Adam rose from his daytime slumber. He came out of his room in his boxers and began looking for something to eat in the kitchen, rummaging through the cabinets before he veered toward the fridge. He silently pumped his fist in the air when he found all of the Thanksgiving leftovers in there, and I sat there giggling as I watched him.

Spinning around to face my direction, he lifted his chin towards me and spoke, "I'm going to heat this up. You want some?"

I shook my head. "No thanks."

"Are you sure?"

"Yeah, I'm not that hungry yet. I'll eat later. Thank you, though!"

Adam shrugged before popping a container of food into the microwave. After making himself a plate, he stood at the kitchen counter and ate over the sink. "What are you up to tonight?"

*Shit*. I was hoping he wouldn't ask me that—I really didn't want to have to lie to him. "I'm not sure," I replied casually. It was technically true. I didn't know where Logan was taking me or what we'd be doing tonight.

"Well, don't be too much of a hermit. I'm sure Rachel would love to hang out with you." He threw it out as casually as he could. "You know, if you need a girls' night or something."

I couldn't help but smile at him. "Thanks, Adam. I really like her."

Adam's face morphed into something like wonder. "I know, isn't she amazing?"

"She really is. I'll reach out to her and set something up soon. Text me her number?"

"Sure." He seemed satisfied with this. "By the way, have you heard from Noah?"

*Whoa.* Hearing Noah's name was like a shock to the system. I shook my head and said, "Not a peep." I wasn't surprised that I hadn't heard anything from him. After the way I left, he was probably too angry with me to ever reach out without a really good reason. As if *I* were the one who'd done something wrong.

I honestly hadn't even thought much about Noah since we left for Breckenridge on Wednesday. My mind had been completely consumed with Logan.

Funny how quickly things could change. It was another really obvious sign that I was settling with Noah, because I clearly hadn't been very invested.

"Good, I was hoping not." Adam put his plate and fork into the sink and rinsed them both off. "Alright, I'm going to go shower and get ready for work. Enjoy your show."

I settled back into the couch and focused on *The Real Housewives of Beverly Hills* as he disappeared into his room.

An hour later, Adam walked out of the door to head to work and I threw myself into action. After turning off the TV, I practically ran into the en suite bathroom in my room and started the shower. As soon as the water was warm enough, I jumped in. I scrubbed my body with my favorite strawberry-scented soap and then shaved every inch of my legs. I washed my hair and let the conditioner stay in for a couple extra minutes to help give it some shine.

After my shower, I spent about thirty minutes blowing my hair out with a round brush, and when I was done I had to admit—it looked good.

I fished out a hydration mask from my toiletries tub and placed the slick sheet over my face. It smelled like jasmine and felt amazing on my skin. The instructions noted that it needed to stay on for about twelve minutes, so I used that time to put lotion on the rest of my body.

When I removed the mask, I let the remaining moisture on my face air dry while I got dressed. I'd chosen a casual-chic outfit that included a beige turtleneck crop top, a pair of comfortable black jeans, and cute black ankle boots. I had a black leather jacket to throw on before I left, so I went to hang it by the front door to grab when Logan got here.

Once I was dressed, I had about fifteen minutes left until six. I spent the remaining time I had putting on makeup, giving myself some extra *umph* around the eyes with my black eyeliner and gold shimmer eye shadow. When I was done, I looked at myself in the mirror and smiled. I felt good. Confident. Ready for this.

Then came a firm knock at the door.

Excitement prickled under my skin as I raced to the entry-way, almost slipping on the hardwood floor in my socks. When I reached the door, I unlocked the deadbolt and swung it open to find Logan standing on the other side, and he looked . . .

My god, he looked *amazing*.

He was wearing a black crew neck sweater, nice jeans, and dark brown boots. His cropped hair was styled a bit to the side, and it hit me again how much of a *man* he was—no longer the boy that I knew so long ago. It almost made my chest ache.

"Hi," I said, realizing as the word left my mouth that just three days ago I was opening this very same door to find Logan on the other side of it. So much had changed in just seventy-two hours.

Logan gave me a lopsided grin that radiated within me. "Hey, Mills." He leaned in for a quick kiss on the cheek as he walked into the apartment. "You ready?"

I nodded. "Yep, I just need to turn off the lights in my room real quick—one second!" I bounded back to my room to make sure everything was turned off, and then met Logan back at the doorway where I grabbed my leather jacket. "Let's go," I said, smiling up at him.

I was *so* ready for this.

Logan stood patiently next to me out in the hallway as I locked the door. As we walked toward the elevator, he reached down to grab my hand, lacing his fingers between mine. I looked up at him and smiled, feeling the heavy pitter-patter of my heart as it raged inside of my chest. When we reached the end of the hall, he pressed the button for the elevator.

A moment later, the elevator chimed before the doors opened and revealed a woman inside. It was the same woman who had sneered at me earlier this week when I'd first shown up to Adam's apartment. Her eyes found Logan first, and she grinned at him appreciatively, giving him a quick once-over with flirtatious eyes. When those eyes settled on me, her face visibly fell in confusion.

I smiled brightly at her, giving her my best impression of Julia Roberts on Rodeo Drive with dozens of luxury bags in my hands. Except we were in a beautiful high rise in Denver, and I had an incredibly sexy man on my arm.

The woman cleared her throat before looking down and swiftly moving out of the elevator. Logan and I stepped in, and as we turned around to face the closing doors, I caught the woman looking back at us. In the last moment before the door shut, I shot her a victorious wink.

"What was that all about?" Logan asked, grinning out of the side of his mouth.

"Oh, nothing." I shrugged. "Some women never leave their 'mean girl' era. And retribution can be sweet." I glanced up at him.

He shook his head. "Remind me to never piss you off."

"I'm sure you will. And I'm sure I'll piss you off too. But that's what make-up sex is for." I winked.

I watched as his pupils dilated, eyes darkening as the elevators opened to the building's beautiful lobby. I noticed Charlie at the door, making small talk with an elderly couple. *Shit.* I didn't want him to see me with Logan and risk him saying something to Adam about it. Looking around, I spotted a side door with an illuminated exit sign and pulled Logan toward it.

"Good call," Logan whispered down to me.

Outside, the air was cold. Thursday night's storm had hit the city just as fiercely as it'd hit the mountains. There was still a lot of snow on the ground, and Logan was careful to lead me through it as we walked to find his car in the lot. The heels I was wearing were comfortable, but I didn't trust myself on icy ground so I was thankful to have him to lean on.

I was so focused on the ground that I didn't notice Logan's car until he was opening the door for me. I looked up and saw his old, black Chevelle, still in gloriously mint condition. "You still have this?” I exclaimed, my voice suddenly a higher pitch in my excitement.

Logan chuckled softly. “Yes.”

I beamed up at him before I stepped in to sit down. He shut my door and walked around the front of the car while I looked around, soaking in the immaculate interior. The black leather seats were a bit worn but comfortable, the center console was so clean I could have eaten off of it, and the carpeted floor looked like it had very recently been vacuumed.

“Here, let me get the heat going for you,” he said as he hopped in and started the ignition.

“I’ve always wanted to ride in this car with you,” I said, still blown away that *this* was what he’d decided to pick me up in tonight. I hadn’t seen much of him over the last few years, but he’d been driving a black, two-door Bronco that he’d bought in college when I’d hung out with him and Adam last. I guess I figured that he’d sold this.

“What do you mean? I’ve driven you around in it before.”

I scoffed. “Yeah, around the block maybe. A total pity ride.” I shook my head, lightly giggling. “I remember you used to take girls out on dates in this thing, and I was always so jealous.”

Logan gave me a side-eye. “You were like, thirteen, Mills.”

“Yeah, but that was around the time you and Adam became too cool to hang out with me and I was definitely a sore loser about it.”

Logan as he steered the car out of the parking lot, and I spent the next ten minutes absorbed by his driving, completely mesmerized with how effortlessly he shifted the manual trans-mission. I don’t think I’d ever seen him look so comfortable doing something, and it was sexy as hell.

"You're staring."

I blushed. "Hard not to." Logan smiled at this. "Where are you taking me, anyway?"

"A fancy shmancy seafood restaurant downtown." His voice was low and matched the rumble of the car's engine. "We'll be there in about five minutes."

I could feel my mouth water. I loved seafood, and I hadn't eaten anything since breakfast. I watched Logan drive for a few more minutes and, sure enough, we soon pulled up to a cozy building with a dark green paneled exterior and an expansive patio. Tall heaters were mixed amongst the small tables, and edison lights hung beautifully from rafters above.

"Wait here," Logan said before he got out of his side of the car. A moment later, he was opening my door and holding out his hand, just as he'd done at the grocery store in Breckenridge.

"I could get used to this," I teased.

"Good." He said it as if it were simply a matter of fact, and I felt that single word well up inside of my belly like an inflating balloon.

Logan kept a hold of my hand as we walked into the restaurant. He gave his name for our reservation at the host stand, and the beautiful hostess led us to a small table in the back corner of the main dining room.

The lights were dimly lit and there were candles on every table. The waitstaff wore black ties, and maroon wallpaper with gold-foiled accents covered the main wall behind the bar, which looked to be made of white marble. Fancy shmancy was right.

Logan pulled my chair out for me to sit down before he took his seat across from me. He was a vision in this low lighting. "How did you find this amazing place?"

His eyes literally glittered. "I helped the owner of the restaurant restore a classic car, one of many in his collection."

"Wow, cars can really yield some great connections, huh?"

Logan laughed softly before nodding toward the menu. "Order whatever you want. I'm thinking oysters for an appetizer?"

"That sounds amazing."

We spent a few minutes looking over our menus before our waiter came to get our orders. We both ordered a drink, and I chose the shrimp scampi risotto while Logan ordered a ribeye steak and lobster tail. My mouth was still watering at the selection, and even more so as I watched the man sitting across the table ordering his food.

Once we were alone again, Logan's attention focused back on me. "Mills?"

"Yes?"

"Do you realize that you and I are on a *date* right now?"

This got my heart going. Were we going to talk about this? Now? "I kind of can't believe it . . ." I shook my head, grinning.

"Me either," he said.

"The last few days have been rather surprising," I continued.

Logan huffed. "You have no idea, Amelia."

"Oh?" I said, hoping that he would elaborate.

His expression became a bit more serious. "I just never thought this would actually happen."

"But . . . you've thought about it?"

Logan was contemplative for a moment before he finally answered, his voice low. "More than you know."

His words sent a ripple of pleasure straight through me.

"So what does this mean?" I dared to ask. "What do we do now?"

Logan lifted his shoulders in a small shrug. "This date is a good start," he said. "I think it might be a good idea to lay out some ground rules, though."

Ground rules? "Like what?"

"No sex, for starters."

I looked at him, deadpanned. "*What?*"

Logan chuckled. "We can't possibly try to navigate through whatever this is"—he motioned between us—"if we're having sex like we did in Breckenridge."

I stared at him, unable to form adequate words to respond with.

My silence must have told him enough, because he went on. "Amelia . . ." His voice was soft. "That was the single best night of my entire life, make no mistake. But you are one of the most important people to me. One of so few. I couldn't live with myself if I let sex get in the way of that."

I considered this for only seconds before I knew that he was right. Two nights ago, we'd let our hearts and bodies consume each other—but what if it wasn't enough to sustain us? We had so much to figure out.

"I was somewhat worried that you would want this to be a friends-with-benefits thing," I admitted.

Concern etched in his brow. "I would *never* use you like that, Amelia. I hope you know that."

I nodded. "Okay, so no sex." I felt my body diffuse a little. "What else?"

I watched as Logan rubbed the scruff on his chin with his hand. "We shouldn't tell anyone. Not until we know for sure what this is."

I already knew it was going to be a really big deal if and when my family ever found out about us . . . but I hadn't actually thought through what it would be like to tell them. Would they be happy? Would they lose their minds? Logan was right —we needed to make sure we were ready for that.

If this didn't work out, I would never want anyone in my family to look at Logan differently. I had to make sure that never happened, and right now, the safest thing for him was to keep this hidden. "I definitely agree with that. We keep it a secret until . . . ," I shrugged, "until we can't anymore."

The waiter came by with our drinks, dropping a large glass of white wine in front of me and a lowball of whiskey in front of Logan. He also set a large platter of oysters on ice in the middle of the table, and they looked incredible.

Logan reached over to grab my plate, dropping four shells on it and squeezing a slice of lemon over them before handing the plate back to me to serve himself. "Ever the gentleman," I mused, holding my glass of wine out to cheers him.

He shot me that breathtaking, lopsided grin of his. "Thank you for being here with me, Amelia." He held out his glass. "To the future," he said, clinking his glass against mine. I felt more hopeful than I had in a really long time. Here I was, sitting in this gorgeous restaurant with Logan, the possibility of a future that I'd given up on so long ago reigniting before me. It was a future that I could dream about again.

Just a mere week ago, I was willingly settled on a path of life that was just "okay." I wasn't brave, I wasn't passionate, and nothing about my relationship with Noah was particularly remarkable. But Logan . . .

With Logan I saw magic. I could see beyond the stars. He made me feel wholly alive, and some part of me had always,

always hoped for this. A beacon of hope that may have dimmed, but had never extinguished. I knew that it was only a chance—nothing was guaranteed—but it was the chance of my life.

We both took a sip of our drinks, and then dug in to the exquisite oysters in front of us, stealing glances at every opportunity.

# Chapter Seventeen

AFTER WE FINISHED ONE OF THE MOST INCREDIBLE dinners that I could remember, we were back in Logan's car. It had gotten much colder outside as the night set in and I was thankful for the hot air blowing from the vents. "Where to now?" I asked, looking over at Logan as he rubbed his hands together, seeking warmth from the friction. I had to stop myself from rogue thoughts about how else he could warm up his hands.

Oblivious to my train of thought, he looked over at me and smiled weakly before looking down at the gear shift. *Is he nervous?* "I'd like to take you to see my shop," he said carefully, "if you're up for it."

I felt my own face light up as I reached out to press my hand against the crook of his arm. "Logan, I would *love* to see the shop. That sounds amazing."

His eyes met mine again with a flash of relief and I realized that Logan was feeling vulnerable about this. Taking me to see his auto shop was important to him, and I could just kick myself that it had taken me this long to be a part of something so meaningful to him. Logan pulled out of the lot and onto the main road, and as he drove I found myself running through everything I'd missed. All the ways I should have been there for him these last few years.

Growing up, Logan had never outright asked me for anything—not exactly. But it also wasn't a secret between us that he came to me with the big things in life. It was our thing, an unspoken rule, an alliance seared into our souls. Adam was his best friend, but . . . I was his person. And I'd let my feelings and insecurities come between us to the point that I wasn't here to celebrate him for such an important milestone.

He was a business owner. He'd carved out success for himself, despite *everything*. I'd seen him here and there over the last couple of years, but our communication always stayed tucked inside of a safe zone—always very surface level. It hadn't felt natural to me, and I was sure it didn't to him either, but I had been more focused on keeping Logan at a safe distance so that I could protect my heart. Plus, I was with Noah, and I honestly didn't know how to approach a friendship with Logan that stayed within certain boundaries.

I vowed, right here in the car next to him, to never let myself stray from our friendship like that again. Regardless of what happened now. Even if we didn't succeed with this chance to be together. Even if it broke my heart and ruined me. Logan was anything but malicious, and I knew I couldn't keep blaming him for things that didn't work out the way I wanted them to. He deserved unwavering love and support, and I cemented it into my heart that I would always give that to him. No matter what.

It only took ten or so minutes before Logan was pulling up to a large brick building that sat along the main road. Floor-to-ceiling glass windows showcased a dark front lobby, and six black rolling doors lined along the side of the building, giving access to the numerous vehicle bays. "Holy shit, Logan. This is huge." A large sign hung proudly on the building above the bays, and though the light behind the sign was turned off, I could still make out the words. LOGAN'S AUTO SHOP. The sight of it caused the corners of my eyes to burn with welling tears. I looked toward Logan in the driver's seat and saw that he was watching me.

"I'll help you out." He nodded to my passenger door before he opened his own. When he got to me, he held out his hand for me again. I took it and briefly reveled in the familiarity of his skin against mine. The comfort of it.

I saw my breath as I stepped out of the car and into the freezing night air. "Let's get inside where it's warm," he said, intertwining his hand with mine as he led the way. He unlocked the deadbolt with the keys in his other hand and opened the glass door, letting me past him to step inside first.

Inside, the shop was warm from a heater still running. The smell of motor oil flooded my nose. It was thrilling to think about the hard work that went on here every day—a whole team of smart and capable mechanics who, under Logan's supervision, worked together to make things better for people.

"Logan." I could hear the wonder in my own voice. "This is amazing!"

I watched as he, too, looked around the lobby that we stood in, absorbing the environment as if he didn't spend most of his time here already. "Thank you. I've been working really, really hard to make this place meaningful."

"Meaningful?" I asked.

"Yeah . . . I have the privilege of *employing* people, Mills. Guys who don't have a lot of other options—real good guys. I get to provide them with a stable opportunity. A stable income. And our customers, we really help them here. This is an honest garage, we do good work."

I could feel my heart fluttering for this man, this incredible man, who was such a light in the world. "I'm really fucking proud of you, Logan." I reached out to hug him, sliding my hands underneath his arms and pressing my cheek to his chest. I craved the feel of him, in this moment of raw intensity. "I'm not at all surprised that you're having success here. You're an amazing person with integrity, and this is what you were made to do."

I felt his arms wrap around me in a firm embrace. "Thank you, Mills." His lips came down to kiss the top of my head in a way that was casual but deeply intimate, causing butterflies to soar throughout my chest and stomach.

He pulled away from me, taking my hand again as he led me behind the counter. "Come on, I'll show you around." Logan proceeded to give me a tour, showing me the various bays that were dedicated to different services. There was a car lifted up high in one of them, allowing easy access for work to be done from underneath. In another, a car's motor had been removed from the front. "This one's been a hell of a project trying to figure out, but one of my guys, Manny, finally found the problem in one of the condensers," he explained, as if I had any idea what a condenser was.

He then took me to a small room in the back that served as his office. There was a computer on a desk with a second monitor showing what was obviously security camera footage.

A small, black sofa sat along the wall, and filing cabinets stood together along the opposite wall. "I don't spend a whole lot of time here—I'm usually out working with the guys—but this is where I handle all of the accounting and other admin stuff."

I pictured him sitting at the desk in here at the end of a long, hard day, processing invoices and crunching numbers and keeping the foundation of this place strong. Finding words that adequately described the pride I felt for him was nearly impossible.

"Are those yours?" I asked, pointing to a pair of gray coveralls that were hung on a wall anchor.

Logan looked to where I was pointing, confusion flashing on his face. "Yes . . ." he replied, looking back at me.

"I'm going to need to see you with those on"—I raised my eyebrows at him—"like, really soon . . ."

Logan let out a bark of laughter. "Behave, Amelia." His smile was bright, reaching the amber of his eyes. Golden circles shined from his irises. He really was a beautiful man, I thought, as I watched his face turn more serious. "You know, I'm so grateful for everything I've been able to do here. I know it's where I'm supposed to be, professionally speaking, and it's an amazing feeling to be able to do what I love and call it a job. But . . ." He hesitated for a moment before continuing again. "I feel like a piece of my life is still missing. And as much as I've always tried to fight it—" He took in a breath. "I know damn well that piece is you." I could hear the splintered edges in his voice, the emotion seeping out roughly from his throat.

A new wave of tears stung my eyes. "Logan . . ."

He reached out to take both of my hands into his. "Thank you, for everything you've done for me, for everything that you still do to make me feel confident in chasing my dreams. I wouldn't be here, standing in *my* office, inside of a business that *I* own, if it weren't for your support every single time that I've needed you." He was studying me with intensity. "And I'm sorry . . . I'm sorry I wasn't there for you in the same way. I'm sorry that I tried so hard to convince myself that my feelings for you weren't worth pursuing.

"I was scared—I'm *still* scared—of what it would mean if things don't work out. I'm not sure that I could take losing you." He began shaking his head, as if to ward off his pestering fears. "I can't lose you." His voice was much quieter. A desperate plea.

I saw the shine of tears form in his eyes, and the pressure squeezing my chest became almost too much to bear. Logan had just broken my heart into a thousand pieces with his words, and then sealed it all back together again with pieces of his own, permanently welding himself to me.

Closing my eyes, I stepped closer to him, breathing in his scent of cedar and citrus. "Logan, I believe in this." I kept my voice as strong as possible, despite the wild emotions surging through me. "I believe that we can do this, and I'm so thankful to finally have this chance with you. I know that it's scary . . . I'm scared too. But . . ." I looked up into his eyes, willing him to hear my words. Willing him to see straight into my soul. "We can't let fear stop us from trying our best to be happy. Or stop us from what could be the best experience of our entire lives. We already have a foundation of love and trust between us, and I think that, no matter how this shakes out, none of that will ever falter. *We* won't let it, okay? Promise me that, moving forward, we tackle our fears together. As a team."

Logan nodded, and I watched as his eyes dropped to my

mouth. "Okay, Mills. I promise." There was a rasp in his breath that tugged low in my belly.

And then I was rising to my tip toes, desperate to close the gap between us. Pressing my lips against his, I felt his hands rise to my waist, sliding around to my back. He pulled me in closer, deepening what I'd only meant to be a soft, quick kiss. His tongue slid against my lips before I opened them for him, and the groan from the back of his throat sent lightning strokes through me.

He pulled away from me, his breathing rapid, and pressed his forehead to mine. "I already want to cancel the no sex rule," he said, his voice gritty like sandpaper.

"Then do it," I encouraged, pressing my hand to his cheek. I knew I should support his rules, but right now—I could only hope he'd be willing to break them.

He groaned again. "You're going to be the death of me." He pressed another hurried kiss to my lips before taking a step back, creating half a foot of space between us. He studied me for a moment, his chest still lightly heaving from the pull of our bodies. "This is a risk we take together. You're right, we do this as a team, through the highs and the lows." He nodded, as if he were speaking more to himself than to me. "The only way this really works is if we go all in. I won't hide my feelings from you—not anymore. I promise."

"Thank you." I smiled, prying my eager mind away from the curve of his throat, the broadness of his shoulders. "Now, tell me more about this place. How many employees do you have?"

He smiled at my subject change, and then started walking out of the office and back to the shop floor. "Let's see . . . There's Jessica and Camila who both work part time at the front desk. Jess is in college so she needs flexible hours and Camila is the sister of one of the mechanics. She fell on some hard times and needed a job, and I was more than happy to give her one. And then I have eight guys who work on the cars. I was thinking, if you're serious about helping me with some marketing, maybe you could come in one day this week and meet everyone." He said it casually but I knew this was important to him.

"That sounds perfect," I said to him. "And maybe we can also make out in your office a little?"

Logan huffed out a surprised laugh. "Mills! It would be during business hours . . ."

"I know," I retorted, throwing him a quick wink.

He shuffled his feet. "My god, woman," I heard him say under his breath.

I pulled my phone out of my purse to check the time, seeing that it was only eight-thirty. "Come on," I said, holding my hand out for his. "I want you to take me to get some ice cream."

THIRTY MINUTES LATER, we sat in a plush booth at a local diner with a massive snickers milkshake sitting on the table between us. "I feel like I'm fourteen again," Logan mumbled before he took a pull from one of the straws.

I put my lips around mine and joined him for a drink. Chocolate and caramel flooded my mouth, sending endorphins straight to my brain. When I was done, I licked my lips before saying, "You certainly don't look fourteen." Flickers of a younger Logan illuminated in my mind. The boyish grin that drove me crazy. The long, unkempt hair beneath his backward hat. The wild rage that could fly out of him on a hairpin trigger. I ached for the boy I once knew, but also fiercely longed for the man in front of me now.

Logan hummed. "When can I see you again?" His eyes bounced from the cherry falling deeper into the melting whipped cream to my eyes. His question sent my body floating. It elated me that he was already trying to secure our next encounter.

"Depends," I responded nonchalantly.

"On what?"

"On when you want me to come in for my field trip." I took another sip of the milkshake, getting some of the snicker chunks up through the straw.

"How about Monday?" It was as if he were injecting helium straight into my bones.

I thought about my schedule for the week. I needed to work on new brand guidelines for Bite of Life, and I had to build next month's social media calendars for a few other clients, but all of that could easily be done after Monday. "Monday sounds good to me."

Logan dipped his head in approval. "Okay, good. I'll have some things to work on first thing in the morning, but I should be available in the early afternoon."

"Okay, I'll be there around eleven?"

He nodded, before his face grew serious as he considered me. He reached his hand out to cover mine, lightly rubbing his thumb along the side of my pinky. "I'm already counting down the hours."

I felt a pitter patter in my chest that only he had the ability to create.

After we finished our dessert, Logan reluctantly drove me

back to Adam's. I'd have liked to say that we fully respected our new rule to leave sex off the table, but we definitely played with fire as Logan pushed me up against the front door and kissed me so deeply I almost forgot who I was. It was a kiss full of promises, a blazing reminder of the twin flame burning within us.

Much to my disappointment, Logan finally peeled himself off of me and said goodnight with a chaste kiss to my forehead. "Sleep well, Mills."

"Thirty-seven more hours," I responded wistfully.

I heard his low chuckle from the end of the hall as I watched him press the elevator button.

# Chapter Eighteen



THE ELECTRICITY IN THE AIR WAS SO THICK AND palpable, I could feel it weave between my fingers as I reached out to grab the cold bottles of beer from the bartender's hands. The little dive bar was crowded with college students fresh off of finals who were looking to unwind and get lost in the night before heading back to wherever they came from for summer break.

I handed my credit card to the bartender, asking her to keep my tab open, and then made my way back to our little table in the corner. Scarlet and Ivy cheered as I approached and Danny whistled his approval, his bright eyes locking on the bottles in my hands.

A shiver of excitement ran up my spine. It felt like the beginning of one of those nights—a night that would sear into my memory to be thought of and admired later. Like a right of passage that I would only really be aware of after it was over. I was twenty-one and had just passed all my finals. Junior year of college was officially over, and as I looked around, it felt like every single student had ventured into this little college bar to celebrate. To let loose. To get drunk and rowdy.

Classes had definitely been difficult, but with a lot of late nights spent studying in my tiny bedroom, I'd ended the year with straight A's. It was my best semester yet, and I was ready to burn off some of my pent-up energy.

I set the bottles of beer down on the table and wrapped my arms around Danny's neck, stealing a quick, salty kiss. We'd been dating for almost five months now, and while our relationship wasn't perfect, he was always a good partner-in-crime to go out with on nights like this.

Danny was a year older than me and had just finished his engineering degree. He'd be graduating with the rest of the senior class early next week. I knew he was probably going to get raucous tonight, and I saw it as a challenge, eager to keep up. "Cheers," I said into his ear, clinking my bottle against his.

He looked up at me and grinned, pressing his bottle to his lips and taking a long sip before he pressed those very same lips to mine.

"Get a room, you two," Ivy said, laughing as she threw a crumpled napkin at us. Her long braids were flecked with gold beads, and she looked like dynamite in a slinky white dress.

"Speaking of which," Scarlet inserted, a smile playing on her lips, "Ivy, you're my wing woman tonight. Let's find some good men, shall we?" She pushed a red curl out of her face and held up her bottle of beer toward Ivy, who tapped it against her own.

"Done and done," Ivy replied.

I'd been living with Scarlet and Ivy in student housing all school year, and while I wouldn't have necessarily said that we'd developed any sort of rock solid, lasting friendship together, they were definitely a pair that I could have fun with. We'd all be moving out at the end of the week, so tonight also served as our last hurrah as roommates.

The lights in the bar dimmed considerably as a spotlight shone on a small stage in the corner. The music that had been playing overhead stopped as a man stepped onto the stage, microphone in hand. "Good evening, everyone! My name's Ryan and I'm here to host karaoke night!"

Cheers erupted around the bar as Ryan chuckled and took a small bow.

"Alright, I love this enthusiasm—I can tell we're going to have a lot of fun. So listen up, we're going to let the house music play for another few minutes, but if you'd like to get on the mic, you can come on over and submit your song in this basket." He held up a brown wicker basket above his head for everyone to see.

"Ohhh, Amelia," Scarlet exclaimed, reaching out to grab my arm. "You have to sing!"

"Yes! You absolutely have to," Ivy echoed.

"Uh . . ." I hesitated. "In front of all these people? I don't know about that . . ."

"Come on," Scarlet whined. "You're pretty decent when you sing around the apartment!" My face flushed. I never realized anyone had been listening to me sing. Knowing that Scarlet was—I felt slightly embarrassed. I also knew she was a damn liar because I could barely hold a tune; Adam and Logan always teased me for it.

I looked around and watched as a handful of other people stood up to request a song. And then my eyes found Danny's, and I could see the dare glinting in his blazing blue eyes. "Come on, Amelia. There's nothing to be scared of." A lazy smile spread across his face. "Show us what you can do up there."

I sighed and made a show of rolling my eyes, but I could feel my cheeks pulling toward my ears as my own smile grew. I was never really one to put myself out there like this, but tonight—tonight I'd wanted to take risks. So what if I couldn't hold a tune. Tonight was about breaking away and finding an opportunity to just *live*. I recognized the fear that held me back, but decided not to let it control me. "You fuckers owe me," I said as I scooted off of my chair and walked up to Ryan and the basket. I could hear the table behind me erupt in another round of cheers, and I rolled my eyes again.

There was a low table near the stage that held the big song book, and I flipped through it for a few minutes before I found a song that I knew would match Danny's dare perfectly. That would help me lean into my fear. To let go of some control. He wanted to see a show—dammit, I would give him one.

I wrote the request on a small white slip of paper and dropped it into the basket and caught sight of the bar. If I was going to do this, I would need a few more shots.

TWENTY MINUTES and three shots later—*whoops*—I heard Ryan say my name through the sound system. "Alright everybody, get ready for this next song. We have a bit of a *dangerous* one, so I hope you're all ready for it . . . Amelia, come on up!"

My friends broke out in loud applause as I got up to make my way over to the stage. I knew I should be feeling more nervous, but the tequila had worked wonders in boosting my confidence. As I reached Ryan, he handed me the microphone and helped me step onto the low stage. I made my way to the center of the platform, looking up to the crowd.

With the spotlight shining on me, it was difficult to see the surrounding bar and all of its patrons. I suddenly felt extremely exposed as a jolt of nerves crashed through my stomach. There was nothing but silence as we all collectively waited for the music to begin playing. I heard someone cough in the corner, the rattle of ice as the bartender made a drink.

Just as the jazzy music began to play, I noticed the door of the bar opening. The frame of the man who walked in seemed familiar to me and as I squinted, I realized it was Logan. I felt myself gasp in a small breath. I hadn't seen Logan in a few months—not since going out with him and Adam for New Year's Eve and watching him kiss a random brunette at midnight which, truthfully, had crushed me. He wore a white T-shirt and dark pants tonight, his long, unruly brown hair peeking out from underneath a backward Rockies hat. He looked . . . Well, he always looked good. He made his way directly to the bar, completely oblivious to the fact that I was on the stage, and another surge of embarrassment swept through me.

Just as he reached the bar, I began to sing "Dangerous Woman" by Ariana Grande. I'd meant for the sexy tune to be a total joke—what I'd thought was a hilarious response to Danny's dare. But now, as I started to sing, watching Logan order a drink, I felt the familiar vulnerability that always seemed to rear itself within me when I was around him.

In an attempt to regain my composure, I closed my eyes and focused on the song's opening lyrics.

*Don't need permission*

*Made my decision to test my limits*
*Cause it's my business, God as my witness*
*Start what I finished*
*Don't need no hold up*
*Taking control of this kind of moment*
*I'm locked and loaded*
*Completely focused, my mind is open*

Opening my eyes again, I immediately found Logan's face. He was sitting at a high-top table in the center of the bar's lounge, watching me. Even through the dimly lit view of the bar, I could see surprise in his eyes and a small smile playing on his lips. He looked positively delighted, like he was tickled to have stumbled upon me, to witness this moment. I felt my own smile bloom as I continued singing.

*All that you got, skin to skin, oh my God*
*Don't ya stop, boy*
*Somethin' 'bout you makes me feel like a dangerous woman*
*Somethin' 'bout, somethin' 'bout, somethin' 'bout you*
*Makes me wanna do things that I shouldn't*

I remained locked in Logan's eyes, watching as he took a sip of his beer. When he moved to set the bottle back down on the table, I could see his eyes slowly shift from delight to something else—a much darker expression that I'd seen before. A dangerous look that had plagued my mind for years. One that I'd questioned over and over again, as if it maybe wasn't ever actually real. That perhaps I'd made it up, telling myself stories —crazy things—to sooth the continuous wounds that he'd inflicted on my ego. But here it was, right there on his face. Proof of his predatory hunger.

Like he was a man starved.

It was the look he gave me right before he kissed me many moons ago. The look he gave me on my prom night. The look I swore I'd caught him giving me numerous times over the years, in many quick moments, small flashes, before he'd always reverted back to his steady expression of control.

*I wanna savor, save it for later*
*The taste of flavor, cause I'm a taker*
*Cause I'm a giver, it's only nature*
*I live for danger*
*All that you got, skin to skin, oh my God*
*Don't ya stop, boy*

My body had begun to move, invigorated by his attention. If he was a man starved, I was his last supper served on a silver platter. I moved in slow, sultry sways as I stared into his dark, honey eyes.

Like a moth to a flame, I was enraptured. I was performing. For *him*. And he made no attempts to conceal the way his body reacted to it. His mischievous eyes locked in on me, his chest rising and falling a bit more rapidly, his hand tightly gripping his bottle of beer.

It made me feel good. Seeing him reacting this way to me— it made me feel alive. I was once again swirling inside of his orbit and the familiar rush of it was all-consuming.

My whole life, Logan had always been around. And as much as we'd both tried like hell to deny it, there was a dangerous undercurrent of desire that threatened to drown us at any moment. It always felt so damn good to give in to that feeling, to lose the mask of the platonic relationship that we'd worked so hard to protect, and give into the deep longing that always *was*.

*All girls wanna be like that*
*Bad girls underneath, like that*
*You know how I'm feeling inside*
*Somethin' 'bout, somethin' 'bout*
*Somethin' 'bout you makes me feel like a dangerous woman*

I ran my left hand up my body as I continued to sing for him. Watching as he kept his full attention on me. Turning the lyrics of the song into a siren's cry out for him.

No one else in the bar existed at this moment. It was just Logan. It was *always* just Logan. I yearned to feel him against my body again. I yearned to taste his tongue as it swept through my mouth again. So many thoughts. So many dizzying thoughts that had never stopped running rampant inside of my mind.

He was here, in this moment of my need to let go. The wicked flame in his eyes matched the fire that burned inside of me, coursing through my entire body. Fully ignited again. Always for him.

As the song ended, the entire bar shifted into a heavy silence before the crowd began to applaud, the sound of clapping ripping me back into reality. Logan seemed to have also been jolted back into awareness as his eyes flicked from mine to the table in front of him where a girl was whistling. His gaze fell back on me and he began clapping his large hands together.

His unfiltered smile was a rarity that I didn't get to see very often, and it took my breath away.

"Damn. That was . . . everyone give a big hand to Amelia for that performance!" Ryan's voice filled the bar through the sound system. I turned to step back down from the stage and was shocked to find Danny standing next to Ryan near the steps, waiting for me. His eyes were blazing with something I didn't quite recognize, something that didn't match the forced smile he gave me.

*Oh, fuck.*

"Hey babe," he said as his eyes moved briskly in Logan's direction. "That was really something."

I smiled back at him, but my body was suddenly riddled with nervous energy. I made an attempt to ease the expression on my face, but the wave of emotions that flowed through me was likely as obvious as a literal elephant in the room would have been.

I made the terrible mistake of flicking my eyes to Logan again, noting the hint of confusion on his face as he watched me falter, before I returned my gaze back to Danny. He didn't miss the move, and his expression sank.

"Thanks, Danny." My voice was breathy and tight. I didn't know what else to say. Everything that had just happened between Logan and I was certainly not fair to him, and the guilt of that tore through me.

There was no going back, though. And I knew it. The look on Logan's face during that song was all the proof I needed that he felt the same way that I did, at least tonight. We were drawn together like magnets. Even if it was fleeting, even if I'd caught him off guard in an unexpected moment of weakness—

hell, even if this was all it ever would be—it was enough for me to know that I wouldn't be able to focus on anyone else.

It was something that I'd tried so damn hard to convince myself wasn't real. It would have been easier if it weren't real, this incessant tugging. I'd tried to move on from it, to run from it, to be with nice guys like Danny who may not have been the loves of my life, but who were at least reciprocating their feelings in a meaningful way.

I sighed, deigning myself to the honesty that I know Danny deserved. "Look . . . I'm sorry. I didn't know he'd be here tonight."

Danny's eyes lit with surprise before the hostility set in. "So, you know him?" His voice dripped with anger.

"Yes. I know him," I replied, keeping my tone matter-of-fact.

Danny scoffed. "Have you been seeing him this whole time?" The hurt in his tone was obvious, and I felt myself sink further into how shitty I was feeling.

"No—it's not like that. I've never been *with* him, not really. But I've known him my whole life and . . . it's complicated. I thought I'd moved on, that I didn't carry these feelings anymore. But . . ." I paused. "I guess I do. I'm so sorry."

Danny turned his angry eyes back toward the direction of the table that Logan sat at, no doubt bristling in an attempt to intimidate him. I kept focus on his face, stopping myself from looking over at Logan again. I didn't want to make this worse.

Danny looked back at me with a viciousness that I never would have expected to see coming from him. "Good luck with that, Amelia." The words spit out from his mouth like venom, and it caught me by surprise. "Actually, good luck to him, because you're a fucking shit girlfriend anyway."

Danny moved past me, heading for the bar's exit and bumping hard into my shoulder as he went. He clearly never expected anything like this to happen, and was probably embarrassed that someone he was dating could be interested in someone else. He was smart, good looking, and had girls ogling him all the time—this sort of thing didn't happen to guys like him.

Taking a deep breath, I turned and faced Logan again. To my surprise, he was standing in front of the table he'd been sitting at, as if he'd been about to approach me. Or, more likely, had been about to approach Danny when he saw him purposely bump into me.

He stood frozen as he regarded me carefully. His expression was a mix of guilt, frustration, and longing. I didn't miss the slight shake of his head as he looked down at his shoes, took in a visible, chest-expanding breath, then turned around and walked out the door.

# Chapter Nineteen

"WHAT A FUCKING PRICK," MACKENZIE SCOFFED with disdain. She had a certain way of speaking in which she enunciated every syllable, and hearing her call Noah a prick felt especially dramatic because of it.

"I know, right." I picked up my glass of champagne—because it was brunch, after all—and took a long sip. Mackenzie shook her head and picked up her own glass.

"Are you okay?" There was real concern on her face. It wasn't the first time she'd given me this look, either. I'd been on the receiving end of it when I told her about Paul's groping hands the day after prom night, when I got so sick with the flu freshman year of college that I missed almost a week of classes, and after our graduation trip to Mexico when I was an emotional, blubbering mess—even though I never truly let her in on what caused my broken heart.

"Yeah," I said, taking in a breath. "I'm actually *really* okay. As pissed as I was that night, I feel like it all happened for a reason. I know that's so cliche to say, but I just wasn't supposed to be with him, you know?"

Mackenzie took off her sunglasses, braving the sunny November daylight with bare eyes, and studied me carefully. "Wow, you really are okay, aren't you?"

I chuckled. I knew not to be offended. Noah was an almost three-year relationship, after all. "Yeah, I am."

Her look intensified as her eyebrows furrowed together in maximum-level scrutiny. "Spill it, Campbell."

I met her gaze, mustering up some bravery. If there was a true time for girl talk, this was it. "Okay, but you *have* to keep this a secret," I implored.

Mackenzie rolled her eyes. "Millie, come on."

"I mean it, Mack." I kept my face serious.

She threw up her hands. "Okay, okay, I promise. I won't even tell Eric."

I nodded my head in approval. "Okay. So . . . ," I started, playing with the edges on the napkin in front of me. "I sort of slept with someone."

"*What!*" Mackenzie screeched. "Amelia, you broke up with Noah five days ago, and we've had, like, *Thanksgiving* since then. How in the world are you already pulling men?"

Her response was so ridiculous that I giggled before taking another long sip of champagne. Mackenzie was locked in on me and I knew I wasn't going to be able to keep it in any longer, so I closed my eyes and just blurted it out. "I slept with Logan."

After a few seconds, I squinted open my right eye to see Mackenzie staring at me, frozen, before she finally reacted. "I'm sorry, Amelia . . . Did you just say you *slept with Logan*?"

"Yes," I confirmed, opening my eyes back up in surrender.

"As in, Logan Davis?"

"Yes," I repeated.

"As in, the third Campbell sibling?"

I scrunched up my face in a flair of annoyance. "Okay, Mackenzie, don't make it weird. He's obviously not my brother."

She threw up her hands in mock surrender, a sudden burst of energy bounding out from within her. "I know, I know, but . . . damn! Amelia! You can't expect me not to be completely shocked by this. How did it even happen?"

I paused for a moment, trying to figure out an adequate way to explain how we'd gotten here. Logan found me in a snowstorm outside of my parents' house in the middle of the night and proceeded to sweep me off my feet and into his bed? It *was* the truth, but it left so many holes—there was a pretty extensive history that I'd always kept secured inside of a steel trap within my heart. I didn't want Mackenzie's first impression of this potential relationship to be that it was some sleazy, drunken hookup. A fierce protectiveness was already welling up inside of me.

I took a deep breath before I spoke. "Truthfully, this thing with Logan goes back really far. I've . . . I've been in love with him for as long as I can remember." I kept my eyes down at the table. "I don't know when or how it started, but for a long time I dealt with it by shoving the feelings as far down as I could and convincing myself that he didn't feel the same way."

"Wow," I heard Mackenzie expel through a breath. I finally looked up and met her eyes, seeing so many conflicted emotions staring back at me. "What changed? Does he have feelings for you too?"

I felt the pull of a smile on my face.

"He admitted that he thought he was doing the right thing this whole time by ignoring what he felt between us. And that he wants to give it a real chance."

Mackenzie's face softened and she tilted her head as she continued to watch me. "Wow, Millie . . . that's one of the most incredibly tortured but amazing love stories I've ever heard. You both have really been pining for each other this whole time?"

"Yeah, it looks that way. But you really can't say anything to anyone." I threw a small thread of authority in my tone, which was so unlike me. "In order for this to work, we need to keep my family out of it, and if Eric knows . . . I feel like it would only be a matter of time before Adam found out."

Mackenzie huffed. "You're right about that. Eric is the worst gossip." She shook her head before smiling at me. "This is such crazy news, Amelia. I'm literally speechless. Wait . . . why don't you want to tell your family? Isn't this a good thing?"

I hesitated for a second, wanting to adequately explain the fear that was so deeply rooted in Logan without jeopardizing his trust. "It's a chance, but we don't know for sure where it'll lead us. And if for any reason it didn't work out, Logan would be really affected by something like that if my whole family was involved. He'd worry about losing us, and he doesn't have any other family. It's what's kept him from acting on this for so long, and I would hate for the pressure from a fear like that to get in the way of this opportunity to be together. It's just better for us to wait until we know for sure, and then we'll tell them."

I watched a golden clump of hair fall in front of Mackenzie's face as she nodded in understanding. "Makes sense, and it gives you guys room without feeling any pressure from anybody."

"Yeah," I said breathily. "Low pressure all around." My voice was confident, but inside I felt a sudden wave of nausea as I realized how desperately I needed this chance to work. I needed Logan more than I cared to admit.

Mackenzie lifted her champagne glass and held it up toward me over the table. "Cheers to you and Logan, and to your happily ever after," she said with an encouraging smile.

My heart welled up at her words as I picked up my glass as well, softly clinking it against hers. "Thank you, Mack."

We both sipped our champagne, Mackenzie watching me through the side of her glass. After setting our glasses back down on the table, she began talking again. "You know, Amelia, love is the easy part. Falling in love, being in love—it's one of the easiest things to do if you're with the right person. I can see the worry on your face, and I get it. But Logan is a good man. He's always been the responsible, guarded one. He's smart. And the way he used to look at you—it all makes sense now. Trust him. He'll see it through to the other side. Don't worry about it all so much that you forget to enjoy the fall."

"The way he used to look at me?" I asked, caught on those words. "What do you mean?"

"Like . . ." she started, pausing to find the words. "He was always watching you. No matter what he was doing, or what was going on around him, his eyes were always searching for you. He would visibly settle when you were in his line of sight. I always thought it was just a protective urge. Brotherly, like something that Adam would do. But now . . . I don't know. I think it was something more."

We both stayed silent for a moment as I absorbed her

words. I'd always felt Logan's eyes on me in the same way that I was completely aware of him, a magnetic pull between us that I thought only I felt.

This realization caused a bout of frustration to ignite within me. I felt anger at his father for hurting him, for crushing his soul as a little boy. If Logan hadn't been so fearful, so careful, perhaps we could have had this chance so much sooner.

We could have had so much more time.

"Okay, Millie, I have news." An air of excitement suddenly surrounded Mackenzie, and I remembered her text the other day mentioning that she had something to share.

"What is it?" I asked curiously.

Mackenzie picked up her champagne again and put it to her lips, tilting the glass so that the rest of the contents poured into her mouth. As she did, one of her fingers was wiggling around, catching my attention. And there it was, right on her ring finger. A big, fat diamond.

"Holy shit! Mackenzie! You're engaged?"

Her eyes practically sparkled. "Yes! Eric proposed on Thanksgiving in front of my whole family. It was so romantic." She clasped her hands together at her chest, practically swooning.

I reached out to touch her arm, briefly squeezing my hand around her. "I am so, *so* happy for you, Mack. I can't think of two people more deserving of a fairytale wedding."

"Thank you, Millie. You're my best friend in the entire world, and you've been there with us since the beginning." She paused for a moment, and I noticed a tear slip down her face. "Would you please be my maid of honor?"

I felt myself gasp as tears of happiness burned in the

corners of my eyes. "Oh my god, Mackenzie, *yes!* Of course I will!" I stood up from the table and moved around it to where she was rising from her own chair and pulled her in for a hug.

As we held on to each other, rocking back and forth with tears of joy streaming down our faces, I couldn't help the fantasy of this exact moment at some point in my future, when I could ask Mackenzie to be *my* maid of honor, and knew that the only man I wanted to reach that moment with was Logan.

I WALKED into Adam's apartment later that evening and caught something delicious wafting from the kitchen. I shrugged my coat off and hung it on the hook by the door and then shimmied out of my cute winter boots. When I rounded the corner to see what could possibly smell so good, I found Rachel at the stove frying what looked like some sort of balled meat. She turned to look at me as I came into the kitchen and smiled brightly. "Hey, Amelia!"

"Hey," I said right back. "I feel like I keep finding you in the kitchen when something smells amazing. What is it?" I asked, nodding toward the frying pan.

Rachel bounced up on to her toes before she answered, "Chicken croquettes! They're like, fried balls of pulled chicken —so good."

"Huh, that sounds delicious. Can I help?"

"Actually," Rachel answered, eyes bright blue, "do you want to throw together the salad?"

"Sure," I said, stepping over to the counter.

Rachel instructed me on everything needed for the salad before jumping back to the stove to flip around the croquettes.

We were working side by side in a comfortable silence when I remembered Adam's nudge from yesterday.

"Hey Rachel, I meant to ask Adam for your number but now that you're here, let's swap info. I'd love to get lunch with you one day soon if you're up for it?" I turned over my shoulder to look at her.

"Oh my gosh, yeah! That would be great!"

"Cool," I said, focusing back on the carrots I was chopping.

The front door opened, followed by the sounds of boots shuffling off, and then Adam was bounding his way into the kitchen with two bottles of wine in hand. "It smells like heaven in here, Rach," he said, holding out the two bottles. "I got two reds, hope that's okay?"

Rachel beamed up at him. "Perfect."

Adam set them both on the counter before turning my way. "What's up, sister?"

"Hey, no work tonight?" He'd worked the last two nights since we got home from Breckenridge.

"Not tonight, but I'll work most of this coming week." I made a quick mental note of this. "What have you been up to today?"

I added the sliced carrots to the wooden salad bowl next to me on the counter. "I had brunch with Mackenzie, and then did a little apartment hunting around the city."

"Oh nice, find anything worth pursuing?"

I shrugged. "Everything I like costs a fortune. And everything in my price range is a dump. When did it get so expensive to lease an apartment?"

Adam chuckled. "Denver is a gorgeous city, and people

have been transplanting here from all over the country for years. Everything is expensive."

I frowned at the tomatoes.

"How's Mackenzie?" Adam asked. "I haven't seen her since . . . damn, I actually don't think I've seen her since Mexico."

"She's great—her and Eric just got engaged, and she asked me to be her maid of honor."

Adam's face lit up at the news. "Wow, he finally did it, huh?"

"Yeah, he proposed on Thanksgiving."

"I'll text them both and give them congratulations. And I better be invited to that wedding—you think they'll have an open bar?"

I giggled as I shook my head, wondering how old Adam would have to get before he finally lost his inner party animal.

"These croquettes are done!" Rachel flitted toward the dining table with a platter in her hands.

I quickly poured dressing on the salad and mixed the vegetables around. "Salad is ready, too," I shared as I brought the large bowl to the table and set it down next to the platter. Adam followed behind me with a bottle of wine and three glasses expertly cradled in his hands.

We all took seats around the table and filled our plates. I stuffed my mouth with a forkful of croquette and moaned. "Oh my god, Rachel, this is so good."

She giggled. "Thanks! I made them for Adam a few months ago and he loved them, so I wanted to make them again. They're honestly pretty easy."

I looked over at Adam and saw him chewing with his eyes closed for a moment before he finally opened them and caught me watching him. "Why have we never had these before?" I asked.

He shrugged. "Our mother clearly deprived us—that wicked woman."

Rachel clutched her chest as a fit of laughter overtook her, which caused Adam to grin at her. I could tell that he liked making her laugh. Inside of my chest, my heart swooned for them.

"So, Rachel," I said as soon as her laughter died down. "Do you have a traditional work week?"

"Mostly. Depending on the project I'm working on, sometimes the hours can get a little wonky, but right now it's a normal Monday through Friday. What about you? You get to kind of make your schedule whatever you want it to be, don't you?"

"Yeah, it's part of why I went freelance. I love the freedom. For the most part I work from home, but sometimes I'll schedule in-person meetings or site visits. I'm actually going to Logan's shop tomorrow to get a lay of the land so that I can help him with some marketing."

"Oh!" Adam interjected, his attention on Rachel. "That reminds me. I need to text him and see if he's free this weekend for that concert."

This piqued my interest. "Concert?"

Adam's eyes flicked to me. "Yeah, Mumford & Sons are playing at the Red Rocks and I was going to see if he wanted to double date with us."

Liquid acid spread through my belly and up my throat, my chest suddenly unbearably tight. I tried to keep my expression as neutral as possible as I asked, "Oh, Logan's dating someone?"

Adam dipped his head and gave a torturous confirmation. "Yeah, remember Mara, from high school? They reconnected earlier this year, I think."

*Mara.* Flashes of the tan, blonde-haired goddess tore through my mind as my heart completely sunk. I felt a panic rise inside of me, its long talons crushing my throat. I stared down at the shine of a reflection on my plate and tried to count to ten, tried to calm myself down, but I was absolutely spiraling. "I don't feel well, I'm going to go lay down," I said, needing an exit from this table.

I heard Rachel gasp. "Oh no! It's not the chicken, is it?"

I shook my head, "No, the food is great, Rachel, really. I just think I might be coming down with something . . ." I scooted my chair back from the table, nearly knocking it over in the process. "I'll just put my plate in the fridge for later." I tried so hard to muster up a smile on my face, but I don't think it worked. I shuffled into the kitchen, placing my dinner on a shelf inside the fridge and then headed to my room, swiftly shutting the door.

I sat down on the edge of my bed and let my head fall between my knees. The panic within me wasn't letting up, and I knew I needed to get control of my breathing before I had a full-on panic attack. It took everything in me to force myself to breathe in for five seconds, and breathe out for five seconds. I repeated this over and over again until I could feel myself begin to calm down.

I needed to talk to Logan. I needed to hear this from him. And if it was true, if he was seeing someone else, I knew that it would completely break me. But I needed to hear the truth, and I needed to hear it from him.

I would just ask him tomorrow, as soon as I got to the

shop. I would take him to his office and tell him to be honest with me.

*This is a risk we take together.*

His words from last night echoed in my mind. He couldn't possibly hurt me like that, could he?

*I won't hide my feelings from you, not anymore. I promise.*

Did that include feelings he had for someone else? I felt my pulse begin to rise again and promptly shut the question down in my head. There was no point in spending the entire night catapulting myself into dangerous thoughts. I knew that we were playing with fire as it was and if it didn't work out, one or both of us was going to get really hurt. I just couldn't imagine the hurt being intentional. I couldn't imagine Logan, *my* Logan, toying with my heart like that.

So I would ask him tomorrow. Demand that he be honest with me. And pray like hell that Adam was wrong. Because if he wasn't . . . Well, I wasn't sure I could survive that kind of heartbreak.

# Chapter Twenty

After barely sleeping all night, I woke up in the morning feeling rather irritable. I'd hoped that ordering the biggest coffee offered from the café on the corner would help, but instead it made me feel jittery and nauseous.

Since I wasn't due to Logan's shop until eleven, I spent the morning getting ahead on some of my other work. I spread myself out on the couch in the living room with my laptop and some paper sketches that I'd started for a few holiday ads. One was for a local boudoir photographer who was offering special pricing for Christmas, and another was for the hardware store downtown who wanted to target holiday shopping for dads.

Adam and Rachel emerged around nine, both of them wearing workout clothes. Apparently, there was a gym somewhere in this building. Adam invited me to join them but I preferred to exercise outdoors where I could get lost in nature and fresh air. With the way I was feeling today, a nice long hike in the snow sounded like heaven. I made a mental note to make that a priority in the next few days.

As nervous as I was to see Logan, a huge part of me was also really looking forward to it. I held tightly to the belief that he wouldn't intentionally hurt me, and that he wouldn't still have Mara in his life if he was . . . doing what he did with me in Breckenridge. But I also owed it to myself not to sweep this under the rug and to confront the potential issue—we promised to be honest with each other and to tackle any fears together.

By the time ten o'clock rolled around, I was anxious and antsy and no longer focused on what I was doing. Logan's shop was about a twenty minute drive away, so I packed up my work stuff and put it all back into my room—in a neat pile on the foot of the bed because my bedroom didn't have a desk—and got ready. I'd decided to wear a simple black sweater, my nice jeans, and a pair of black ankle boots in an effort to look nice but comfortable. I put on a simple gold chain necklace and kept the makeup to a minimum before packing my computer and a notebook into my bag and heading out.

The drive to Logan's shop was quick. There wasn't a whole lot of traffic to worry about in the middle of a weekday, so I made it in about fifteen minutes. The parking lot in front of the building was almost full, but I found a spot in the deserted lot out back.

Once inside, an older hispanic woman was behind the front desk, her smile bright as she looked up at me. "Good morning, how can I help you?" Her question was somewhat muted by the sound of an air compressor and power tools coming from the bays.

"Good morning," I said warmly. "I'm looking for Logan, I have a meeting with him at eleven."

Her face lit up in recognition. "Oh, yes! You must be Amelia?" I nodded. "He told me to go ahead and send you back—I think he's in the third bay right now working on something, but he should be done soon."

"Thank you!" I turned to my right and saw that all six bays had cars in various stages of disassembly. Men in matching gray coveralls moved methodically as they worked on each one of them.

When my eyes finally landed on Logan, something deep within me stirred. He was bent over the open hood of a black sports car, working a wrench somewhere inside of the engine. He was wearing those damn coveralls with the sleeves rolled up, and I watched as his forearm flexed obscenely as he turned the wrench over and over again. I felt mildly jealous of whatever it was that he was working on, because I wanted him working on me instead.

One of the guys next to him caught sight of me watching Logan and bumped him on the shoulder, pointing in my direction when Logan looked up at him. I watched in heavy anticipation as Logan's face turned in my direction. The change in his expression when his gaze landed on me was unmistakable—the brightness of his honey eyes ticked up a notch, his features relaxed, and his mouth curved up at the corners.

He was cinnamon whiskey and loud engines and the first snow of the season. My heart beat fiercely for him.

With a tilt of his head, he nodded toward his office, indicating for me to meet him there. I walked along the perimeter of the bays to where his office door was tucked behind large stacks of tires. The door was closed, but when I turned the knob it opened easily and I let myself in.

It would be a few minutes until Logan got there, so I took some time to look around at everything, knowing I was being undoubtedly nosy. The shine of a small silver frame on the corner of his desk caught my attention, so I moved to go pick it up.

It was an old Campbell family picture depicting all of us in front of the house that I grew up in. I remembered when the picture was taken in the fall of that year, so long ago, around Halloween. Logan, Adam and I stood proudly in front of a huge pile of leaves that we'd raked into the middle of the lawn, and my parents stood on either side of us. My mother had asked a neighbor to snap the photo, wanting to catch the moment. Logan and Adam looked like they were about ten or eleven, which meant I was only six or seven.

I had no idea how or why Logan had the picture, but the fact that it was here in his office broke open a fissure in my chest. I studied all of our faces and wasn't surprised to see genuine smiles. Even on Logan's. I realized that this was taken before my parents had gotten involved in his home life, so he was still living with his father at that point. I looked for any signs of distress in his expression, but his face was angled at me as I threw leaves up into the air.

"Hey." Logan's deep voice rumbled from behind me and I almost jumped out of my skin.

I turned to look at him, feeling caught in my snooping. "Hey," I responded, waving the frame toward him so that he could see. "I'm sorry, I just . . . I noticed this on your desk."

His eyes were soft as he watched me. He was leaning against the door frame, a smudge of oil on his chin. A stark white undershirt was peeking out beneath his coveralls at his chest, where the first button was undone. "Don't be sorry." His eyes flicked to the picture in my hands. "That was a good day."

I felt myself smile, despite the nerves still raging inside of me. "Yeah, it was . . . how did you get it?"

"Your mom was looking through pictures when I was at the house a few years ago. I saw that one and remembered how good I felt that afternoon, just being a kid running wild in the leaves. I asked her if I could keep it."

I looked back down at the frame and then set it back on his desk, keeping my eyes on it as I heard Logan's movement behind me, feeling him take a few steps in my direction. His arms snaked around my ribcage and he pivoted me around to face him. "I can't stop thinking about you," he murmured. His eyes were bright and his smile was disorienting—it was almost enough to make me forget about the panic in my bones but, nope, it was still there, chipping away at my resolve.

My tension must have been written on my face because Logan's features suddenly transformed, his eyes focused and a small frown played on his lips. I could feel his arms around me stiffen. "What's wrong, Amelia?"

I blinked. "I . . . um . . ." I hesitated, finding myself incapable of bursting this bubble. I wanted to rewind the last thirty seconds and pretend like nothing was wrong. His arms around me tightened as he took another small step closer to me, as if closing the distance between us could eliminate any threats.

"Amelia." He said my name again, and this time it sounded like a plea. "Tell me."

I let out a breath. "Adam said he wanted to invite you to a

concert." My voice was only a whisper. "He wanted to invite you . . . and Mara . . . for a double date."

Logan briefly closed his eyes, and my heart hung over the edge of a cliff until he opened them again, and I could see his panic subsiding. "Is that what this is about?" And then he pulled me into a hug, pressing the whole front of his body to mine. My face rested on his chest and I could feel his heartbeat was steady, providing a sort of comfort. "Amelia, I haven't been with Mara in months. Your brother is an idiot. I'm so sorry."

I felt his hand cup the back of my head, his fingers winding into my hair, as my whole body melted into him. "Fuck," I said. I didn't know if I said it to him or to myself, but it was a much needed release of tension from my throat.

"I'm sorry," Logan said again. I could hear the rumble of his voice through his chest. "Adam and I haven't kept each other updated as well as we used to. I should have told him that I ended things . . . I should have mentioned it a while ago."

I squeezed my arms tighter around his waist and sighed. "You have nothing to be sorry for. It's not like you could have anticipated him telling me something like that."

"Maybe, but this was avoidable." He pulled away so that he could look down at me. The gold rings in his irises were captivating, even as he frowned. "Amelia, I could feel the worry seeping out of you. You were scared. I don't want to *ever* cause those kinds of feelings. Not from you."

"It wasn't your fault, Logan," I pressed. "Look, I knew in my heart that you wouldn't intentionally hurt me . . . I just wanted to bring it directly to you. We made a promise."

He looked into my eyes for what felt like endless seconds before he pulled me back in for a hug, pressing his lips to my forehead before he rested his cheek on the top of my head. I heard him sigh. "You're so perfect, Mills," he murmured into my hair. "Do you know that? Do you know how perfect you are?"

I felt my nose skate along his neck as we swayed in place, holding fast to each other. "I'm not perfect, Logan. But these feelings I have for you sure feel like they are."

A small groan escaped from his throat. I felt a flash of stubble against my chin and Logan's lips were on mine, searing me with a warm, soft kiss. I slid my hands up his chest to the collar of his coveralls and pulled him down further into me.

After a moment, he pulled away and chuckled. "Looks like you got your wish."

My wish? I looked at him, confused.

"Making out in my office during business hours." He looked at me pointedly with arched eyebrows. I started giggling when I realized he was referencing my words from Saturday night, and watched as his face bloomed into a full smile.

"You should do that more often."

"What?"

"Smile," I said as I reached up to kiss his cheek. "Now, Mr. Davis, would you be so kind as to teach me the ways of this business so that I can learn what opportunities exist for me to help you?"

"Yes ma'am." He waved his arm toward the open office door, gesturing for me to go first. "Let's start at the lobby. I'll introduce you to Camila and she can go over our customer intake process."

Logan trailed closely behind me as I made my way back to the front of the shop. I could feel the stares from the mechanics around us, but it felt more like curiosity than anything else.

"Camila," Logan addressed the receptionist, "could you

please walk Amelia through our process when a new customer walks or calls in? She's going to help us with marketing, and I'd like to make sure she understands how people are currently finding us."

Camila lit up from the inside. "Of course, Logan."

He grabbed the nearest chair from the waiting area and set it down next to Camila for me to sit in. When he disappeared back to work, I put all of my focus on Camila as she showed me their customer database.

I spent almost four hours at the shop that afternoon, immersing myself in every customer touchpoint that they currently had. Logan was doing an incredible job already, and the sense of pride I felt for him only grew as I learned more and more.

At lunchtime, Logan sent one of his mechanics, Andre, out to get lunch for everyone, giving him his credit card without hesitation. It was clear that Logan trusted his employees, and they all seemed to have a mutual respect and appreciation for each other.

This somewhat surprised me, as I knew it could be difficult to create a positive work environment when so many people with different backgrounds and experiences came together. I remembered my time at the agency where dealing with toxic coworkers was the norm . . . but not here. The brotherhood amongst the mechanics was obvious, and the same treatment was extended my way simply for being Logan's guest.

When Andre returned with lunch for everyone—a delicious assortment of tacos and burritos from a local Mexican restaurant—the entire shop closed down to enjoy lunch together, finding places to sit inside the front lobby. I took the opportunity to observe Logan in his element, passing around food to everyone and making sure everybody got their fill. At one point, he looked over as if just to visually check-in, giving me a quick wink before his attention was back on Andre, who was telling everyone about his birthday party that evening.

"Y'all better come through," he said, sweeping a look across the whole room, his gaze landing on Logan. "Especially you, boss."

Logan chuckled. "Andre, I'm too old for birthday parties."

Andre, who looked to be six and a half feet tall and had tattoos on almost every inch of skin except for his face, shook his head adamantly. "Nah, sir, you need to be there. Bring your friend, it's all good." And just like that, everyone's eyes were on me.

"Ha!" one of the other guys, Manny, cackled. "Andre's calling out the boss's new friend."

Logan's focus shifted from Andre to Manny, giving them both a quick glare. "Leave my friend alone. Also, her name is Amelia."

Andre lifted his hands up. "I mean no disrespect, sir. Manny is a wise ass. My invitation comes from a good place, I hope to see you both there." He nodded toward me. I wondered how old he was turning. He definitely seemed more my age than Logan's. He was handsome too—not exactly my type, but I'm sure he had no trouble with the ladies.

Logan looked at me, the question swimming in his eyes. "I'm down," I said, shrugging. "Why not?"

Logan's face ignited into that megawatt smile again, the one that made me feel weak, before he looked back to Andre. "There better not be any funny business at this party."

When I'd seen everything I needed to see to get a good idea of how to elevate some of their customer communication, I put my laptop back into my bag and set off to find Logan. I took my time walking through the bays, watching all of the mechanics as they worked on the various cars.

In one bay, Andre and another guy—Cameron, I think— were jacking up a minivan. In another, Manny was taking a wheel off of a Prius. I found Logan back in the third bay, elbows deep in another engine with his tongue stuck between his lips in concentration. An older man was clutching a handful of shop rags, waiting for Logan to give him a cue.

"Hey," I said as I saddled up beside him. "Don't stop what you're doing, I don't want to interrupt."

Logan shook his head, pulling his hands out from the hood of the car. "It's okay, I was just about to clean up. Are you heading out?"

"Yeah, I think I got what I needed and I don't want to be in the way. But I wanted to check in about that party later and see if we're really going?"

"If you want to go, we'll go. No pressure."

"Let's go, I want to get to know everyone better."

"You got it. Does Adam work tonight?" he asked.

"Yes, he was off last night but said he works most nights this week."

"Okay, I'll come pick you up when I'm done here. I'll text you after I get home and showered." He leaned in for a quick kiss, making me blush in front of the older man who was still standing beside him, watching our entire interaction.

"See you later," I said before I turned around, finding my way back to where I parked my car. I felt everyone watching me again, only this time I knew it was because they'd seen Logan kiss me. Guess they all knew I was more than a friend, now.

It was exhilarating that Logan had shown affection for me

like that in front of his whole team. I knew we were keeping things quiet from my family for now while we figured this out, but he'd had no problem with his employees knowing. It felt like a big move, and my heart was almost bursting out of my chest in response.

I made it out to the parking lot and into my car, catching myself in the rearview mirror and seeing a flush on my cheeks before putting the car into gear and peeling away.

# Chapter Twenty-One



It was a warm day in May, and I could already feel small beads of sweat beginning to slide down my spine beneath the stiff, black graduation gown. Thankful that I'd decided on the chunky wedges to go with my dress instead of my nude pumps, I stepped into the soft grass and made my way toward the organized rows of white folding chairs.

The entire football field at CU Denver had been converted for tonight's graduation ceremony and a large, stainless-steel stage stretched across the furthest end. A few members of faculty had already taken their seats upon the big stage, and were peering down on all of the hustle and bustle as the arriving graduating students worked to find their respective seating sections.

Seating for the ceremony had been organized by degree program, and a reference guide of the seating chart had been emailed to all students a few days prior to the event. I pulled the folded piece of paper out of the small clutch that hung from my wrist, having just printed it before leaving to head over here today. Squinting down at the impossibly minuscule letters on the paper, I saw that students who were graduating from the marketing program were seated within a larger cluster of students who were graduating with business-related degrees in the left column of chairs toward the middle rows.

I found the area for marketing students and made my way to the first row, figuring students with a "C" last name would be assigned to seats toward the front of the section. Quickly finding a chair marked "Campbell, Amelia," I took my seat and exhaled.

I glanced at the slender, gold watch on my wrist and saw that it was half-past four. The graduation ceremony would begin at five o'clock sharp, and the stadium was only about halfway filled. I knew when I left my apartment a half hour ago that I was going to get here much earlier than necessary, but the worry of being late and unsure of exactly where I'd be seated had given me anxiety all afternoon.

My parents, who were always severely punctual as well, would likely be arriving at any moment. I took my phone out of my clutch and sent a text to our family group thread to let everyone know the general area that I was seated in. Within moments, I began receiving their responses.

MOM

We're on our way, sweetie! 🩶

DAD

I'm so proud of you! See you soon.

ADAM

Wait, your graduation is tonight?

I rolled my eyes at that last text. *Seriously, Adam?*

ADAM

Just kidding. Logan and I are on our
way, too!

I felt my breath catch as I read that second message from my brother. *Logan was coming.* Not that him coming to my graduation was surprising—Logan was family, and he was usually a part of big family moments like this. I just didn't really think through the possibility of him being here tonight, and was completely unprepared to see him.

After he walked into that karaoke bar when I was on stage a year ago, I did my best to completely avoid him where possible. I even worked to avoid *thinking* about him after practically drowning myself in thoughts of him for so many nights, haunted by the sight of him walking out of that bar door.

I'd been hurt and disappointed that he didn't reach out to me at all after that night. Especially knowing that the fire burning in his eyes as he watched me perform was proof of his desire, and that it had fully matched the licks of flame that I'd felt inside of my own body.

At some point along the way, this had all become a bit of an unhealthy (and unspoken) cycle between us. We'd have a moment together—a magical, stars-aligning, blinding dive into the deepest of dangerous temptations that clearly existed some-where within both of us. But then Logan would pull a disap-pearing act, only to reemerge later out of the dust seemingly unscathed, acting as if nothing had ever happened.

It made me absolutely crazy.

After ending things with Danny that night last year, I'd decided to hit the brakes on dating in general and to instead just focus on myself and my studies during this last year of college. It wouldn't have been fair to date anyone with what I was battling inside of myself when it came to Logan anyway, and I wasn't the type of girl to play with someone's heart.

After successfully avoiding him for so long—it wasn't lost on me that I was probably only so successful because he'd been avoiding me too—I'd finally seen him again during the holidays. In typical Logan fashion, he slipped firmly back into his big brother role and didn't give me *any* acknowledgement of what had happened that night downtown.

It was just like five years ago when I'd picked him up in the middle of the night. We *kissed*. Like, genuinely had a full-on, heated make out session full of a raw need and a hunger that I had certainly never felt before. And then, *poof*, it was over. And Logan made it clear that he wanted to go on with life as if it had never happened.

It all felt like a cosmic joke—and with *Logan*, of all the men in the world.

I would always love him, and I knew that he'd do anything for me. But we needed to keep our relationship on the platonic side of the fence. Anything else was just way too risky, and I knew that I wouldn't be able to survive the inevitable fallout. He was way too important to me to casually mess around with. Not to mention that Adam would likely murder both of us slowly with a butter knife.

Snapping back to reality, I noticed that the seats around me had filled with more students. I looked down at my phone and saw that it was now four forty-five, and I had a new text from my mom.

MOM

We're here - look up! ☺

I looked up into the stands to the left of me and spotted my family amongst the crowd of other onlookers. As soon as my eyes landed on them, they all began cheering and waving their arms around. My mother was dressed to the absolute nines in a gorgeous summer dress and a classic sun hat shading her face from the bright sun. Long, brown curls curved from underneath her hat and around her face with an elegance that I could never quite pull off. The smile on her face was a mile wide as her eyes connected with mine, her hand waving back and forth with motherly gusto.

Next to her, my father wore a white, button-up T-shirt with dark slacks, looking sharp as usual. I could sense his eyes twinkling down on me through his aviators.

In front of my parents sat two familiar-looking young men, both dressed a bit more casually than my parents but dashing nonetheless. Adam's dark hair was cropped short from a recent haircut, and my heart warmed at the dimples that formed in his cheek as he smiled down at me.

And next to him was Logan, whose beautiful, golden brown waves had grown much longer since I'd last seen him, easily reaching past his shoulders now. The look worked for him. Instead of appearing grungy or unkempt, he looked like a goddamn movie star. He wore his usual white T-shirt and black jeans, and I noticed that his biceps were stretching the sleeves of his shirt. His smile was lazy as his eyes locked in with mine. I didn't miss the mischievous wink.

My heart roared.

*Stop it, Amelia.*

Looking back at my parents, I took in a deep, grounding breath. It had been a few weeks since I'd been back home, as the last few weeks of school were crammed with endless studying sessions and difficult final exams. But now, seeing my family gathered here together for me, I felt myself swelling with pride as the enormity of my accomplishment began to sink in.

I was graduating college.

I'd done it. I'd made my family proud.

While my collegiate career may not have involved the grueling work that it took to become the next neurosurgeon in the family, there was no doubt that I'd worked really hard for my degree. In the occasional moments of weakness against my own self-esteem, I'd start to feel like my choice to study marketing instead of something as glorified as medicine—or law or engineering or biochemistry—might have disappointed my family.

They'd never given me any indication of having bigger expectations for me, but the pride that my father so obviously felt when Adam declared his decision to follow in his footsteps was no secret, and sometimes I found myself comparing my journey with Adam's. He'd always been the golden child. The smart one. The one who so effortlessly achieved everything he tried for, whereas I always had to work *really* hard for the things I set out to do.

I knew that I was following the right professional path for myself, but that didn't take away from those occasional bursts of self-doubt and anxiety that I wasn't doing enough to be as impressive or successful as Adam.

But in this moment, for what was possibly the first time in my life, I truly allowed myself to feel the collective pride of my family shining on me like the warm rays of the sun above us.

Had it always been there? Had I been the one too full of my own fears to recognize that it existed? The thought prickled at my mind as I smiled back at them.

Just then, the wail of a microphone screeched through the stadium as the school's dean began his welcome message, kicking off the ceremony.

Two hours later, I threw my cap up into the air alongside the thousands of other graduates around me. In the fleeting glow of dusk, the wave of black hats flying above the crowd looked eerily like a colony of bats raining down into the stadium. The roar of applause all around me was thunderous. Families poured their love and accolades into the entire graduating class, and the swell of the electric energy was palpable.

It was the most incredible feeling—I was completely high from it.

A couple of tears escaped down my face as I moved my way out of the row of seats I was sitting in, heading toward the edge of the field where my family was waiting for me. As soon as I was within reach, Adam scooped me into his arms and swung me around, lifting me off my feet and squeezing my body against his with a firm embrace. "I'm so fucking proud of you, Millie," he said, kissing the side of my head.

"Thanks, Adam," I responded, barely able to say the words out loud from the unyielding constriction of his hug.

Adam released me, only for my father to immediately catch me in his own grasp. I felt his strong arms wrap around me as his warm breath tickled my ear. "Congratulations, my beautiful girl. Your mother and I are unbelievably proud."

I felt my mother wrap her own arms around both of us, sighing into our group huddle. "So proud, dear." I could tell by her rapid intake of breath that she was fighting tears welling in her own eyes, as well.

With a final squeeze, my parents released me. It was then that I noticed Logan standing in front of me, a cluster of white lilies clutched in his hand. As he approached me, I couldn't help but feel swallowed by the large form of his body, and as he pulled me into a light embrace, the smell of cedar and citrus filled the air around me.

"Congratulations, Mills," he murmured softly in my ear, sending a chill up my spine. He pulled away and replaced the space between us with the bouquet of flowers. Their blooms were larger than my hand, light orange pollen dusting their centers.

"They're gorgeous, Logan." I looked up at him as I took them. "Thank you so much." A new wave of tears burned in the corners of my eyes, threatening to spill over.

He threw me that delicious, lazy grin again, and I had to work *very* hard to keep my thoughts from going back to places that they shouldn't.

My father clapped his hands together firmly as he took in the crowds around us. "Alright—getting out of here is going to take some collective patience, but we better get a move on. Who's hungry?" He turned and began walking toward the parking lot, affectionately pulling my mother under his arm. Adam, Logan and I trailed after them.

"So, what's next?" Adam asked, as we stepped back onto the concrete of the outer concourse.

"I have a few interviews with marketing firms in the city that have new graduate programs, so I'm hopeful that I'll have a job landed pretty soon. I might move back in with Mom and Dad for a few months while I save for my own place." After living with various roommates all throughout college, I was looking forward to getting out on my own.

I heard Adam whistle beside me. "Smart girl. Save money while you can," he replied, sounding just like our father.

"You're not even going to celebrate?" Logan asked, looking over at me.

"Celebrate graduating?"

"Yeah. You can't just go right into work—you'll have work for the rest of your life."

"Well . . ." I started, staring down at the beautiful flowers in my hand. "Mackenzie actually called me yesterday about a graduation trip to Cabo—I guess a few people are pitching in to rent a house on the beach. I was thinking about going but, I don't know . . . I've never been out of the country before."

When I didn't hear either of them respond, I looked up to find Adam looking wide-eyed at Logan over my head. I turned to look at Logan, who had a huge smile on his face as he looked back at Adam.

"What?" I asked, looking back and forth between them, feeling uneasy at the look on their faces.

"CABO!" they both yelled, high-fiving each other right over my head.

"Oh my god, you guys are so embarrassing." I shook my head, facing forward as we made our way into the expansive parking lot.

In front of us, my mother turned around from under my father's arm with a curious look on her face. "What are you kids yelling about?"

I had just opened my mouth to answer, but Adam beat me to it. "Amelia is going to Mexico, and I think it's imperative that Logan and I go with her to . . . look out for her safety."

I rolled my eyes. "Oh come on, I don't need babysitters. I'm a grown adult."

"It's a foreign country, Millie. It would be wrong of us *not* to accompany you on such a big adventure," Logan argued, his eyes twinkling with wicked delight.

As we reached my parents' SUV, my father turned around to look at all three of us before zoning in on me. "Amelia, you're going to Mexico?" His eyebrows were furrowed, as if he was attempting to diagnose a complex neurological disease.

I sighed. "Mackenzie invited me to Cabo on a graduation trip with a small group of people. I haven't decided anything yet, and I shouldn't have opened my mouth in front of these losers."

"Well, if you do end up going, it wouldn't be a terrible idea to have your brother and Logan around with you. It would certainly make your mother and I feel better."

"Dad, I'm twenty-two years old. I can handle a vacation with my friends."

Adam stepped in front of me and grabbed my shoulders. "I'll buy you all of your drinks for the entire trip."

That definitely perked my ears up. "*Every* drink?"

He nodded enthusiastically.

I glared at him for a solid minute before sighing. "Deal."

Adam and Logan started jumping up and down around me, hooting and hollering and fist bumping each other. I rolled my eyes again and looked back toward my father. "I'm parked down a bit further. Where are we going to dinner? I'll meet you guys there."

# Chapter Twenty-Two

Andre sure knew how to throw a party. Or at least, his friends knew how to throw one for him. Beautiful Spanish music played through a sound system that had been set up outside as people danced on a slab of concrete near where Logan and I sat together in a camping chair. We were two of what felt like a hundred people in the deceptively large back-yard of the tiny bungalow home that Andre lived in with his sister. The music was turned up loud enough that I would have been worried about a noise complaint, but it seemed the whole street lit up with activity at night—much more activity than I would have expected on a Monday evening in late November.

We were in a part of the city I didn't frequent much growing up. I'd always heard stories about East Colfax and the crime that happened here, but tonight I was seeing the old neighborhood in a different light. The houses all around us were lit up with colorful Christmas lights, and I could hear similar, joyous music playing from the other houses around us.

Logan and I had gotten here less than an hour ago. We were a bit late because Adam left for work later than usual, and I had to wait until he left before I texted Logan that it was safe to pick me up. I felt a little guilty about all the secrecy, but I knew it was for good reason. Hopefully things between Logan and I would keep progressing in a positive way and we could eventually shout about our relationship from the rooftops for everyone to hear. For now, though, I was rather enjoying sitting in his lap in front of his employees.

When we arrived at the quaint white house with yellow shutters, we could hear the party from across the street where Logan had parked the Chevelle. Logan—who looked absolutely edible in jeans, a white henley and a brown leather jacket—held my hand on our way up the front walkway. The door to the house opened before we had a chance to knock, revealing Manny holding two cans of beer stacked in a one-handed grip. "What up, boss man!" he shouted.

Logan chuckled. "Manny, you already look halfway to hell-bound."

Manny's smile widened, the skin around this dark brown eyes crinkling. "Nah, boss, I'm cool. Just burning off a little steam, you know?"

After Manny gave us a quick tour of the house, which was decorated on the inside with a gorgeous Christmas tree and a garland along the kitchen counter, he opened the back door where the party was unfolding. I recognized a few of the mechanics from Logan's shop gathered together in a corner of the yard, but there were dozens of other people milling about as well—it definitely wasn't a small party.

Logan had found a free chair and pulled it over to where the rest of the shop's team was sitting around a makeshift fire near the dance floor. He sat in it, and then patted his lap for me to sit on him, and we'd been hanging out here and people watching ever since.

Eventually, the man of the hour made his way over to us. Andre looked sharp in a black long-sleeved button-up and black pants. His dark hair was shaved close to his head, and his gray eyes glinted beneath an expression of mischief. My attention caught on his neck, where a bold tattoo of a skull with roses for eyes and a pair of what looked like hawk wings spread out from the sides. It covered the whole front of his throat, the realistic wings spreading out to behind his ears.

"You all came—" he nodded toward our group huddled around the fire—"thank you, it truly means a lot to me to have you here." He eyed Logan and I sitting together and grinned out of the corner of his mouth. "Would you or your friend like a drink, boss?"

Logan looked at me in question, and I nodded. "Amelia will have one, thanks. I'm okay though, I'm driving."

Andre's gaze moved to me. "What would you like? We have beer, tequila . . . I think my sister has a margarita mix going in the kitchen . . ."

"I'd love some tequila, please."

Andre's grin turned into a smile. "That a girl. Ice?"

"No, thank you, just straight up is fine." I could see Logan's eyebrows raise in my peripheral vision. "What?" I said, looking at him.

His smile matched Andre's. "Nothing, I just didn't realize you were a tequila-straight-up girl."

Shrugging, I leaned back against him and settled my head on his shoulder. One of Logan's mechanics, Cameron, sat up straighter as he watched Andre walk away. "What about the rest of us? I'll take a tequila, too!"

Without pausing, he called back, "Get your own fucking tequila, Cameron," over his shoulder.

Everyone around us laughed as Cameron's face flushed red. "Aw, don't mind him, Cam," Manny said, slapping him on the shoulder. "It's his birthday . . . he just wanted to pay respects to boss man and his lady friend."

I felt Logan's arms around me tighten as he sighed quietly into my hair. I turned to face him. "You okay?"

He nodded. "I'm good." His face shimmered under the holiday lights, like the dream that he was. I considered for a moment that all of this might actually *be* a dream, that I would wake up in the morning and realize I dreamt up this chance with Logan. Just to make sure, I cupped his face in my palm. I needed to feel him, the coarse stubble of his chin against my wrist, his pulse beneath my fingers.

"What?" he asked, bemused.

"Nothing," I whispered, before pecking him on the cheek with a quick kiss. I heard his soft hum as he again tightened his arms around me with comfortable pressure. His nose grazed the back of my neck and it sent chills up my spine.

Andre came back a moment later with a very generous glass of tequila. "Here you go, Amelia." He handed it to me with a gleam in his eye. I was slightly caught off guard that he'd called me by my name, since all of Logan's employees had only called me his "friend" up until this point.

"Thank you, Andre," I responded. He turned his attention to Logan then. I registered the respect and admiration in his expression as he dipped his head again. "You sure you're okay, boss?"

Logan's velvet voice rumbled behind me. "I'm great, Andre, thank you. Don't worry about me, just enjoy your party. It's your birthday."

Andre grinned just as a bout of cheering sounded from the other side of the yard where a group of people were gathered around a keg. It looked like someone might have been about to do a keg stand. Andre rolled his eyes and grumbled, "Dammit, Chino," as he started in their direction.

I looked around along the circle of Logan's employees as I took a sip of my tequila. It was smooth, lightly burning my throat as I swallowed it down. I felt the warmth of it in my belly.

Manny was poking the wood that was burning in the fire with what looked like a tire iron. He seemed to be swaying from his seat on the ground, the two beers from his earlier grip long gone now. Cameron, whose face was mostly hidden in the shadow of the hood from his sweatshirt, was picking black nail polish off of his fingernails as he watched Manny's assault on the firewood. The older mechanic who was helping Logan earlier, Ernesto, sat quietly and unmoving in a chair closest to the back wall of the yard. I thought for a moment that he might be sleeping, but his eyes were open and watchful.

Neither Jessica nor Camila had come—both of them citing prior commitments—and a few of the other mechanics had migrated to the beer pong table along the far wall of the yard to play with Andre's other friends.

Our small group by the fire was quiet, a rather far cry from the rest of those in attendance at this party. Between the dancing, keg stands, and drinking games, everyone had definitely come here to let loose and celebrate.

I took another long sip from my glass of tequila, relishing

in the way Logan's thumb slid up and down my ribcage. I could get used to this . . . this electricity. This vibrancy. The color and sounds. Logan had, through his shop, cultivated a little corner of the world for himself, and I felt incredibly lucky to be a part of it with the people around me.

I turned around to tell Logan that I was going to the bathroom. "Are you okay on your own?" he asked, visibly contemplating if he should get up too.

I nodded my head. "Yeah, Manny showed us where it is. I'll be fine, promise." I handed Logan my drink and bounded toward the back door to the house, eager to get into the warmth.

Inside, things were much quieter. There were a couple of girls talking quietly in the living room, and a man in the kitchen who seemed to be looking through the cabinets for something, but otherwise the house was empty. I made my way down the short hallway to where Manny pointed out the bathroom earlier.

After I was done and washed up I retraced my steps, heading back through the house when the sound of a woman's voice stopped me in the kitchen.

"Who the hell invited a white girl here?"

I hesitated, wondering if I'd heard her correctly. Turning to look in the direction of the voice, I saw three girls standing at the kitchen counter. One of them, the taller one in the middle, was glaring at me. She looked to be about my age if not slightly younger, wearing a black thermal long-sleeved shirt with a red flannel wrapped around her waist. Dramatic eyeliner lined her narrowed eyes.

"I'm sorry?" I responded, confused at her hostility. A shorter woman to her left pretended to make herself busy by opening a bottle of wine, looking uncomfortable with the situation. The other girl standing on her right simply looked back and forth between the two of us with a perplexed expression.

"You heard me. Who invited you?"

I looked around me to find another source of her obvious frustration, because it couldn't have possibly been me. I didn't even know this person and she was looking at me like I'd knocked her down in the middle of a supermarket. When I didn't see anyone else lurking behind me, eager to take responsibility for the attitude being thrown in my direction, I turned back to face the woman who was still glaring at me. "Andre invited me. Why?"

A heated look of pure hatred flashed through her eyes before I heard someone approach from behind me. "For someone so concerned about Andre's guest list, I'm having a hard time remembering *your* name being on it, Leticia." I turned to find Andre's sister, Marisela, behind me with her arms crossed over her chest as she shot the woman—Leticia—a stern look.

Leticia grumbled and flipped her hair behind her shoulder as she turned on her heels to make her way out the door and into the yard.

I stood awkwardly frozen in place, having absolutely no idea what had just happened. "Um . . ." I'm so sorry, I don't know who she is or why that happened . . ."

Marisela's face transformed into a softer expression as she unfolded her arms and waved a hand out in front of her. "That had nothing to do with you, that was all her. Leticia and Andre used to be a thing but they've been broken up for almost a year now and she still tries to piss all over his life. She was probably worried that you were here as his date because you're new and she doesn't recognize you."

"*Oh* . . . I see." I nodded my head in understanding.

"Hey, you're here with Logan, right?" she asked, tilting her head as if she was just now really looking at me.

"Yeah, Logan brought me," I repeated rather lamely. "I was just on my way back out to him."

Marisela smiled, bright white teeth flashing against her dark mauve lipstick. "He's a good man. Andre was really struggling before Logan hired him." A look of anguish crossed over her eyes. "We lost our oldest brother, Gabriel, three years ago and . . . Andre took it really hard. Lost his direction in life. But when Logan hired him, things seemed to start turning around. Andre is focused again . . . driven. I feel like I have my brother back.

"Anyway, I'm so grateful to Logan for coming into his life. I know working at his auto shop has given him purpose, and words could never express how thankful I am." She smiled. "It's nice to see Logan with a girl—a pretty one at that. Enjoy yourself tonight." She pressed her hand to my shoulder and walked away, leaving me standing alone in the kitchen with tears threatening to escape from my eyes.

I wasn't at all surprised to hear that Logan was making a positive impact in someone's life, but hearing Marisela's words made my heart squeeze. Logan was truly one of the best people on the entire planet, and having come from pain and heartache like he had, I was so proud he'd turned out to be such an amazing man.

He'd made it. He'd truly made it.

Finding myself back outside, my skin felt warm despite the frigid night air. It might have been the buzz of tequila, or the way Logan was looking at me as I approached him, but I felt like I was floating, gently falling back into his lap like a snowflake.

The warmth of his arms wrapped around me again. It felt like home. "Everything good?" he murmured into my hair.

I thought about telling him about Leticia's wrath, or about Marisela's kind words, but decided to save it for another time. Right now, I just wanted to sink into him. "Everything is perfect," I whispered back to him. I took my drink back from his hand and took another sip, watching as the flames in front of us danced. I noticed Manny and Cameron were gone, only Ernesto still sitting in his chair across the fire. "Where'd the others go?"

"Andre came and grabbed them for the beer pong tournament. I think they're playing."

"Oh. Should we go watch?"

"No." Logan answered quickly, making me giggle because I agreed. I wanted to stay here, in his lap, forever.

"Thank you for bringing me here."

I heard the rumble of a hum from Logan's chest, felt the vibrations of the sound dance along my back, even through the fabric of my coat. After a moment, I felt the whisper of his breath against my ear. "We'll stay for a few more minutes, Mills, but I have to admit that I'm itching to get you alone."

A sudden heat rose to my cheeks that had nothing to do with the fire in front of us. I nodded my head, eager for the same.

We sat there together for another fifteen minutes or so while I finished my drink, anticipation welling inside of me for wherever Logan was going to take me next. Somewhere deep inside of my mind I was reminded of his no sex rule—but there were plenty of ways I could still enjoy him.

I was just about to tell him I was ready to go when he began stirring beneath me. We both stood up and I was surprised his legs weren't asleep after I'd been sitting on them for so long. But if it had been uncomfortable for him at all, he hadn't let on.

Grabbing my hand, Logan started walking toward the other side of the yard where the beer pong tournament was being held in dramatic suspense. Manny and Cameron stood together on one side of the long table while Andre and someone I didn't recognize stood on the other side. There was only one cup left for each team.

"You ain't gettin it in, bro!" Manny yelled across the table as Andre lined up his toss, the white ping pong ball tucked tightly in his tattooed fingers. He displayed a pretty high level of control considering he was likely beyond a healthy level of tipsy. With a firm flick of his wrist, the ball flew across the table to land inside of the red solo cup, and everyone erupted into loud cheers as Andre threw his hands up victoriously.

Logan took the opportunity within the chaos to approach Andre, patting him on the arm in congratulations before leaning in to tell him we were heading out. Andre pulled Logan in for a side-hug, followed up by a firm handshake. It always amused me to see how grown men showed each other affection.

Andre turned to me and leaned in close enough for me to hear him say, "Thank you for coming out tonight, Amelia. It means the world to me to have you both here."

"Happy birthday, Andre!" I smiled back at him. "I'm sure I'll see you again soon."

He threw me a sly wink before saying, "I have no doubts." Logan patted his arm a final time before saying goodbye to the rest of his team.

# Chapter Twenty-Three

We drove deep into the lower downtown region of Denver where pedestrian traffic was plentiful and cars typically stayed clear. Logan parked along the main road and swiped his credit card at the meter, pushing the button for the three-hour maximum option. I raised my eyes at him in question, and he deadpanned, saying, "I'm not rushing my time with you over a parking meter," which made my heart soften into gooey marshmallow fluff.

The entirety of 16th Street in the downtown district had been decorated with beautiful Christmas lights. They adorned all of the trees, had been spread across the window and door trim of every business, and covered all of the lamp posts in sight. It was . . . magic. There was really no better word.

Logan took my hand into his, and we strolled at a leisurely pace along the brick sidewalk. I had no idea if he was leading us in a particular direction, or if the goal was to simply get lost in the lights together, but either way I could feel a deep contentment within my soul. Like this was all inevitable—being here with him, in this moment, with our hands intertwined together.

I could do this forever.

"So"—I raised my eyebrows—"you finally got me alone."

He kept his eyes focused on the ground in front of him but I noticed a slight flush to his cheeks as he answered. "Yeah, it looks that way, doesn't it?"

"Thank you again, for bringing me to the party with you."

"Of course. I'm glad you came. Sorry we didn't know a whole lot of people there, but it was good for me to show face for Andre. He's a good guy." We walked under a tunnel of multicolored Christmas lights, the ambience of their glow dancing along Logan's face in a beautiful whirl.

"Andre seems nice. They all do. You've created a good team, Logan." I remembered Marisela's words from earlier. "You know, Andre's sister stopped me in the kitchen earlier and practically raved about you . . . about the good influence you've had on Andre's life. Something tells me you might have that effect on all of them." I looked up at him again.

His eyes flicked to mine before they refocused on the pathway in front of us. He shook his head slightly. "I don't know what she said but I'm not doing anything special. I just . . . I wanted to find people that I could trust to work with me at the shop. And you'd be surprised how many good people there are who just need a little bit of a budge in life. I enjoy the ability I have to give an opportunity to someone who might otherwise be overlooked. Andre was one of those guys.

"On paper, it seemed like he'd be unreliable. Maybe even a liability. But when I got to know him and after I heard his story, it was obvious that he just desperately needed something to sink his teeth into. He was one of my first hires, and he really helped me make the shop what it is today. He's bright, and has great ideas for business, you know?" His chest rose before he let out a sigh.

"And the others?" I asked, curious.

"Manny was a high school dropout. His parents were junkies and barely around, so he started working at a really young age to help his siblings survive. He has a passion for cars and knows more about them than anyone I know. He can take apart and rebuild an engine like it's nothing and can diagnose complex issues much quicker than the rest of us could, which helps customers get their cars back quicker.

"Cameron comes from a rich, conservative family who own a few big ranches throughout the state. Unfortunately, they basically disowned him when he came out to them a few years ago. He and Manny worked together before at a super-market and had kept in touch, so when we were hiring more guys, Manny reached out to him. Cameron doesn't know much about cars or being a mechanic, but he's definitely eager to learn. I don't think it's his passion by any means, but it's a steady paycheck while he gets himself back on his feet.

"Camila's husband died two years ago, and she learned that they were in severe debt after he passed. She thinks her husband kept it from her so that she didn't have to worry, but that obvi-ously backfired in the end. Ernesto is her brother, and he asked if she could pick up a few shifts at the reception desk as sort of a temporary gig so that she could pay some of those bills. She's really great at it, and great with our customers, so I made her a permanent employee shortly after she started."

I felt a little breathless at the amount of heartache that Logan's team had collectively endured, the pain of which seemed to fit the mold of Logan's own. We were silent for a moment as we continued walking, the cold air curling around us as he held my hand firmly. There were only a few other people walking along the street at this hour on a Monday night, so it felt like we had the entire city to ourselves.

"I don't think this world deserves you, Logan."

Golden eyes flashed to me. "What do you mean?"

"You have every right to struggle. You have *every* right to be angry at the world, to want to take from it and get yours." I hesitated before I said my next words, wanting to get them right. "I know you've never had things easily handed to you. So much pain is wrapped up in your childhood. You were dealt a fucking shitty hand. I just . . . I'm so proud of the man that you've become. I would never have held it against you if you let it all win, but you didn't. And you still found this incredible way to not only thrive in what you've created for yourself—completely on your own—but to help others beat the odds as well. The world just doesn't deserve you." I shook my head. "You're too good."

Logan stopped walking and faced me, an expression that I didn't quite recognize marring his features. "I'm not good, Mills." The conviction in his lowered voice surprised me.

"Like hell you aren't," I retorted.

"No, Amelia. Listen. I've done plenty of bad things. Things you don't even know about. I've hurt a lot of people. I let my pain and heartache get the best of me for a long time, and I'm only now finally starting to make up for it. Don't let what things look like in my life today confuse you, sweetheart. I'm plenty bad, too."

"Logan, you would never intentionally hurt anyone." I shook my head defiantly. "I don't believe it."

"Oh." Logan chuckled darkly. "I wish that were true, Millie." He took a deep breath, focusing his gaze somewhere above my head. "Only three things in my life have ever truly scared me. The first one has long been dead and buried. The second is becoming the first. And the third is that, in doing so, I'd lose the one thing I've ever actually loved.

"Those second two fears . . . they consumed me for a very long time. They still do, although I have a little more control over how I respond to the pressure of it all. But I know my place in the world. I was born into a home built from darkness and hate. I don't even remember my mother, and my father— well, you know enough.

"There isn't exactly a whole lot of good for me to carry on. I'm the only living Davis man from a long line of mean, ruthless Davis men. It's in my blood, and I can *feel* it. I can feel the anger and rage inside of my bones, and some days it takes everything I have to quiet the noise.

"You've been one of the only things in my life that can actually help with that." His gaze met mine as he flashed a small smile, though it didn't quite reach his eyes. "Since we were kids, you've had this way of . . . I don't even know, Amelia. Seeing me. Feeling me. You were like this bright light, casting away all of my dark corners. I found myself needing to be near you more, chasing after that light for warmth. Without you around me, everything was always so damn bleak. And as we got older, I realized it wasn't just your light that gave me hope. It was your strong mind. Your selfless heart. God, you were such a fucking spitfire. Still are."

He looked to the ground, seemingly lost inside of his mind, swirling in the memories of our past. Flashes of those memories reared inside of my own mind, where I could still vividly see a younger version of the man in front of me, looking like he carried the entire world on his boyish shoulders.

To hear him say that he'd felt it too, this pull between us, and that he'd needed it to overcome his hard, dark days—it left me feeling a sudden overwhelm of guilt for not seeing it for what it was. I was so damn worried about whether Logan felt something for me simply to lessen the sharp edges of my young vulnerability, and I missed the demons playing out inside of the very boy that I was pining for.

"Sometimes I'd daydream about what it would be like to have you." His voice ripped like a current through my heart. "Quiet mornings making toast. Afternoons making you laugh. Nights under the stars making love. But then the dreams would turn on me . . . because I knew I'd never let myself have what I so desperately wanted. I was way too damn scared to fuck it up.

"So I kept you at a distance—turning on myself in a vicious cycle that became almost muscle memory. Get angry. Need to release it. Sit at a bar and drink until I could muster up enough of an attitude to start shit with someone, just so I could fight. I was reckless. Night after night after night, I hurt so many people in my attempt to numb you out of my head."

Just like that, I was a puddle at his feet. And then a different memory came to the surface. "The night you kissed me," I said, my voice just above a whisper.

Logan's eyes flashed in recognition before he dipped his head. "I found out that my dad was dead, and the first thing I wanted to do was call you. But I didn't know how . . . . I didn't know what to say. I didn't know how to articulate my feelings and I was so *angry*. I was worried about what you would think of me and I didn't want to be a burden or make you nervous. So I went to that club instead. I probably drank a whole bottle of whiskey over the course of that night. Got in a fight with a random group of guys who were just trying to enjoy themselves. And then I ended up calling you anyway."

My mind sputtered as I tried to wrap my head around everything Logan was sharing with me. I knew he struggled back then, but not to this extent. The guilt deepened. "You could never be a burden, Logan. And you've never made me nervous. All I've ever wanted was for you to be happy . . . for you to feel like you *deserve* to be happy."

Logan let out a long breath. His eyes held so much remorse. "I've made a lot of mistakes, Amelia. I don't honestly know what I deserve, but I'm doing what I can now to right a lot of wrongs. To be a better man."

It surprised me how differently Logan viewed himself compared to the way I saw him, but I understood how the pain of his past could tilt his reality. Stepping into him, I reached out to touch his face, running my fingers lightly down his cheek and across his jaw. "You deserve to be happy, Logan. Don't complicate it. It's not something you have to earn.

"I'm in awe of you. I'm proud of you. And this," I said, dragging my hand down to his chest, "this heart of yours . . . It's big. You may have had a reckless streak—hell, you may have more—but it doesn't change the composition of the man that you are. You are fundamentally good, and you deserve to be happy."

We stood there locked in each other's eyes for what felt like endless seconds, the entire world around us having completely faded away. It was only Logan and I and our beating hearts and this undeniable need for each other.

I pressed myself up onto my tip toes and lightly pressed my

lips to the corner of his mouth. And then I pressed them against the other side as I felt his arms wrap around my waist.

"You make it hard to breathe, Mills." I pulled my face away from his and looked up into those honey eyes that felt like home. Logan's mouth found mine in a kiss that was slow and soft, unhurried in the way that it just might last forever. I sighed into his mouth, feeling my body melt against his.

And then his arms were urgent as they pulled me closer so that I was flush against him. His hand moved up to my head, tugging my hair back so that he had better access to my mouth. Flames ignited inside of me as his tongue plunged past my lips and pressed against my own. It was a kiss that almost knocked the wind out of me.

I felt my toes curl within my boots as he pulled away. His hands raked down my back as he let out a breath. "I'm having a really hard time controlling myself right now." His voice was downright guttural.

*Then don't*, I thought to myself. "Well"—my breaths were quick and shallow—"I'm pretty sure that kind, old woman over there would rather not see you ravage me in the middle of the street."

Logan huffed out a laugh. "You never know, she might have a kink for this." He pressed his mouth to my neck, sending shockwaves of heat through me. I giggled as I peered over at the woman across the street who had stopped walking and was undoubtedly watching us with a scowl on her face.

I threw her an apologetic smile as Logan continued his delicious assault along my jawline. "Mm, Amelia." He sounded a bit breathless. "I lose my damn mind when it comes to you."

His words hit me square in my chest. Pressing one last kiss to the sensitive spot behind my ear, he straightened and looked down at me through his dark lashes. Now I was the one who was breathless as my eyes caught on a small freckle on his cheek. The words I suddenly needed to say rose up inside of my throat. "I love you, Logan." I watched his face change in response, his eyes locked on mine, his lips parted in surprise. "You don't have to do anything to earn it. You don't have to erase the mistakes of your past to be worthy of good things today."

"Amelia . . ." he started, but I quickly pressed my finger to his mouth.

"I'm not looking for you to say anything back to me. In fact, I don't want you to. Not yet. I think it's important that you decide to love yourself and break away from the chains of your destructive inner dialogue, because you owe that to yourself."

Logan's lips pressed together in a firm line, as if he wanted to argue against my words. But he kept himself quiet, instead lifting his hand to gently tuck a stand of my hair behind my ear.

"I'm not going anywhere." I pressed my hands against his chest, needing to feel him, to ground myself within him. "I'm right here, and I always will be. I promise you that. But you need to figure out how to love yourself. How to go easy on yourself. Okay?"

Logan's eyes were focused somewhere on my coat as he searched for words. When they lifted back up to mine, they were full of warmth and adoration. "Okay, sweetheart." He nodded. "But I might need you to help me along the way."

Wrapping my arms around his neck, I again pressed myself up for a kiss. "There is nothing more I'd rather do than help you see yourself the way I do."

# Chapter Twenty-Four



On the first Thursday of June, three weeks after graduating from college, we took a three-hour flight from Denver to Cabo San Lucas. In the days leading up to the trip, Adam and Logan were positively beside themselves with excitement. If you didn't know any better, you would have assumed that this graduation trip was for *them* by the way they extensively researched excursions, mapped out the best local restaurants, and completely overhauled the shared packing list that I'd created with things like "multi-person unicorn raft" and "hella sunscreen."

I had to admit, though, that once I got settled into my seat on the airplane, my own excitement kicked in. I'd never been to Mexico before, and after what felt like a lifetime of schoolwork and studying, I was ready to fully let loose and enjoy these next few days with my best friend.

In total, we had seven people in our group. Mackenzie, who'd originally intended for this to be a small girls trip, had invited Nora and Gwen from her education program at CU Denver. Once Mackenzie's brother, Trevor, found out that Adam and Logan had forced themselves into the trip, he declared that he was coming too, despite Mackenzie's best attempts to stop him.

Trevor was a year younger than Adam and Logan but had known them well enough growing up, and was able to get the trip's details from them with a simple phone call—making it impossible for Mackenzie to thwart his plans. Once she finally gave in to the reality that the guys were coming with us on this vacation, Mackenzie decided to also invite her boyfriend, Eric. Unfortunately, he had to pull out of the trip at the last minute because he got hit with some sort of summer flu.

The house that we'd rented was right on the beach with a back patio overlooking the gorgeous Pacific Ocean. On one end of the patio was a built-in fire pit with chairs seated around it to enjoy in the cooler evenings, and on the other side was an array of lounge chairs to lay out on during the warm, sunny days.

The house had three bedrooms inside of the main structure, and there was also a detached casita on the property that was built out as a fully-loaded studio unit. Adam and Logan had called dibs on the casita as soon as we confirmed the booking on the house. Mackenzie and I were sharing the primary suite inside the main house, Nora and Gwen would share the second biggest bedroom, and Trevor would have the third bedroom all to himself.

I'd met Nora a few times over the years at various college parties with Mackenzie. They'd met in their first week of classes, both of them in the education program at CU Denver. Nora was a bit of a wild child and could certainly hold her own when it came to partying. Her almost six-foot stature was a force to be reckoned with when she started drinking. She was a lot of fun to be around and I'd always enjoyed hanging out with her.

This trip was my first time meeting Gwen, who was a petite blonde with an adorable pixie cut who looked like a little fairy next to Nora's tall frame. Gwen was two years older than us and had just finished her master's degree in education. She'd been a TA in one of Mackenzie and Nora's classes during their third semester and they'd both instantly clicked with her.

The weather in Cabo couldn't have possibly been any better on the day that we arrived. The sun was out, the air wasn't too warm, and both the sky and water were crystal clear. We'd decided to keep the first night in Cabo low-key, staying at the house to build a fire in the fire pit. We figured it was more responsible to just hang out on the patio all night, to save our "vacation energy" for the next full day. Starting a three-night trip off by diving right into the local bar scene was probably not the best idea.

It didn't stop Adam from getting absolutely hammered, though. We'd started pouring cocktails around six that evening, and by nine o'clock Adam's face was completely flushed. Before I knew what was happening, he'd launched himself up from his lounge chair and began running down the patio steps that gave access to the beach. He was somehow totally naked as he plunged himself right into the ocean.

Not one to be outdone with any party tricks, Nora was just as impulsively flying down those same steps, discarding her clothing along the way as she attempted to remove each article mid-stride. Her long, blonde hair whipped behind her as she ran right into salty water. Those of us who remained on the patio simply watched them, stunned, as they both screamed and splashed at each other in the waves.

"Fifty bucks says those two hook up this weekend," Trevor said as we all watched Adam push Nora underneath the water.

"If he doesn't *drown her* first," Mackenzie responded with disdain. She still wasn't super happy about any of the guys being here, and I didn't blame her. It wasn't exactly ideal to have your older brother with you on a weekend party trip.

Trevor, Mackenzie, Gwen and I were seated around our small fire with margaritas in red solo cups. Logan had been lying on a lounge chair next to Adam before Adam had so abruptly decided to go skinny dipping. I glanced over in that direction now and caught Logan looking at me. There was a desperate look in his eye—something wild and ferocious—but he blinked and it was gone. I sent a small smile his way, and he smiled back before briefly turning his attention to Adam and Nora in the water, and then he laid his head on the lounger and looked up into the night's starry sky.

I looked back into the fire, recognizing a similarly burning flame within my own belly.

The next morning, Adam and Logan were up bright and early, yelling at everyone from the hallway that it was time to go snorkeling. When everyone ignored them, they began opening all bedroom doors and throwing inflatable drink holders at us.

"What the fuck are they doing?" Mackenzie grumbled from her side of the bed. "How is your brother even vertical right now?"

I threw my pillow over my head in protest.

After extensive persuading, everyone was out of their beds and congregating in the kitchen in their swimsuits looking half asleep as we all rifled through the assortment of snacks for something to eat. "Do you think it's too early for beef jerky?" Nora asked. She looked a lot like one would look the morning after drinking tequila and swimming naked in the ocean.

"I don't think it's ever too early for beef jerky when you're on vacation," Gwen answered. She didn't look tired at all. In fact, she looked positively radiant as she bounced through the kitchen in a bright yellow sundress. Her hair was adorned with little hair jewels that glinted in the sun. How in the world had she had the time to do something like that?

"Perfect," Nora replied as she began ripping open the package of a bag of jalapeño flavored jerky.

I grabbed a banana and a bottle of water and walked toward the back patio, wanting to take a moment to myself to enjoy the incredible morning horizon. Slipping out the back door, I made my way down the steps to the beach.

I stood there for about fifteen minutes, ankle-deep in the warm ocean as I ate my banana, soaking in the beauty of this beach. Of this sky. Of this whole place. A collection of small, white fishing boats floated lazily in the distance. Other vacationers were walking along the shore line, looking for shells in the sand. It was serene, and I felt thankful to be on a trip like this at all, celebrating such a pivotal moment in my life.

Hearing a low whistle behind me, I turned to find Logan walking down the steps from the house, a bottle of sunscreen in hand. He looked amazing in a white T-shirt and black swim trunks, hard muscles gliding along his frame as his body moved toward me. His dark brown hair was all wild waves underneath his backward hat, and the sight of him quite simply took my breath away.

"Hey." He grinned as he reached me on the shore. I could almost see his eyes twinkle through his sunglasses. Or perhaps I was simply imagining it. "Here, put this on. You'll get burned really quick out here next to the water." He held out the large tube of sunscreen.

"You came all the way down here to bring me sunscreen?" I asked, looking from the bottle in his hands back up to his face.

"We have a long day in the sun ahead of us, and I don't want you to get hurt," he said simply, as if there was nothing else to consider. As if this wasn't actually a really thoughtful gesture, but merely a standard transfer of resources.

I smiled at him, suddenly feeling as if I were floating rather than sinking into the wet sand. "Thanks, Logan." I took the sunscreen from his hand and watched as he swiftly turned and walked back to the house, content that his mission was accomplished.

Before long, the seven of us were climbing aboard a boat that was run by a local company who brought tourists out to sea for various excursions. True to their word—that they'd practically screamed from the hallway—Adam and Logan were taking us all snorkeling. Each of us grabbed rental gear from a large bin and found a place on the boat to sit. I tried not to think about how many faces had been in the snorkel mask in my hands. The driver of the boat introduced himself as "Fancy Pants" and offered everyone a beer.

Mackenzie looked up at him, squinting in the sun. "It's, like, nine thirty in the morning."

Fancy Pants shrugged. "Suit yourselves."

We boated out to the Cabo Pulmo National Marine Park, a reserve with a thriving coral reef and plenty of wild marine life to explore with our snorkels. After a brief training run-through at the stern of the boat, we all jumped into the warm ocean and scattered around, looking for some marine action.

It didn't take long before I was completely transfixed by the bright colors of the hundreds of fish all around me, following various schools of them around the reef. The whole scene was like a fluttering, underwater rainbow. It was pure magic.

As I watched a big, beautiful sea turtle glide out into the ocean beyond the reef, a scene straight out of something on the National Geographic channel, I glimpsed a sudden movement in the water to my left. I instantly panicked, thinking that I was about to be eaten alive by a menacing reef shark. I swung my head toward the commotion and saw a flurry of bodies and bubbles. *Uh oh.*

I quickly kicked my legs to push my head above the water's surface so that I could see what was going on. Were we in danger? Was there an apex predator nearby? Instinctually, I began swimming for the boat.

I reached it in record time, thanks to a kick of adrenaline. As I pulled myself up onto the back deck, I heard Gwen let out a loud scream. "It fucking HURTS!" I could tell that she was in full-fledged panic mode.

I heard another voice, one that was low and soothing. "Gwen, you're okay. Look at me." Pause. "Deep breaths." Pause. "See, you're okay."

Logan. That was Logan's voice.

I stood up, stumbling on my feet as the boat rocked in the water, and noticed Adam and Nora swimming toward the boat as well with concerned faces.

Turning back to Gwen and Logan, I saw that she was lying on one of the boat's bench seats, holding her leg in the air. Angry, red blisters were spreading in a cluster of welts on her calf. Logan was kneeling in front of her, attempting to calm her down.

"What happened?" I asked.

Logan turned to look at me briefly before refocusing on Gwen in front of him. "Jellyfish, I think. She was swimming next to me and I realized something was wrong, so I helped her back to the boat and carried her over here."

"You carried her?"

He shot me another quick look, eyebrows furrowed together in confusion. "Yeah, why?"

"What's wrong?" Adam asked, pulling himself up from the back of the boat right behind me.

"Jellyfish sting," I responded. *Why did I sound so flippant?*

"Oh man, that looks bad," Nora said as she nudged past me toward her friend who was now panic-crying and squeezing her eyes closed, as if pretending like she couldn't see the wound would help the pain go away.

Logan turned to Adam. "Do you know how we can help her?" *We.* I felt a surge of frustration at his words.

Fancy Pants suddenly appeared at the stern. "You need vinegar! Hold on," he said, pulling up the lid to a floor compartment in the boat. He pulled out a gallon jug of vinegar and reached out to hand it to Logan.

"Gwen, I'm going to pour a little of this vinegar on your leg, okay?" he said gently, watching her for permission. She kept her eyes closed but nodded her head. Logan tilted the open jug of vinegar so that liquid began slowly pouring onto the welts on Gwen's leg. She winced, but stayed focused on taking the deep breaths that Logan was now encouraging her to take. I suddenly felt like I needed a few deep breaths, myself.

Adam called out to Trevor and Mackenzie, who were still about thirty feet away from the boat and unaware of our current turn of events. When they looked up from the water,

Adam motioned for them to come back aboard so that Fancy Pants could bring us home.

Once they reached the boat, Trevor and Mackenzie pulled themselves up out of the water and everyone sat around Gwen, looking for opportunities to help her. I knew with zero doubts that I was being absolutely ridiculous, but the storm that was raging inside of my body felt all too familiar, and I wasn't prepared to deal with it right now. Not here. So I wrapped myself in a large beach towel and sat down on the side of the boat, staying near the back and away from Gwen and Logan.

# Chapter Twenty-Five

I arrived at Logan's house just as the first rays of the morning sun began rising out of the horizon. The air was bitter cold as I got out of my car and shut the door, but I knew that once we made it to the hiking trail and got our bodies moving we would warm up. Still, I'd put on an extra scarf for good measure and was wearing my heavier knit beanie over my ears.

It had been three days since I'd seen Logan. After spending that incredible night downtown, we both jumped right into a heavy work week. The shop had kept him busy from sun up to sun down these last few days, and I used the time to catch up on things I needed to get done for my clients.

We texted each other every day, but I'd felt an overwhelming need to see Logan yesterday as I was wrapping up a campaign outline for a local flower shop. I sent him a text to ask when he might have free morning to go on a hike with me—

also feeling the urge to get out into nature—and he responded within seconds, *Tomorrow?*

Adam worked at the hospital last night and I'd left the apartment before he got home, but if he later asked where I'd been this morning, it would be easy to tell him the truth. I was hiking.

I stood for a moment at the sidewalk, taking it all in. Logan's house was endearing. The exterior was painted a cozy, dusty blue with white trim around the large windows that flanked either side of the front door. There were brick steps leading up to a front porch that looked like it might wrap around the whole house. A wooden porch swing hung on the right side, and I found myself picturing us sitting side by side on it in the summer, rocking lazily as I curled into the crook of his body, his arm wrapped around me tight.

It was a place that was truly his. Where he began and ended each day. Where he was, undoubtedly, his purest and most honest self. I wanted to know the secrets contained within the walls. The noises he made when he dressed in the morning. Is that what he was doing now? Did he brew himself coffee? Make himself breakfast? Or did he merely go through the motions to get out of the house and on with the day before him?

Taking in a deep breath, I skipped up the seventeen steps it took to get to his front door and knocked. It had been only three days since I'd seen him, and yet my body was rattling with anticipation. Was it normal to feel this crazy about someone? I had no idea, but I didn't care either way as long as it meant I could have Logan.

Immediately, the sound of barking came from within. I'd almost forgotten that Logan had a dog, a fact that was still bewildering to me. We'd never had pets growing up—unless you counted the sea monkeys that Adam and I had for about two weeks when he was in fifth grade and I was in first. That was, until one unfortunate day when I'd spilled the plastic container that held them all over my bed, and that was the end of that. My mother was allergic to dogs and my father was against cats, so we were forced to grow up in a home without animals. I'd never been to Logan's grandmother's house, but I was fairly certain there were never any pets there either.

I heard the swipe of the deadbolt turning before the door swung open to reveal a yawning Logan. His face was still swollen from sleep, his eyes not quite all the way open. His hair was adorably unkempt, sticking out in all directions. From the looks of it, he'd managed to put on clothes suitable for a winter hike, although I was pretty certain his shirt was on inside out. The unmistakable smell of hazelnut coffee filled my nose. *So he did brew himself coffee*, I felt satisfied to know.

"Good morning," I said.

Logan regarded me for a moment before responding. "Any chance I can convince you to lie down with me instead of going on this hike?" His voice was deliciously raspy. All of his hard work at the shop must have been catching up to him because he looked tired.

"As tempting as that sounds"—and I did mean *tempting*—"you made rules."

"Cuddling isn't against the rules."

I felt a flush to my cheeks at the thought of lying next to Logan, possessively wrapping my limbs around him. I'd give just about anything to slide under the sheets next to him in his bed. But I knew that wouldn't be enough. The hunger I felt couldn't be satiated with cuddling.

The truth must have been evident on my face, because Logan's eyes darkened before he cleared his throat and moved out of the way. "Come in, it's freezing out. Have a cup of coffee and then we can go."

I stepped over the threshold and into his house, and was immediately ambushed by a fifty-pound gray tornado at my feet. The impact against my shins nearly knocked me down to the floor, but I felt Logan's hand wrap around my arm, holding me upright.

"Hook! No!" Logan commanded firmly. Immediately, the tornado stilled and transformed into a politely sitting pitbull. He panted excitedly as his tongue hung out the side of his mouth, and it was then that I realized he was missing one of his front legs.

I bent down to say hello to him, scratching a patch of white fur on his chest as he began licking my arm, making me giggle. "Hi, Hook! Nice to meet you." His name suddenly dawned on me. "Oh my gosh! Captain Hook!" I smiled up at Logan. "That's amazing . . . I loved Peter Pan as a kid."

Logan was leaning against the wall by the front door, watching me with an amused look in his eyes. There was the slightest uptick in the right corner of his mouth. "I know."

Those words hit me like a sucker punch.

He pushed himself off the wall and held his hand out to lift me back into a standing position. "Let me show you the house, and then we can drink our coffee."

I nodded silently, my thoughts still stuck on Hook's name. Had Logan really named his dog after my favorite movie from twenty years ago?

I followed him through the house as I soaked in the details of every room. The living room was charming and comfortable with a worn leather sofa, low wooden coffee table and a large flatscreen television. Down a narrow hallway were three bedrooms—one was converted into an office space with a deep mahogany desk, one looked to be a guest room, and finally at the end of the hall was Logan's bedroom.

I felt a thrill rush through me as I looked inside and saw a king-sized bed against a dark gray wall. The room held minimal decor, but didn't look empty or unfinished. A sleek, black dresser stood against the far wall, and an armchair perched in the corner of the room next to a reading light. A small, black bookshelf full of books was pushed up against the wall near the chair, creating a charming little reading nook. I thought of my own book collection, and how nice it would be to sit in that chair together at the end of a long day, a soft blanket pulled over both of us as we read our books.

I turned to meet Logan's eyes, finding that he was watching me. "I like this room," I said, raising my eyebrows with mock flirtation. Although, despite making light of the moment, there was no doubt that I was feeling the tension in the air. The sudden need to slide my hands under Logan's shirt was almost overwhelming.

I watched as he gave me that sexy side grin that he was so good at. "Is that so?"

"Mhm. It suits you."

He dipped his head and looked down at his feet before his eyes found mine again. "I'm glad you like it." His tone was teasing, but I could see the desire mirrored in his eyes and I felt my mouth go dry. He tilted his head back toward the hallway behind him. "The coffee is still warm, would you like a cup?"

"Absolutely."

We made our way back through the house and into a big,

lovely kitchen. From the dishes in the sink, it was clear that he cooked for himself. It made me happy to know that he'd created such a comfortable home.

There were already two mugs set on the counter next to the coffee pot, and I watched him pour coffee into each of them before turning around to hand me one. We both took a seat at the breakfast table, the hazelnut coffee wafting into my nose.

"So, hiking?" Logan asked.

"Yeah . . . There's a state park about twenty minutes away that I like to go to. It's quiet, and the red rocks surrounding the trailhead are amazing. I try to get out there a couple times a week—sometimes I feel like I do my best thinking when I'm out there."

Logan nodded. "Sounds perfect."

# Chapter Twenty-Six

THERE WAS ONLY A LITTLE BIT OF SNOW ON THE ground, so the rocks we were climbing over weren't too slick or icy. The morning air had already gotten significantly warmer beneath the rising sun that was peeking over the red rocks to the east. Already, the fresh air was doing wonders for my soul.

We'd been hiking along the trail for about a quarter mile so far, and I was impressed with how well Hook kept up with us. He moved as if he didn't have a disability, bounding along the trail with four-legged confidence. It was clear that Logan had worked with him and kept him active.

"Oh, hey," Logan huffed out as his long legs stepped over a boulder, "you'll never guess who brought his car into the shop yesterday."

I tried to think of who Logan could be talking about, but my mind came up blank. "Who?"

"Your ex." Logan's voice was mildly sinister.

I stopped in place and turned around to look at him. "My ex?"

"Yep." His eyes were playful, his tone daring.

"Noah?"

Logan's brows furrowed. "No, not Noah. But, to be fully transparent, I would probably pummel him if I ever saw him."

Confusion hit me. "Oh . . . then who?"

"Your first love," Logan answered, cocking a brow, as if this should be an easy guess. He must not know that *he* was, most certainly, my first love.

"I give up." I shrugged. I didn't like this game. An uneasiness was spreading within my belly, a tightrope threatening to snap.

Logan rolled his eyes. "Paul! Remember Paul? Your prom date?"

I felt my face drop. "Oh." I turned back to the trail, taking a large step forward. "I would *not* call Paul my first love."

"You wouldn't?" Logan sounded genuinely surprised.

"No, I definitely wouldn't." I could feel a twinge of irritation coming to the surface as I stepped over a fallen tree.

"Wait, Amelia. Stop," Logan gently urged behind me. I took a few more steps up before I felt his warm hand wrap around my shoulder. "Amelia." His voice a sliver more demanding now. "Stop."

I halted in place and turned around to face him. It was likely that I threw a glare at him from the way that his face fell. "What?" I could hear Hook's tail thumping wildly against the ground at our feet.

"Mills," he said, studying my face. "What happened just now? Why are you upset?"

I stared back at him for a number of seconds before I felt

my shoulders collapse. Blowing out a breath, I finally answered. "Paul was *not* my first love. He wasn't a love at all. He was . . . a total asshole."

Logan narrowed his eyes. "I thought you really liked him?" The confusion on his face was evident.

I shook my head. "No. Maybe I tried to at one point, but he proved to be rather unlikeable."

"But," Logan pressed, "you went to prom with him. And you . . . you let him give you a hickey."

I felt my eyes widen in shock. "*What?*" He clearly had no idea what happened that night, but how could he? It's not like I ever told him. "Logan, Paul tried to force himself on me on prom night. He was upset that I wouldn't do *more* with him and he made it very hard for me to go home. That wasn't a hickey, that was a bite mark. He bit me after I tried to walk away from him."

I saw a flurry of emotions shift through Logan's features. His nostrils flared as his right eye twitched, a vein in his neck protruding with enthusiasm. He balled his hands into tight fists before releasing them and placing them on his hips, only to let them fall again at his sides. "Why didn't you say anything? Why didn't you call me that night, Amelia? I would have come for you." There was something in the tone of his voice. Something that hinted at violence and broken bones. It sent a steep awareness through me.

"I don't know, I . . . I didn't know what to do. He didn't really make me nervous until we were parked in front of the house." I took in a breath. "He didn't want me to go inside, he didn't want the night to end. He said I *owed* him after all the time we'd spent together." Logan scoffed and shook his head as more anger filled his eyes. "I was home though, and I was able to run inside. And then I found you and Adam in the base-ment with those girls and . . . I felt jealous and ashamed and I didn't feel like you would want to hear it."

"Amelia." Logan's voice was insistent. "I always wanted to hear it. I hated knowing you were with him that night. You looked so damn pretty, and I hated knowing he was dancing with you, holding your hand. I hated that it wasn't me. Trust me, I always wanted to hear *anything* from you." He combed his fingers through his hair in frustration as he looked at the ground before his eyes rose to meet mine again. "I'm sorry I misunderstood. I was so focused on being angry that I failed to see what was right in front of me."

"You couldn't have known. There's nothing for you to be sorry for. I just . . . I don't want you to think he was my first love. He wasn't."

Logan huffed out a breath as he nodded. "I'm going to fuck his car up. I'm going to fuck *him* up."

I threw my hands out toward him, grabbing his shoulders. "No, Logan. No you're not. You're not going to risk your busi-ness because of something that happened a long time ago. He's not worth it. He's not worth an ounce of it because it's only going to hurt you in the end."

His body was still stiff with discomfort, and I could tell this was really bothering him, so I pulled his hand in mine and started moving us onward, hoping the physical activity would help him calm down.

We spent the next fifteen minutes or so in silence as we continued through the trailhead, our hands remaining inter-twined. The air was still chilly, but fresh in a way that nurtured my body. Eventually, I thought of a question that would steer the subject away from Paul.

"What happened between you and Mara?" I asked, hoping my curiosity wasn't too nosy. I had been surprised to hear her name come up again and wondered how she came back into Logan's life after all this time, and if he might still have feelings for her.

"She came into the shop, not knowing that I owned it. Her car had died on the side of the road and she didn't know what to do, so she walked through our door and asked if someone could help her tow it. We don't normally tow cars—the business doesn't have a tow truck or anything—but I heard her question from where I was underneath a van and decided to see if I could help.

"When I walked up to the front lobby I saw that it was her." I felt him hesitate, fumbling in his mind for the right next words. "I noticed she had some bruises on her arms . . . small ones, in a row. I recognized the familiar way it looked. Fingertips, from a hand squeezing."

I felt my breath catch, not expecting anything like this. But I stayed quiet, giving him room to tell the story.

"I hadn't seen her since high school, over ten years ago. But we both recognized each other right away and I told her I would help. I borrowed a truck from one of the guys and was able to tow her car back to the shop, and then I took her to lunch while the guys took a look at it.

"She opened up to me while we ate burgers and explained that she'd been trying to leave her boyfriend for awhile. He was getting pretty handsy with her and she was fearful of him. She was finally able to pack all of her things and leave after a bad fight, and she was staying on a friend's couch trying to navigate through her next steps. All she had was her car and whatever was in it. I don't know . . . after hearing that, I felt compelled to help her."

I nodded as I looked up at Logan, squeezing his palm in silent support as we continued on the trail.

"I made it a point to check in on her and be there for her, and after a few lunches—and then eventually a few dinners—we just sort of stuck together."

"Wow." I could feel my voice was tight. I knew an experience like that was probably really triggering for Logan. "Is she okay now?"

"Yeah, yeah," Logan quickly responded. "She's okay. She got a place of her own outside of the city and she's pretty much back on her feet. We never actively talked about dating again, it just sort of happened. I think we fell into an old routine from when we were younger. But we realized before long that it wasn't working and I finally told her that we'd do much better as friends."

"Why wasn't it working?" I heard myself ask before my brain could catch up to my mouth. "Sorry, that's probably a little invasive . . ."

"No, it's okay. It's a fair question." He gave me a small grin before he looked back down to his feet, Hook still marching faithfully at his side. He didn't answer right away, and I thought maybe he wasn't going to before I heard him say, "She wasn't you."

I felt the beat of those words in my heart like a kick-drum.

# Chapter Twenty-Seven

I woke up the next morning to a text from Logan.

LOGAN

My legs are sore.

Smiling at the screen, I typed a reply back.

Me: Big baby

I put my phone back down on the nightstand and covered my face with one of the many soft pillows that adorned the bed. Logan and I hiked for almost four miles yesterday morning, only turning around because he had to get to work. It had been one of the best mornings I'd had in a long time, wandering through the red rocks with Logan and Hook, like a beautiful glimpse at our potential future. Taking the pillow back off of my face, I sighed as I stared at the ceiling. I already wanted to see him again.

The bright, morning sun was shining through the bedroom window, casting a beam of light onto the bed. It was a bit blinding, so I sat up and put on my socks, figuring it was time to get up anyway.

I opened the bedroom door and made my way to the kitchen, finding Rachel cooking breakfast in a plush, pink bathrobe. Her face was fresh and free of makeup, and her hair was loose around her face. "Good morning," I said, causing her to jump and clutch her chest.

"Oh my gosh—you scared me," she said through shaky breaths. A brown lock of hair fell down in front of her eyes, and I watched as she tucked it behind her ear.

I threw her an apologetic glance. "I'm so sorry, I didn't mean to."

A smile grew from her lips as the panic left her eyes. "That's okay, not your fault. Are you hungry? I'm about ten minutes away from being done with this and Adam should be home from work any minute."

I took a look over her shoulder at the assortment of breakfast items cooking on the stove. Scrambled eggs, bacon, biscuits and gravy . . . it all smelled like heaven. "Yeah, that sounds amazing." I went to the fridge to pour myself a glass of orange juice and took a sip. "I'm going to jump in the shower, but if Adam gets back before I'm out, don't wait for me. Go ahead and eat."

"Alright! Take your time."

I went back to the bedroom with my glass of juice and shut the door behind me. Just as I was about to enter the bathroom, I heard my phone chime with an incoming text. I made my way back toward the nightstand to find another message from Logan.

LOGAN

I think I might need a massage 😊

I could help you arrange a massage.

You could???

Yes. I know a masseuse with GREAT hands.

Who?

Giggling, I brought my phone to the bathroom and started the shower, making the water temperature nice and hot. After taking off my pajamas and kicking them to the corner of the bathroom, I used my phone to snap a couple of mirror selfies and sent them to Logan. It didn't take him long to respond.

LOGAN

Holy hell

Amelia

Best. Text. Ever.

My god, woman. When can I see you?

Knowing that I had this effect on Logan made me feel unabashedly sexy. His obvious want for me and our overall sexual chemistry was nothing like I'd ever experienced before. I typed a quick response before I set my phone on the bathroom counter.

Tonight. Please.

I stepped into the hot shower, letting the water cascade down the front of my body. Goosebumps rose all along my skin from the blissful warmth. I heard my phone chime from the bathroom counter, and I smiled to myself.

Something about knowing that Logan and I were strung together with this desire and anticipation made me feel utterly euphoric. I'd spent so much time in my life yearning for exactly *this*, yearning to be his, that to actually have it all coming true felt nothing short of miraculous. I heard my phone chime a second time and I again giggled to myself, feeling like a young teenager with a heavy crush.

The thing was, it *wasn't* just a sexual attraction. It wasn't just some lustful fantasy coming to fruition. It was *Logan*, someone I cared so deeply for and had for as long as I could remember. The amount of genuine love and respect we already had for each other was understood completely, and so to be on this journey with him—with someone I already felt so close to —it made everything that much more real. It made the possibility of our future together that much more . . . inevitable.

I spent the next fifteen minutes enjoying the scalding shower and my favorite eucalyptus soap, feeling immensely grateful for the way things were going in my life. After I finished washing away the suds, I turned off the water and grabbed a plush towel to dry myself off with, making a mental note to thank Rachel for stocking the apartment with such luxuries because there was no way in hell Adam would have purchased nice towels like these on his own.

Stepping out of the shower onto a soft bath mat—another Rachel item, no doubt—I picked my phone back up to see Logan's responses.

LOGAN

Done. Just let me know when and where.

I can come to you if it's safe.

Other than picking me up for our first date, Logan hadn't been to Adam's apartment since he showed up for the ride to Breckenridge before Thanksgiving. It felt safer to avoid any close proximity to Adam while we navigated through figuring out what we were actually doing with our relationship. But . . . I couldn't help but think of Rachel out there in the kitchen cooking breakfast and wishing that Logan could be here too, enjoying the morning with me as Rachel did with Adam.

I didn't need any more time to figure out if this was what I wanted. If Logan needed more time, of course I would respect that and give him as much of it as he needed. But I knew, without question, that I wanted to spend the rest of my life with him. I was all in.

Was it too soon to tell him? I mean, it had only been six days since we decided to take this chance together, and six days was hardly enough time to decide that you want to go endgame with someone. But Logan was hardly just someone.

I figured it was probably better to be honest with him about my feelings, since that was part of this whole agreement, anyway. We spent enough time in our lives not sharing our real feelings, so to hold back didn't feel right.

Tonight. I would tell him tonight.

I threw my phone on the bed and got dressed for the day, deciding to stay comfy in an oversized T-shirt and sweats since I'd just be working from home on the couch today. I put my hair into French braided pigtails so that it would be fun and flirty later after it dried, and then I made my way back out to the kitchen.

Adam was home, sitting at the table with Rachel as they ate their breakfast. Rachel was laughing at something he'd just said, pure adoration in her eyes as she looked at him. It made my heart melt, and strengthened the feeling of wanting to share every morning like this with *my* person. "Well aren't you just the cutest lovebirds," I sing-songed to them as I went to make my own plate at the stove.

"Good morning, sister." Adam's tone was cheerful, but he sounded tired. He'd been working almost every night this past week, which was a lot because his shifts were usually about twelve hours long.

"How was work?" I asked.

"Good. Long. I can't wait to hit the sack."

"I bet. Are you home tonight?"

"No, the neurology department is pretty short-staffed right now and we have quite a few patients on the floor, so I need to be there. If I can bump up a few surgeries it will really help alleviate our limited capacity with beds."

Rachel shook her head. "I keep telling him he needs to take a break. He's going to work himself to death."

Adam threw Rachel a smirk. "Babe, I can handle it, okay? I'm a strong surgeon, and they need me."

I was reminded of what it was like growing up with a father who so willingly gave himself to his patients. There were so many times that he was away, missing big moments in our lives, but I knew he was *saving* lives and it made it all worth it. He was a hero, and Adam was following right along in those footsteps.

"I don't doubt your strength, honey. But I would like to

see you have a night off soon so you can give your body and mind a break." Rachel's tone was firm but gentle, delivered with a smile. I liked knowing that she wasn't afraid to speak her mind to my brother. Adam was undoubtedly kind and considerate, but when it came to his work and being the best, he could be very stubborn. He needed someone like Rachel keeping him in check.

I loaded up my plate with food and joined them at the table, listening to the two of them go back and forth as they talked about work. Soon, Rachel got up to get ready for her own day, saying that some of her prosthetic prototypes were going into testing next week and she and her colleagues needed to make a few modifications to the design. She disappeared into Adam's room to take a shower.

Adam finished his plate shortly after, and after putting his dishes in the sink he, too, headed toward his room. "I'm going to pass out, Millie. But I'll see you later?"

"Yep," I smiled. "I'll be around today."

Adam nodded in response before he shut his bedroom door behind him. I finished the eggs on my plate before I hurried back to my room, grabbing my phone to text Logan back.

> Come here. It'll be safe.
>
> And Logan... I'm done with your rules.

I'D SPENT the last hour making pan-seared scallops and pasta as I waited patiently for Logan to get here. Before I started cooking, I spent a little time cleaning up the apartment and getting myself ready, putting on comfortable jeans and a tight sweater. I'd taken my hair out of the braids I'd put in this morning and was pleased at the beach wave effect they'd left.

After he finally texted me that he was on his way over, I put some garlic bread in the oven and cleaned up my mess in the kitchen before setting the table for two. I couldn't help the giant smile on my face as I set two plates out, knowing Logan would soon sit at the table with me to enjoy a home cooked meal. And then for dessert, he could enjoy *me*. My body positively ached for him, and the anticipation had me feeling a bit breathless.

It wasn't long before I heard a firm knock at the door, and when I swung it open, Logan was instantly lurching himself forward to kiss me. His hands cupped my face as his mouth hungrily consumed mine. He smelled like cedar and motor oil and the mix of both was sexy as hell.

He steered me backward into the kitchen with his body, kicking the door shut behind him. "You drive me completely insane, Amelia," he murmured into my ear. "I couldn't focus on anything today except getting to you as fast as I could."

I smiled, relishing the moment. His mouth found my neck and he not-so-gently nibbled at my skin as he lifted me up onto the kitchen counter. My hands eagerly swept over his chest as my legs wrapped around his hips, and I couldn't help but feel the spark of immense relief at having him close to me like this again. To feel his body against mine—I didn't know that I would ever get enough of this high.

Logan was just as eager as I was, pulling up the hem of my shirt and swiftly taking it off of me, exposing the black lace bra that I'd put on for him. I started unbuttoning his work shirt, and when I glanced up I saw that he was smiling brightly at me, a funny look in his eye. "Are you cooking?"

"Yes."

"For me?"

I feigned annoyance at his interruption, rolling my eyes. "Yes."

He nipped at my chin, but his eyes were alight as he hummed his appreciation. "It smells amazing."

"No, Logan, *you* smell amazing."

He shook his head as he nuzzled back into my neck. "No, I'm dirty."

I pulled myself back from him to look into his eyes. His hair was a bit unkempt, his smile lazy. "Show me." My voice came out raspy and full of need.

Instantly, his eyes darkened as his focus sharpened. He stood up straighter, looking down at my mouth before his eyes fell further down to my bra, as if just noticing it. He hooked a finger beneath one of the straps at my back and slowly slid it down my skin. "I like this," he whispered, before his mouth was on mine again.

I finished unbuttoning his shirt and tore it off from him, throwing it to the ground before I wrapped my arms around his neck and pulled him closer as he kissed me deeply. Logan's hands roamed my legs as I began working his belt and the button on his jeans. He groaned into my mouth and it was like lightning down my spine. The tremors of his wanting were evident as his hands grazed higher along my thighs.

My attention was caught on the zipper that I was sliding down his pants and the tongue that ravished my mouth, so I didn't hear the twist of the doorknob or the creak in the wood as the front door opened. I also didn't hear the three or four footsteps it would have taken to get a good view of Logan and I in the kitchen. But what I *did* hear immediately shook me to my core.

"What the *fuck*!" Adam growled.

Before he'd even gotten the words out, Logan stepped away from me to face his best friend. As he moved, his pants slid lower down his thighs. He quickly reached to pull them back up and began fastening the button as he kept his eyes on my brother. "Adam . . ." His face was in utter shock, twisting into fear and then shame.

"What the fuck are you doing with my sister?" Adam's face was contorted with fury and so much hurt. And then, within seconds, the worst thing that could have possibly happened, did. Adam charged toward us, locked in on Logan who was still trying to buckle his belt, and punched him square in the jaw.

The sound of his fist making contact with Logan's chin was all I could focus on for the next several moments.

"*Adam!*" I screamed.

My brother turned to face me, his face full of fury and disappointment. "How could you let this happen, Amelia?"

His words surprised me. I knew that Adam would have needed a little bit of time to get used to the idea of Logan and I being together—and he ideally wouldn't have found out by walking in on us like this—but the outright anger he was displaying was unexpected. "What the hell is wrong with you, Adam?" I shoved past him and put myself in front of Logan, who was holding his face in his hand. I pulled his hand down so that I could see the damage and found that his lip was bleeding and his jaw was red. Logan pulled his hand out of mine and turned away from me, running his hand up through his hair. When he came back to face me, his eyes caught on mine and the evident pain that flooded through him tore my heart wide open. "Logan." My voice was barely above a whisper as my eyes filled with tears.

He shook his head, breaking our eye contact to look down at his feet for a moment before lifting them to find Adam behind me. "I'm sorry," he said quietly before his eyes flicked to mine and he said the words again. "I'm so sorry."

He moved to pick his shirt up from where I'd thrown it on the floor minutes earlier. Then, he walked right out of the apartment, shutting the front door firmly behind him.

I turned to face my brother. "God *damn* you, Adam!"

He furrowed his brows as he yelled, "*Me*? Amelia, are you serious? I walk into my own home to find my best friend with his tongue down my little sister's throat, and you want to damn *me*?" He scoffed, turning to storm out of the kitchen before he suddenly stopped in the middle of the living room and turned around to storm right back. "How long has this been going on?"

I crossed my arms over my chest, feeling red-hot fury spreading through my body. "Since Thanksgiving, not that it's any of your business."

"Not my business? How is my best friend fucking my little sister not my business?"

"Okay, stop with the vulgarity. It's not your business because, at least for now, this is between Logan and I. We aren't ready to tell you guys yet . . . not until we know for sure that this is actually going to be something. We're finally giving ourselves a chance, Adam, but we can't exactly do that if we're too worried about what the family thinks.

"That makes no fucking sense, Amelia. You were literally

*just* with Noah. For *years*, might I add. And now all of the sudden you and Logan are 'taking a chance'? Why would you need to take a chance without us knowing? Why wouldn't you just be honest? Clearly this is just about sex and I am *not* okay with Logan being your rebound! He's my best fucking friend!"

"It's not just sex, you asshole! And we aren't telling anyone yet because he's fucking scared, Adam," I retorted, "of exactly what *you* just did."

Adam's brows furrowed tighter together again as he processed my words. His face still held incredible anger, but I could see the crack of something else, something raw that looked a lot like guilt.

I needed to make sure he truly understood what I was saying—I owed it to Logan to fight for him. "We are Logan's family. We're *all* he has. You think this is easy for either of us? Logan and I are well aware of what we are risking. This isn't just some irresponsible fling, Adam! We have tried so fucking hard to pretend that we don't feel the way that we do about each other for *years*, but you can't control who you love."

Adam's eyes widened in surprise at that last word. I watched as he faltered, taking a step back, as if I'd shoved him with what I'd said. "What?" His eyes were narrowed in disbelief.

"You heard me. I *love* him. And I refuse to let you make him feel bad for loving me back. Because I'm pretty sure that he does." I felt the sting of tears rise up, knowing I was mere moments away from becoming a sobbing mess.

I needed to land the final blow, and I needed to do it soon before I started crying. "He's your best friend. Do you remember what life was like for him as a kid? Do you remember the hell he went through?" I watched Adam's face twist in pain from the memory. "Logan was punished for everything. He grew up scared to want anything. And now, he's finally a man who's learning how to live without that fear, trying to learn how to feel deserving of real happiness, and you just *punched him in the face* over seeing us together." I shook my head in heavy disappointment. "God, Adam. He didn't deserve that."

Adam's face was bright red as shame fell upon his features. I knew I was being harsh, and I knew that he would never intentionally try to trigger any of Logan's past trauma. He knew the severity of pain that would be caused in doing so. But even if it wasn't intentional, he had to know the impact of his actions. This was the *one* chance that Logan and I had, and I'd be damned if I let Adam's irrational response be the nail on the coffin of us.

There couldn't be any coffins, not when it came to Logan and I. This was not a love story meant to die, and certainly not because of Adam.

"Maybe he didn't deserve the punch, but you guys still should have told me, Amelia."

"We *would* have, Adam. But just like you didn't tell anyone about Rachel—even though she was clearly here enough to spread fancy girl shit all throughout your apartment—we also deserved to have the room to figure out our feelings without owing anything to anyone else in the process. We would have told you. I'm sorry you found out this way, but we would have told you."

We stood in the kitchen, hackles raised as we stared at each other, until I could see my words slowly chipping away at Adam's anger. But he was stubborn, and I knew he wasn't going to just let this drop, either. He'd never been very good at admitting fault or being wrong.

I shook my head, reaching up to rub my face in my hands. "Dammit, Adam," I said, moving around him to head to my room. I grabbed my purse and car keys off the dresser before I turned on my heels back out toward the door to chase after Logan.

# Chapter Twenty-Eight

THREE YEARS AGO (AGE 22)

GWEN SPENT MOST OF THE AFTERNOON RECOVERING in a lounge chair on the patio, fretting about the pain in her leg and worrying about a lasting scar. Logan had moved a blue beach umbrella over her so that she was in the shade while she rested, and the gesture sent a swift jolt of jealousy through me. It clearly wasn't only *my* skin that he was worried about.

In an attempt to hide my admittedly inappropriate frustration, I'd gone inside to get some distance and take a shower. While I closed my eyes to wash my hair, I couldn't help but envision Logan lathering Gwen with his prized sunscreen, kneading it into her supple, glowing skin before he declared his love for her and her tiny, sun-protected body. Needless to say, the shower distraction plan was unsuccessful.

It turned out that Gwen's leg was practically healed by the time we got to dinner that night. Although there was definitely still some discoloration, Gwen was back to her happy and perky self just in time for the night's festivities. High praise to Fancy Pants and his fast-thinking vinegar solution, although a quick Google search also indicated that in most cases, a jellyfish sting causes pain that only lasts for one or two hours. But who am I to make judgements?

With Gwen back on the positivity train, the whole gang was feeling optimistic about a great night out. We found a local seafood restaurant that served incredible fish and shrimp tacos, cooked from what their kitchen staff caught that day out on the water. The food was delicious and the margaritas were as big as my head. Despite finishing my entire plate of food, I was feeling pretty tipsy from the one margarita that I'd managed to finish without issue.

After paying our bill, we walked along a strip of bars and restaurants that were centrally located within a mainly touristy part of the city, and eventually found a dimly lit nightclub that Mackenzie pulled us all into. The music was so loud that, once inside, none of us could hear each other without screaming in each other's ears, and I could feel the pulsing beat of the tempo through my bones.

We found a dark booth in the back corner, and a waitress came by to get our drink order as soon as we sat down. Adam ordered everyone shots, making good on his promise to buy all of my drinks during the trip, but I guessed his dinner margarita made him feel generous enough to open a tab for everyone. Typical Adam—he loved to find ways to achieve glory.

I tried not to notice that Gwen slid into the booth's bench right after Logan and was eagerly talking to him on the other side of the table. I couldn't hear a single word of their conversation from where I sat, but I imagined that she was telling him about her life plans for a cookie-cutter future, and how he was the perfect man to help bring those dreams to fruition.

I was *clearly* handling things exceptionally well.

Mackenzie was suddenly pulling on my arm. "Come on, Amelia . . . let's go dance!" She turned to push herself out of the booth and then looked back at me expectantly.

I shook my head and said, "You go ahead, Mack! I'll meet you out there soon, but I want to get a drink first." *Also, I want to keep a close eye on what's currently happening between* your friend *and Logan.*

Mackenzie rolled her eyes, shifting her focus to Nora and raising her eyebrows in question. Nora put up a hand as she scooted out of the booth, "Sorry . . . I gotta pee!" she shouted. "I'll be right back."

Not giving up, Mackenzie turned her attention to Adam. "Adam, come with me? Please? I want to dance!"

Adam grinned at her. "Mackenzie, I would love to accompany you to the dance floor. I'm not sure why you didn't ask me first, to be honest." His face was smug as his eyes twinkled up at her. I had to move out of the booth to let Adam through, and when I turned back to face the table I noticed that Gwen was also scooting over to let Logan out. To my delight, he followed Adam out to the dance floor and Gwen sat back down at the table. He must not have invited her to go with him. My heart soared.

It wasn't long before the waitress returned with tequila shots for everyone, passing them around the table despite the now mostly empty seating spaces. Before she left, I quietly asked her for another one. Gwen, Trevor and I clinked our shot glasses together in the middle of the table before we gulped them down. Gwen choked on hers and shoved a lime into her mouth, eyes watering. "You don't like tequila?" I shouted over the music.

"Not really, no!" she shouted back.

Nora returned to the booth from the bathroom, noticing the shot glasses on the table. I watched as her face fell when she found that ours were already empty. "Thanks for waiting for me!" She sat down next to Gwen and swiftly threw back her shot. Gwen watched her swallow it with a hint of admiration.

Naturally, all of our attention turned to the dance floor, where Mackenzie was swaying to the music with her eyes closed as if she were at a flower festival and not a nightclub in Mexico. Adam and Logan were messing around, flailing their bodies around in movements that could hardly be considered dancing. The raw joy in their faces was contagious though, and I fought back a smile as I watched them. It felt nostalgic, like I was sent back in time to watch them as fourteen-year-old misfits who couldn't take anything seriously.

I heard a giggle behind me, and turned to see Gwen and Nora talking to each other as they, too, watched the guys. I still couldn't hear anything over the music, but I soon figured out what they were giggling about when Gwen bent her head toward me and asked, "Is Logan seeing anyone?"

Dread pooled within my stomach almost instantly.

"Logan?" I rebounded, doing whatever I could to give myself more time. More time to come up with an answer. More time to take grounding breaths so I didn't visibly shoot daggers out of my eyeballs.

"Yeah," she confirmed. "He's so dreamy. And he's like, the *nicest* guy I've ever met."

Flashes of Logan sprang to life inside of my mind—

consoling Gwen on the boat, gingerly pouring vinegar on the angry-looking jellyfish sting on her leg, pulling the big umbrella over to where she lay on the patio so that she was out of the sun. I felt my heart pounding in my chest and I swear my eye might have twitched.

"Um . . . I'm not sure, actually" I mumbled, looking back in Logan's direction in time to catch him bend his knees and twerk toward the DJ in an infuriatingly attractive way.

I heard Nora shout, "Let's go join them out there!" just as the waitress came back with my second shot. Gwen and Nora scooted out the other side of the booth while I slammed my tequila back and caught eyes with Trevor. I'd almost forgotten he was still sitting at the table.

"You look like you're trying to get drunk tonight." His voice was barely audible over the music but clear enough to understand.

"We're celebrating, aren't we?" I asked, smiling in an attempt to play off the jealousy brewing inside.

"Well, in that case"—he paused and smiled—"shall we?" I watched as he nodded his head to the dance floor, where Nora and Gwen were now dancing with Mackenzie.

Turning back to Trevor, I regarded him for a moment before I answered. The second tequila shot buzzed through me, and I could feel the music's tempo a little more as it thumped across my body. "Only if you dance with me."

A crinkle of delight reached his eyes. "I thought you'd never ask, Campbell." He stood up from the booth and reached his hand out for me. I placed my hand into his and got up to follow him over to the rest of our group.

Three things happened very quickly as we reached the dance floor. First, Gwen took a step toward Logan and firmly planted her arms up and around his neck. Second, Logan noticed Trevor and I approaching, and his eyes flicked down to my hand in his. Third, I felt Trevor's breath on my skin as he said softly into my ear, "You know, Amelia . . . you've really grown into a beautiful woman."

I tore my eyes away from the subtle downturn of Logan's mouth and looked back to Trevor, who was pulling me closer into his chest. Our bodies pressed together in a way that felt vaguely uncomfortable just as both of his hands pressed against my hips. He began to move to the beat of the music, looking down at me with a grin.

"Oh, uh . . ." I stammered. After a quick glance back at Logan and Gwen, I saw that Logan was dancing with her and no longer focused in this direction. I snapped my attention back to Trevor, feeling myself fumble through the moment. "Thank you?"

His grin widened as he continued to look down at me, and I noticed his eyes catch on my mouth for a moment before they roamed down to my chest. He wasn't exactly being sneaky about it, and I felt like a gross piece of meat on display. It didn't help that I'd picked an outfit that showcased my chest, but it *certainly* hadn't been intended for Trevor. "You know, I always had a little thing for you." I watched as his eyes made their ascent back up as his hands made their journey from my hips to my ass.

I narrowed my eyes at him. "What?" I couldn't help but scoff, feeling annoyed at this curveball. I was just looking for a noncommittal, friendly dance with Trevor in an attempt to distract myself from Logan. Did I miss something? Like the part where I invited him to fondle my ass?

"Yeah," he said, his eyes stuck on my chest again as his

hands held firmly onto my backside, and I instantly stepped backward and out of his hold. Confusion flashed across his face as he looked up at my eyes. "What's wrong?" he asked.

I narrowed my eyes at him again, and in the process realized that the edges of my peripheral vision were blurring. It was like everything around me was moving in slow motion.

The back-to-back tequila shots were kicking in at a *very* inopportune time.

Trevor was still staring at me, looking confused and perhaps a smidge guilty. *Good.* "Amelia . . . ?"

I shook my head and turned away from the dance floor, beginning to feel unsteady on my feet. *Did the music get louder?* I could feel the bass practically thumping through the inside of my brain, swirling my thoughts around into pudding. I spun around in place until I found an exit sign hanging above a dark door on the back side of the bar and then promptly made my way through it.

As soon as I got outside, I felt like I could breathe again. I could still hear the music beating through the door—but it wasn't as suffocating, and the fresh air helped my mind recalibrate with the rest of my body. I realized I'd gone out a back exit and not the main door where we'd entered, and was relieved that the bar backed up to the beach so that I could orient myself with the ocean. I decided to walk down into the sand and toward the water, craving the bright moonlight on my skin.

Just as my feet stepped into the warm water, I heard the back door of the bar open and shut from up behind me. I closed my eyes and took in a deep breath, praying that it wasn't Trevor coming after me.

Turning to look, I saw it wasn't Trevor, but Logan. He

walked toward where I stood at the edge of the water with a firm determination held in his shoulders, but he stopped his pursuit a good distance away from me. Even in the darkness of night I could see the utter rage in his eyes. It made me freeze in place, my breath catching on an inhale.

"What did he do to you?" he growled. His hands were clenched into fists at his sides and I knew he was on the verge of losing control of his anger. Tendons were practically bursting from his neck.

I wasn't sure that I'd ever seen Logan this lethal before. His eyes bore into mine as his eyebrows scrunched, willing me to answer him. Willing me to give him the opportunity to break from his restraint.

He was reacting. Reacting in a way that sent shivers down my spine, because he was reacting for *me*.

"It was nothing," I stammered. "He just . . . he came on to me, and I didn't expect it." Despite the flickers of pleasure within my body at seeing him respond in this way, I wasn't sure that Trevor truly deserved whatever wrath that Logan undoubtedly had in mind.

I saw his jaw clench and his eyes narrow even further. "Amelia, don't lie to me. He was grabbing your ass like it was already his." His face contorted as if he was experiencing a jolt of pain. "That's not how you come on to someone." His voice was gravely and dangerous. The tension in the air was so thick that goosebumps exploded all over my skin.

I was suddenly yearning to touch him, to feel his raw emotion through his hands as they skated across my body. But how long would this last? How long until he reverted back to acting like whatever this was between us wasn't real? "Why do you care, Logan?" I needed to hear him say it. I needed him to admit what he was feeling at that moment.

He stared hard at me for a moment before answering. "What do you mean, why? You know why." He kept his voice low.

"No, actually, I *don't*." I scoffed. "I don't know why, because you spend so much time pretending like this thing between us doesn't exist." I watched as he took a deep breath and looked down toward his feet, a tell tale sign that he was trying to collect himself. Trying to restrain himself. "Logan, when you found me in that bar a year ago, you looked at me like no one else in the entire world existed. You've been looking at me like that for as long as I can remember. You *kissed* me all those years ago when I picked you up from that bar downtown. And that kiss was the best thing that I've ever felt in my whole life." I inhaled a deep breath, feeling like my lungs could expand more now than they had in years. It felt so good to finally say the words out loud. To speak life into them.

Logan's eyes flicked up to mine. "Amelia." He said my name like it was a plea. A plea for me to understand—a plea for me to drop it.

I felt my stomach coil tightly inside of me, but I kept going, choosing to ignore the look on his face. "And now, when I'm right here in front of you, you spend the entire day taking care of *Gwen*."

Logan's face instantly changed, morphing from regret into something else, something more desperate. "*What?* Amelia, that's not what I was doing," he said, his voice a little more urgent. "She was hurt and I was just trying to do the right thing."

"Why don't you do the right thing with me, then?"

He paused and stared at me, eyes pleading. I watched as his throat bobbed. "That's all I'm ever trying to do, Mills."

I scoffed again. "Then tell me that you want me." I would have been mortified by how desperate I sounded if I didn't need to hear him say it so badly. I needed him to soothe the ache I felt around him by acknowledging that he felt it too. I kept my eyes locked on him, waiting for him to say the words that would finally give me solace. "Logan, tell me that you want me. Please. Tell me that I'm not crazy. Tell me that you want this just as much as I do." He still only stared back at me. I began marching toward him, closing the distance between us. The urge to kiss him, to *remind* him, came over me with such tenacity that I couldn't stop myself. I was being reckless, completely irrational, but I didn't care.

As I approached him, I could see his body tense. He looked away from me, shaking his head. My embarrassment grew with every passing moment that he didn't say anything, that he didn't reach out to touch me, but I held my ground. "Logan," I said finally, willing him to look at me. "Logan, please." His eyes flicked down to mine and I saw a swirl of emotions that I couldn't quite decipher. "Tell me that I'm not crazy. Kiss me. Touch me. Show me." I heard my voice crack. "*Please.*"

When he finally answered, his voice barely above a whisper, there was a shimmer in his eyes that caught in the moonlight. "I can't."

I felt my stomach bottom out as I desperately tried to grab hold to any semblance of reason. "You can't or you won't?"

His beautiful eyes—rich, dark molasses in the night—were locked on mine. I watched as he inhaled a deep breath and then pushed it out between his lips. But he didn't say anything.

I felt the unyielding pain of my heart fracturing into a

thousand jagged pieces as a furious rage rose up to take its place. Here I was, in this fucking place with him, *again*.

I could no longer stand to be near him. I couldn't take him looking at me like he was worried that I was going to break. "Then *don't* do this to me anymore," I spit out. I balled my hands into fists to hide the fact that they were shaking as I backed away from him. "This is over for me, Logan. It hurts too damn much, and I can't do it anymore." I tried to take control of my emotions, to strain my features into a neutral look to hide the fact that I wasn't just breaking, I was absolutely shattering.

I turned away from Logan and began walking away, suddenly feeling completely sober. My head throbbed and my whole body was trembling with adrenaline, but my mind was finally clear. "Amelia," I heard him call out. "Wait . . . please . . ."

Ignoring him, I continued to make my way down along the beach, feeling grounded with the water at my feet. Our rental house was only a mile and a half away from the bar, close enough that I could walk home. It would give me the time I needed to reflect on everything that just happened.

"Amelia, wait!" I heard Logan yell with a firmer voice, but still, I didn't turn around. I had nothing to give him. Nothing more to say.

Logan was like the tide in the ocean, flowing in and out of my heart throughout the cycles of our lives. Just as his waters reached my shore, smothering me with the beautiful essence of him, he was disappearing again into the wild currents that swept him out to sea. I didn't know what stopped him from just admitting the way that he felt about me—what I'd known in my gut was true—but I couldn't keep waiting for him to figure it out. My heart couldn't tolerate it anymore. So I had to let this go. I had to let him go.

As I made the long walk home, I pretended not to notice Logan trailing behind me the entire way. He kept himself a far enough distance back, but made no efforts to hide the fact that even now, he wasn't going anywhere.

# Chapter Twenty-Nine

As I sat on the patio of the apartment in the bitter cold, watching as snowflakes lazily fell across the city, I felt numb. I took a sip of the hot tea from the mug in my hands, barely even registering the burn on my tongue from the scalding liquid. There was a haze on the horizon that mirrored what I felt inside of my soul, a culmination of murky, cloudy shit where something beautiful should have been.

I hadn't spoken to Logan in two days, and certainly not for a lack of trying. He really hadn't wanted me to find him—which, quite frankly, devastated me. After I left the apartment the other night, I got in my car and sped over to Logan's house assuming that he would be there, but he wasn't. I waited for almost an hour, sitting in my parked car outside of his house, but he never showed.

I'd spent the entire weekend lost in my own madness, taking long car rides by myself through the city, showing up at Logan's house again and again only to keep finding that his car wasn't parked in the driveway, and then showing up at the shop to find that he wasn't there, either; Camila told me he had taken a couple of days off. I called and texted his phone numerous times, but never got an answer. Eventually, calls went straight to voicemail, so it seemed likely that he had turned his phone off.

At home, I avoided Adam as much as I could, and it felt like he was avoiding me, too. We hardly left our rooms when we were both home, neither of us wanting to talk to the other. I felt so incredibly frustrated at how he handled seeing Logan and I together, but a big part of me blamed myself, too.

Adam's actions may not have been ideal, but I was the one taking the risk having Logan over for dinner. Regardless of if I thought Adam would have been at work or not, he was letting me stay in his home, and I took advantage of his absence to sneak around with his best friend. In those optics, I could understand why Adam would feel hurt and angry with us.

I sighed. My skin was frozen, and I could barely feel the fingers that were wrapped around my mug, but I didn't care. I welcomed the numbness because it kept me from crying.

I didn't know what to do. I didn't know how to do *this*. The thought of my chance with Logan being over, of Logan deciding that this wasn't worth the risk, cut me to my very core.

But I couldn't blame him. His lifelong best friend punched him in the face. I knew that Logan was worried about the possibility of losing my family, somehow thinking that he could fuck this up enough that everyone would simply choose to walk away from him.

In his mind, he viewed being with me as a catalyst for the end of everything good in his life. Giving in to the temptation of his true desires, of having me, meant potentially wreaking havoc on the people who had kept him safe and who had supported him for all these years.

Our relationship wasn't simple. We were so intertwined in each other's lives already without adding romance to the mix. But that was exactly what we were trying to do, and the minute our feelings for each other reared themselves, we began a slow dance with the devil. And Logan had looked that devil in the eye, thinking that if this didn't work out the way we hoped it would, he might lose the people he loved most.

I thought I could protect him from that with good my intentions. I thought I could show him that love conquered all, and that my family would never turn their backs on him, even *if* he broke my heart. But I didn't stop Adam from hitting him, and the guilt of that tore me to pieces. I didn't protect Logan like I thought I could.

It was almost torture—the need to *do* something, to make all of this okay. But with Logan not speaking to me, I didn't know what to do. I needed to find him so that we could talk about this.

*What if he says it's over?*

I sunk into myself. If Logan said he doesn't want to do this anymore, I would have to find a way to be okay with that, even if it killed me. But I owed it to myself—to both of us—to make one last stand. Logan's fears were getting the best of him, and while that was a dragon he had to slay himself, I could at least try to give him the sword.

The truth was, I didn't just *love* Logan. Love wasn't a big enough word to describe the way I felt about him. The feelings that I had in my heart for him were well beyond the bounds of reality. Beyond the stretches of an entire ocean.

And nothing was over until you stopped fighting for it.

AN HOUR LATER, I parked my car on the side of the road in front of Logan's house. There were no lights shining from the windows, and his car wasn't parked in the driveway, but I wasn't giving up so easily this time. Instead of pulling away and driving home, I turned off the ignition and got out of the car.

The sun was still up fairly high in the sky, but it wouldn't be long before it began to set and the already freezing temperature would drop even further. I tucked myself deeper into my scarf as I began walking up the pathway to Logan's front porch. There was snow around its edges, but underneath the awning the majority of the porch was clear. So was the porch swing, where I decided to take a seat and wait.

Christmas lights were already turned on at many of the houses on Logan's street, twinkling around my vision as I mentally prepared a speech for when Logan eventually arrived. That was . . . if he did.

I spent two hours sitting on the porch swing in the frigid evening air, revolving through an uneasy smattering of emotions and thoughts as I waited anxiously for any sign of Logan. As the sun dipped lower toward the horizon, more holiday lights flicked on along the cozy neighborhood street, a beautiful depiction of joy that was a sharp contrast from the haunting turmoil I was feeling inside.

Suddenly, my mind honed in on the sound of a familiar engine coming from down the street. I turned my head in the direction it was coming from, and saw Logan's Chevelle winding its way toward the house. The silhouette of the man I loved sat in the driver's seat as a small, gray tornado moved around excitedly on the passenger side.

Logan parked the car in his own driveway, no doubt having seen my car in the street. And yet, he hadn't decided to keep driving, to deny me this conversation and leave me here alone to wallow in self-pity. He was making the choice to stay, to see me, and I felt butterflies overtake my stomach in heavy anticipation.

I watched as he opened his car door and stepped out, glowing in the magic of the sunset. Hook bounded his way out the driver's side door before tearing across the lawn in a mad dash and running up the steps to sit patiently at the front door. I shifted slightly on the swing, causing the chains to clink against the wood, and Hook noticed I was there. He came running my way, jumping up on his hind legs to ferociously lick my face.

"Hook!" Logan commanded, and just as easily as his call worked last time, Hook was back on the ground in a calm sitting position. Logan shook his head. "Damn dog. Come on." I watched as he unlocked his front door and opened it to let Hook in as I sat in place, unsure if he was going to invite me in or not. As soon as Hook was inside, Logan shut the door and took a few steps toward me, his heavy brown coat zipped up high around his neck, his dark boots thudding against the wooden porch. His face was indecipherable, giving nothing away as his eyes shifted to me.

I felt anxious. Worried that if I took my eyes off of him for even a second, he would be gone. That this desperate and fiery blaze between us might be as fleeting as the snow, melting before I had a chance to really feel it between my fingers. "I'm sorry for just showing up like this, but you haven't been answering any of my calls or texts and . . . I couldn't take it anymore."

Logan tucked his hands into his coat pockets as he sat down next to me on the porch swing, keeping ample space between us. "Don't be sorry, Amelia. I understand."

"I have a lot of things I want to say to you. And I need you to just listen, okay? Can you do that?"

The hint of a smile played on his lips, and I felt my heart skip a beat in response. "Okay. I can do that."

"Okay." I nodded, before taking a deep breath. "Look. I know what happened with Adam was probably the worst case scenario of things that could have possibly happened during our . . . trial phase. But I know that my brother cares for both of us very deeply, and I think he was just a little blindsided. You didn't deserve that reaction from him, and I'm so, so sorry that it happened. In all fairness, though, I shouldn't have had you over to his apartment like that. It was irresponsible of me to take advantage of his hospitality, so I know that I owe both of you that apology."

"Amelia, that wasn't your fault," Logan cut in. "That wasn't anyone's fault. It just happened. Don't blame yourself." He kept his hand in his coat pockets, kept his body a solid few inches away from mine, and I yearned to touch him, but I shoved the feeling down and continued.

"Maybe, but I still could have prevented it from happening." I sighed, feeling my chest loosen as words began to pour out of me. "Logan—you have a dog with a disability. Employees who have been dealt some shitty cards in their lives. You surround yourself with these mirror images of the way you feel inside—broken and discarded. And then you give those reflections of yourself everything you have . . . to help. And you do. You make them all better.

"You can fix all the broken things in the entire world if you want to, but it's still not going to fix the way you feel about yourself until you tackle *that* head-on. You are worthy of love, Logan. Without a doubt. Love isn't something to be held back just because pain might also exist. And I'm sure as hell not going to hold back from you. I love you. I always have and I always will. I've loved you for as long as I can even remember, and I will love you every single day for the rest of my life. I feel like I just started *living*, finally giving in to this special pull that leads me right to you.

"I want to marry you, have babies with you, grow old with you, and love you harder every single day." I watched as he straightened his back, his amber eyes piercing me with enormous intensity, but I kept going, feeling almost frantic with a desperate need for him to know how much I loved him. "I want to be your family. I don't want you to just be a part of mine, although you'll always have that too, but I want to give you one that's *yours*. I want to *be yours*, Logan. I want to be Amelia Davis . . ."

Before I could keep sputtering out words in my fight to convince him, his mouth was on mine. His arms wrapped around me tightly as he pulled me flush against him on the swing. It was a chaotic, maddeningly beautiful kiss of promises. Of forever. Of *finally*. It was the moment I knew, with clarity and certainty, that Logan really was going to be the happy ending to my story.

"Amelia." He said my name like only he could, curling his voice around my heart. He bent down to kiss me again, pressing his lips to the corner of my mouth. "I talked to my dad yesterday."

I blinked up at him, surprised by his words. "You did?"

"Yes." He dipped his head as a small smile grew on his lips. "I borrowed your thinking space in the red rocks, I hope you don't mind." He grabbed my hand, intertwining his fingers into mine as he gently stroked my inner wrist with his thumb. "I needed to get lost for a minute and clear my head, so I decided to take Hook back out to that trail because I wanted to be close to you, too.

"I've been thinking a lot about what you said that night in the city, about deserving to be happy. And I realized how much my fears have gotten in the way of that. I always knew the fears were there, always a part of me, but I don't think I've truly realized how much control they still have over my life. I was out on that trail and I found this boulder off to the side under a big tree, and I decided to sit and . . . I don't know what came over me, but I just started talking to my father.

"I told him that, wherever he is now, I hope he's free from the pain and anger that he was fighting every day that he was alive. That I like to think he isn't a broken man anymore. The more I talked, the more I felt the weight of it all start to seep out of me." He shook his head. "I spent over an hour sitting under that tree, just talking. I told him about you and that, respectfully, I'm going to do things completely different than he did. That I'm not going to let fear control me anymore. Life's already complicated enough, so I'm choosing to chase happiness, instead." He squeezed my hand, smiling brightly at me. "I'm choosing this, Amelia. I'll choose you every damn day for the rest of my life. And I'm so sorry it's taken me this long to get here, but I promise you, I'll make up for it."

And then his mouth was on mine again, pulling me over his lap so I was straddling his waist. The porch swing rocked back and forth as our kiss became fervent. I felt tears slipping down my cheeks, the salt hitting my lips as his tongue caught mine.

He must have realized I was crying, because he pulled away and brought a warm hand to my face, gently wiping away the proof. "I'm so sorry for leaving you hanging. I never meant to hurt you. I just . . . I needed self-reflection. I needed the space to deal with myself. But I know, without a doubt, that I also *need* you in my life, Amelia. Now that I know what it is to have you, I will never, ever let you go. Come hell or high water, it's you and me. Okay?"

More tears streamed down my face as I sputtered out a sob of joy. "Okay, baby," I whispered, wrapping my arms around his neck.

I watched his eyes flash with surprise as a big smile grew on his lips. "Say it again," he said, so softly I almost couldn't hear him.

"Okay," I repeated.

"No, no. The other part."

I paused, realizing what he meant, a matching smile inching up my own face. I watched as his eyes flicked down to my mouth, wanting to watch me say the word. I wrapped a hand around the back of his head, steadying myself as I whispered, "Baby."

Logan groaned before standing up, lifting me with him as my legs wrapped around his waist. He pushed me up against the front wall of his house and kissed me so fiercely I thought I might faint.

He opened the door and carried me inside, walking straight

back to his bedroom. Hook was chasing after his feet, but once he stepped into his room, he kicked the door behind him. He ran a hand up my back as his mouth devoured me, claiming me forever.

Laying me down gently on the bed, he was immediately on top of me, both of us completely overwhelmed with the sudden, desperate need to get each other out of all of our clothes. If I thought Logan was hungry for this in Breckenridge, he was now a man who was completely, utterly starved.

As I lay naked before him, his eyes raked over my entire body. "You are so perfect, sweetheart." And then he was eagerly pressing himself against me, sliding inside of me in the sweetest, most delicious relief. His mouth came down to kiss my lips, my neck, my shoulder, as the rhythm of his movements drove me completely insane.

His flames stroked against my body, licking my skin until I couldn't take it anymore. I was an inferno in his arms, pinned to the bed by the weight of his hips. He looked at me, grinning like a devil at the obscene sounds that he was bringing out of me, and within moments of watching him watch me, I completely caught fire.

As I was wholly ignited, riding a high that was unlike anything I imagined could be real, I heard the words I'd been waiting my entire life to hear. "I love you, Amelia." I opened my eyes to see the beautiful man above me—my best friend— and watched as he, too, burned for me.


HOURS LATER, we were still wrapped around each other. The combination of his pillows and thick white duvet swallowed us whole, cocooning us from the rest of the world in absolute bliss. Logan was playing with strands of my hair as we quietly existed—simply, irrevocably together.

"Move in with me," Logan whispered into my hair. I felt the warmth of his breath curve around my neck, lighting up my arms with goosebumps.

I paused, soaking in the question. *Did I hear that correctly?* "What?"

He squeezed my hip with his hand as his thumb stroked the dimple at my back. "Move in with me." His voice was velvet, soft and delicate around my freshly stitched heart.

I turned my body, detangling my legs from his as I looked at him in question. "You want me to move in with you?"

His eyes were sure, his face almost completely relaxed except for the little ribbons of vulnerability tracing around his eyes. He placed his hand on my hip again, reassuring. "Yes. I can't think of a reason why you shouldn't."

I felt the drumbeat of my heart igniting. "You can't?" My voice was careful.

He blinked once before his eyes lowered to my mouth, to my jaw, my collarbone and back up to my eyes. "Nope. Can you?"

I considered this. It had only been a week and a half, but Logan was the most sure thing I'd ever felt in my entire life. The thought sent a further pounding in my chest. "No," I finally responded.

His eyes flashed darker, the hand on my hip sliding up to settle on my ribcage. The pad of his thumb stroking along the curve beneath my breast. He bent his head down to softly kiss my shoulder, and then buried his nose into my neck where he breathed me in. "Then it's settled. You're moving in with me." I felt his teeth skate across my skin before his soft lips covered the sensitive spot below my ear, causing my mind to go blank. "Okay?"

Logan pushed himself up to his elbows, hovering over me as his hips again settled between my legs. He looked down at me through heavy lids. I felt a deep desire to count his eyelashes. "Okay?" he asked again, bending down again to kiss me on my collarbone, lazily moving his mouth across my chest.

I felt my mouth go dry, the saliva on my tongue thick and sticking to the roof of my mouth. A familiar tension began pulling low, deep in my tummy. "Okay," I whispered, closing my eyes. My body was entirely focused on the movement of his mouth as it began to tease my aching nipple. I was completely full of desire for him. Full of need for this. He hummed his appreciation as I curled my hands into his hair.

His glittering golden eyes found mine, full of promise and unrestrained joy. *I'm happy*, they said, and it made my chest squeeze. And then we sealed the moment with a kiss.

# Epilogue

## LOGAN, SIX MONTHS LATER

It was already a burning hot day, and it was only nine in the morning. Despite my shower over an hour ago, sweat was already making my shirt stick to my skin, and I knew I would definitely have to shower again before the chaos started later.

The street in front of the house was quiet—in the thirty minutes or so that I'd been sitting out here, I'd only seen one neighbor from a few houses down come out to retrieve his newspaper. After a quick, neighborly wave to each other through the distance, Mr. Jimenez retreated back inside, shutting his door firmly behind him.

Since then, there'd been no movement in my line of sight, unless you counted the birds flying around overhead. It was peaceful, and I always found myself thankful in times like this. Times of quiet and calm. I watched as the bright purple blooms of the wisteria tree in the front lawn swayed in the morning breeze.

Beside me on the porch swing, Hook was snoring loudly, enjoying an early nap. We'd gotten up at the crack of dawn this morning to go for a run, and now he was enjoying his post-exercise slumber. I rubbed my hand along his back, working his muscles with a massage. I always found myself thankful for him, too. Since the day I rescued him, he'd been a loyal, dedicated wingman.

I adopted him specifically because I knew I needed something to love. I knew that, after working so hard to set up the shop and getting that piece of my life up and standing, I needed to start preparing for another major piece that—despite my raging, almost debilitating fears—I'd always secretly prayed like hell for.

Family.

Coming from a home like mine, I didn't learn shit about how to be a good man. I didn't learn how to be a loving husband, and I definitely didn't learn how to be a strong and stable father. Thankfully, the Campbells stepped in when they did and became enough to fill that void. Richard was—and still is—a great example of a good man, and Liz was a much-needed mother figure that I would have never had, otherwise.

A million thank-yous would never even scratch the surface of the depths of my appreciation for them in my life. But as I started to put down my own roots, the roots of a Davis man, I knew that I'd need all the help I could get to learn true patience, trust, and unconditional love. Those things were hard for me because they were tangled up inside of so much fear and doubt in my ability to do things right. I wanted nothing more than to be a damn good man, but I was scared to death that I would fuck it up. That I would turn into *him*.

Adopting Hook threw me into the trenches of an opportunity to learn, and his impact on my life was incredible. Because of him, I started to believe in myself. Within minutes of meeting him, I was wrapped around his little paw. I felt myself constantly worried about his happiness, his comfort, that it became apparent that I—at least for this crazy ass dog—had what it took. My dedication to him, to his handicap and to his quality of life, allowed me to prove to myself that I really can love something. Even love some*one*.

"Whatcha doing out there, handsome?" I heard her sweet voice from the screen door, and instantly felt my breath hitch. After all this time, she still had that effect on me.

"Thinking about you," I responded honestly, and looked over my shoulder at Amelia's face through the screen panel. She rolled her eyes—always so damn sassy—before she pushed open the door and stepped out onto the porch. Her bare legs were heaven from beneath one of my old T-shirts—the one she'd slept in last night—and her long dark hair was a tangled mess. My girl, the late sleeper. The beat of my heart. The most beautiful thing I'd ever seen.

I patted my thigh as she approached the swing, and she sat her fine ass down right into my lap. I wrapped my arms around her and pulled her close, breathing her in. She smelled like a mix of that strawberry lotion she loved to put on and old remnants of my cedar aftershave still on the shirt she was wearing. Strawberry and cedar, my new favorite smell.

"How long have you been up?" She wrapped her arms around my neck and gave me a quick kiss on the cheek. An action that was so casual and second-nature for her. Something I would never forget to appreciate.

"Since six. Hook and I went for a run and enjoyed the sunrise—something you know nothing about," I teased.

She scoffed. "Okay, you know I'm not a morning person." She flipped her hair back behind her shoulder in a small show of defiance that had me silently chuckling. "But I *could* be convinced by the promise of a good sunrise."

"Noted," I said as I leaned in to kiss her, the need to feel her lips on mine overpowering me. She was so fucking radiant in the morning, all doe-eyed and still sleepy. Absolutely edible.

This. This is how I hoped to always remember us when, someday, I looked back on our beginning—on the first chapters of our happily ever after. Amelia, with the warmest damn smile I'd ever seen in my entire life, and a touch so intoxicating that it could drop me to my knees. She was the sweetest nectar of life, as bright as the sun, as stubborn and wild as a hurricane. I didn't know how in god's name I ended up with the right to call her mine, but it was the honor of my life. One that I'd *never* take lightly.

The kiss we shared was lazy. Unhurried. And I loved that it felt like we had our entire life to kiss each other like this.

After a moment, she pulled away and looked up at me, catching me in the vise of her gaze, and within seconds, the rest of the world faded away. Her beautiful green eyes were burning with a look as she traced her fingernails along my arm. "Happy birthday, baby," she whispered as a smile played on her lips.

"Thank you, sweetheart," I said, and kissed her again. I couldn't help myself. I knew I didn't deserve her, but I would spend the rest of my life fucking trying to.

"Are you excited for your party?" Her eyes were already full of excited anticipation.

I chuckled. "I'm still not sure how I let you convince me to invite people over here," I responded, teasing her.

"Well, it's your birthday. And technically, I live here now

too . . . so if I want to throw a party for my insanely hot boyfriend's thirtieth birthday, I'm not really sure that I actually *need* your permission."

A burst of emotion welled up within me at her words. Life really had a funny way of changing just about everything in such a short amount of time. For so long, I hung suspended in such darkness, incapable of allowing myself to be honest with Amelia. And now, her clothes were hanging in my closet, her fancy girl shampoo was in my shower, and there was more love in this home than Hook and I could have possibly mustered on our own.

"You sure have a smart mouth, woman," I rebounded in mock-disapproval. I watched as she bit her bottom lip and I almost threw her over my shoulder and carried her into the house right then. "In all honesty, I'm pretty amazed that you're doing all of this for me, Mills."

I saw a softness come over her as she looked at me thoughtfully. It was a look she'd given me so many times throughout our lives. One that reminded me that she was here with me, no matter what. "Of course I am, Logan. And you better get used to it." She leaned forward and kissed my nose.

"What time are people coming?"

"I told everyone to come around noon, but you know Adam. He'll probably be showing up any minute now to start the party," she said, her sarcastic tone causing her to giggle at herself. She was right though—Adam was never one to show up late to a party, and to him, on time was late.

I had to admit, as much as I was looking forward to having everyone here today, I was *really* happy that Adam was coming. Even after we'd gotten over our fight—the only fight we'd ever had in our entire lives—work kept us both pretty busy, and I hadn't seen a whole lot of him in the past few months. I missed my best friend and, while it might have been a little awkward at first, I wanted to share more about my life with Amelia and make sure he knew how serious I was about her.

A large, black box truck suddenly turned down our street and, to my surprise, pulled in front of the house and stopped along the curb. Amelia jumped out of my lap. "Shit, they're already here. I need to go get dressed!" She raced through the screen door and back into the house.

"Wait," I called after her. "Who's here?"

"The rental company!" I heard her yell from somewhere in the house.

I watched as a man jumped out of the truck and walked to the back, reaching for a handle that slid the rolling door open. "What rental company?" I hollered back.

"For the tables and chairs!" Her voice was muffled, and I could picture her wrestling to get a shirt over her head.

"Where do you want this?" the driver of the truck called from the street as he looked over at me, waving his arms toward whatever was in the back of that truck. Fuck if I knew, sir.

The screen door swung open again as Amelia came flying back outside. "Hi!" she yelled out, smiling down at the driver with an enthusiastic wave.

"He wants to know where we want it," I told her.

Amelia's eyes cut to me before they were back down on the man in the street. "We're going to set it all up out back!" she yelled down.

I turned back to Amelia. "We rented tables and chairs?"

"Yeah, how else will we seat thirty people?"

"*Thirty* people?"

She giggled in response, her smile completely infectious.

"Yes, Logan. Thirty people. And we only have a couple hours to get ready, so let's get moving."

THREE HOURS LATER, the house was packed full of people. More people than I realized I even knew. It felt like everyone from my entire life was here. The Campbells came, and I was glad to see that Adam brought Rachel with him. Just like I anticipated, he'd shown up an hour before everyone else, claiming he was there to help set up even though the only thing he set up was a beer in his hand.

Everyone from the shop was here. Andre had brought his sister, Marisela. Amelia had even gone as far as inviting Mara, who'd shown up by herself but soon made friends with Jessica.

Some of Amelia's close friends were here too. Mackenzie and Eric had shown up with Mackenzie's brother, Trevor in tow. I hadn't seen Trevor since the trip to Mexico, and things didn't exactly end on friendly terms back then—after I threatened to knock his teeth out if he touched Amelia like he had on the dance floor again—but he seemed to be in good spirits here today. Either way, I had my eye on him.

Nora had also come as a tagalong with Mackenzie. I hadn't seen Nora since Mexico either, and last I'd heard she moved to California to be with a boyfriend she met shortly after that trip, but from the looks of the sadness on her face, I wondered if she was still with him or if she might be home for good.

Hook was hands down enjoying the party the most. He'd quickly ousted me as man of the hour—everyone was rather obsessed with him and his charm. I think this was the happiest I'd ever seen him, surrounded by so many new and exciting people to chase around the backyard.

After mingling with everyone, I saw Richard and Liz standing in the corner of the backyard by the grill. I made my way over there, needing to speak with Richard about something important. His eyes caught mine just as I was stepping toward them, and a warm smile flooded his face. "Logan! This is some party."

"It was all Amelia. She put way more effort into this than I even realized. Hey, I was hoping I could speak to you alone, Richard"—my eyes briefly cut to Liz in apology—"it won't be long, Liz, I promise."

Concern swept over Richard's face. "Is everything alright, son?"

I nodded, "Yes, nothing like that, nothing's wrong."

"Well, go on, Richard," Liz prompted.

I dipped my head towards the side of the house where there was a door that led to the garage. Richard walked toward it, opening the door and stepping into darkness before I reached past him and flipped on the lights, stepping in behind him and shutting the door behind me.

Richard walked over to the Chevelle, currently parked on the other side of the garage. "I remember when you bought this. I was actually pretty damn jealous." He chuckled. "But your dedication to this car proved how much more deserving you were of it. I was mighty proud of you for that, Logan." He turned to face me, a familiar twinkle in his eye.

"Thank you, sir. You and Liz have always been extremely supportive of me, and I'm eternally grateful. I'm actually hoping you'll support me in what I'm about to ask of you."

Richard's eyebrows furrowed in curiosity. "Anything you need, son, of course. What is it?"

"Your daughter."

His face lit up in surprise. "Amelia?"

"Yes, sir. I'm crazy about her, sir. And I want to ask her to marry me." I blew out a nervous breath. "I'm hoping that I have your blessing to do just that."

Richard studied me, taking a moment before he responded, and my nerves intensified with every second that passed. He took a few steps toward me, closing the distance between us as he reached out to press his hand to my shoulder. "Logan, I wouldn't trust my daughter in the hands of anyone else. The way you love her so completely is as obvious as the sky is blue, and Liz and I are both thankful that you kids finally figured your shit out and made it happen."

I felt myself catching on his words. "Sir?"

Richard chuckled. "You think we haven't known about the way you two have always felt about each other? Son, we've known for years." He squeezed my shoulder before pulling me into a strong hug. We'd shared plenty of hugs over the years, but each time it happened, it knocked something loose inside of me, some deep, inner wall no doubt constructed in my youth to protect me. As he held me firmly against him, I heard him sigh. "You have our blessing, without question, son."

I felt relief overcome me, feeling my shoulders relax as Richard pulled out of our embrace. His eyes still held a twinkle as he regarded me with what looked a lot like pride. I felt an unfamiliar sting in my eyes, not used to emotions like this coming over me, but his words meant more to me than he could've possibly known. "Thank you, Richard. I promise to take care of her for the rest of my life."

"Oh, I have no doubts, Logan. None at all."

• • •

THAT NIGHT we laid together in bed, the warm summer air flowing through the open windows, both of us completely exhausted from the eventful and fulfilling day. The party extended well into the evening hours, and it felt incredible to be surrounded by so many people who came to celebrate *me*. I wasn't sure if I would ever get used to that.

After Amelia and I practically kicked out the final stragglers—Adam and Andre made fast friends and ended the night in a heated tournament of flip cup in the kitchen—we came straight to bed to curl around each other, leaving the mess in the house for the morning.

As I enjoyed this incredibly meaningful life with her, I found myself constantly feeling like I needed to soak in every single moment—every look, every touch, every sigh that expelled from her mouth—so that I could hold it tight and keep it safe to look back on later. To have a life that was worth wanting to look back on was amazing to me. Something I still couldn't quite believe was real.

I couldn't get enough of this girl. She'd found the light within me, the light that I hadn't been able to find in myself. I spent so much time being angry with the world. Angry at my life. Angry at my father. The demons that came along with such deep anger almost overpowered me. It honestly almost cost me my life on numerous occasions. But in the hellish depths of darkness, when I found myself at the brutal end of my rope, Amelia's wild blaze of furious light bound its way right into my heart, every time.

I didn't know how she did it, but she could settle the riot inside of my soul. The anger and sadness and bitter remnants of hurt. She could soothe me with the tilt of her smile. The soft pads of her fingers on my skin. A spark in her eyes that calmed my bones. She was my North Star, my resting pulse. My quiet peace. The only home I've ever truly known. Finally.

"Marry me," I whispered into her hair, feeling her instantly grow still beneath my hands. I traced my fingers up her arm, feeling her soft skin explode in goosebumps.

"What?" she asked, and it made me smile.

"Marry me, Amelia."

She pulled herself away from my chest to face me, her expression dancing with surprise and an unmistakable joy that made my heart sing. "I promise to give you my very best—" I paused, beginning to feel a wave of emotions welling up inside of me as I looked into her beautiful, emerald eyes. I cleared my throat to keep my composure. "I have to be honest, Amelia . . . standing next to me in this life won't always be easy. I wish I could promise you that it will be, but I still struggle sometimes and I think that's just a part of who I am. It's how I was made, forged in the fire. But I promise to give you my fucking best, every single day. I will never hurt you. I will love you and protect you with everything that I am for the rest of my life, I swear it."

I watched as tears began pouring down her face, collecting on her pillow as she reached up to lightly touch my bottom lip. I wrapped my arm around her, pulling her back close to me, feeling her heart beat wildly inside of her chest as her forehead pressed against my throat. "Logan," she murmured into my chest. My name from her lips was the sweetest sound.

"Marry me," I repeated. "Please."

She turned her face up to me, gently cupping my jaw in her soft hand. I was the luckiest man in the whole entire world to have a love like this. A woman who so completely poured herself into me. So selfless and kind and sure.

Leaning forward, she pressed her smile against my lips as she said the words I was waiting for. "Yes, baby." And then her mouth became an explosion of fury as she kissed me with her soul.

**THE END**

# Acknowledgments

THANK YOU for taking a chance on this debut novel, written by an indie author like me—and for making space in your life to enjoy these characters. Logan and Amelia's love story has been one of the greatest adventures of my life.

Thank you to my whole family for encouraging me and supporting me throughout this journey.

L—because of you, I know how to write about romance like this. I love you 🤍

Mom—thank you for always teaching me to be brave and to chase my dreams.

To my team:

Britt—girl, did we just become best friends?! You have been such a ray of light to work with, and I have so much gratitude for you. Thank you for pushing me. Thank you for believing in this story like you do.

Cat—thank you for bringing Logan and Amelia to life! Your talent is incredible and I'm so thankful to have you in my corner.

Beta readers—Lauren, Lissa, Veronica—thank you for taking the time to comb through this story and to provide such great feedback! Your early excitement kept my spirits high and I cannot thank you enough for being a part of this.

ARC readers—thank you for your support and excitement, and for sharing such beautiful reviews. I'm eternally grateful.

xo, Michaela

# About the Author

Michaela is the author of heartwarming contemporary romance novels featuring diverse characters with strong emotional development. Don't worry - there's always a HEA (and plenty of spice).

When she's not reading or writing she's usually with her family and dogs, enjoying the desert in Arizona.

Stay tuned for exciting announcements at
michaelajeantaylor.com

amazon.com/author/michaelajeantaylor

instagram.com/michaelajeanbooks

tiktok.com/@michaelajeanbooks

goodreads.com/michaelajeanbooks

facebook.com/michaelajeanbooks